I0772932

WARDEN'S JUSTICE

TRIALS OF THE AEGIS

BOOK ONE

AARON HODGES

Edited by Karen Sanders
Cover Illustration by Efosa Promise
Typography by Nikko Marie

ISBN: 9781991018281

ABOUT THE AUTHOR

 Aaron Hodges was born in 1989 in the small town of Whakatane, New Zealand. He studied for five years at the University of Auckland, completing a Bachelors of Science in Biology and Geography, and a Masters of Environmental Engineering. After working as an environmental consultant for two years, he grew tired of office work and decided to quit his job in 2014 and see the world. One year later, he published his first novel - Stormwielder.

FOLLOW AARON HODGES…

And receive TWO FREE novels and a short story!

https://aaronhodgesauthor.com/newsletter

ALSO BY AARON HODGES

Trials of the Aegis

Book 1: Warden's Justice

Book 2: Rogue's Gambit

The Sword of Light

Book 1: Stormwielder

Book 2: Firestorm

Book 3: Soul Blade

The Legend of the Gods

Book 1: Oathbreaker

Book 2: Shield of Winter

Book 3: Dawn of War

The Knights of Alana

Book 1: Daughter of Fate

Book 2: Queen of Vengeance

Book 3: Crown of Chaos

The Evolution Gene

Book 1: Reborn

Book 2: Havoc

Book 3: Carnage

Descendants of the Fall

Book 1: Warbringer

Book 2: Wrath of the Forgotten

Book 3: Age of Gods

Book 4: Dreams of Fury

The Alfurian Chronicles

Book 1: Defiant

Book 2: Guardian

Book 3: Conquest

The Swords of Heaven and Hell

Book 1: Darkstrider

Book 2: Voidlight

The Four Circles

Book 1: Help! My Wizard Mentor Had A Heart Attack And Now I'm Being Chased By A Horde Of Giant Spiders!

The Untamed Isles

The Path Awakens

Kickstarter Recognition

Hello again everyone, and a great big thank you to the 89 amazing backers below who supported the Kickstarter campaign for Warden's Justice! It was a whirlwind 3 weeks and I was really happy at the end of it with the level of support we reached—and now I'm even more excited to reveal some of the epic benefits you unlocked in the stretch goals. I think the full page images inside each chapter heading really turned out well and is definitely something I'll be adding to future campaigns!

In the meantime, however, please enjoy the story of Kaila and Theron as they battle for survival deep in the mountains of the Iron Pinnacles.

Write on, Aaron Hodges

Build Your Own Teir: Esapekka Eriksson, Gregory Ashe, Seamus Sands

Copper: B. Plaga, Jason, Robin Hill, Gianna C., Michael, Jillipop, Greg Levick, John Walsh, David Berry, Vickie Grider, Jasmine C, EJB, Jan Birch, Franchesca Caram, John Idlor, Jesper D, Eric P, ALB

Iron: Patrick Palm, C Taormina, Elizabeth Davis, Noeleen Liapis, MJP, James R McGinnis Jr, Steven Byrd, A. Sturniolo, MJP, Felicitas Odemer, Rosa Thill, Gary Phillips, Jason Lovell

Steel: Serena M, Chris Bristow, Kat Englin, Craig Sisson, Marlene R, TL Walcher

Three Nations Ebook Bundle: Alexandra Corrsin, Bouke de Boer, Anonymous

Ultimate Ebook Bundle: Stephanie Meier, Grace Hoffman

Bronze: Petar Novakovic, Connor Mayo, Ellen Pilcher, Noone, Dr. Charles E Norton III, Eric Vilbert, John Gilligan, Renske Veldkamp, Robert Brown

Silver: In loving memory of Basil Martin, Scott Casey, Annarose Willhite, Brendan Papz, Malfor, Hugo Essink, Gerald P.McDaniel, Marcos Ramirez, Peter "Tonour" Basak, Zeebers651, Jacob Joseph, Izaak, Billye Herndon, Vivian Cicero, Duncan Wilcox, Chris Roeszler, Randy Smith, Scott Chisholm, C Wilson, Elizabeth Haynes, Justise Briones, Katrina Gilles, L. Nabeta, Patricia, NeonPixxius

Gold: Bradley Bolt, Ket, Aletia Brauer

Ultimate Super Duper Aaron Hodges Bundle: Samantha Newberry, S. L. Puma, Aleksandra

Tuckerisation: Julia Deutsch

ARBASTEN
WASTELANDS
TORRSEA
CASCADELANDS
ELGOSS
AR'IMES
IRON PINNACLES
ISELADOR
BERMISH
TAH'RAUS
BRENSHELD
RIVERGATE
THE
KINGDOM
OF FRESIA
VERMILION COAST
BELGROVE
MARSHWOOD

S omething was wrong.

Kaila knew it the moment she heard the footsteps. They weren't the calm, measured footfalls of her fellow citizens, but quick and hurried, betraying haste.

Someone was running.

Kaila Dwyn had lived in the mining village of Elgoss her entire eighteen years, and she could count on one hand the occasions she'd heard an adult *running.* People didn't *run* in their sleepy town. Elgoss was safe, protected by its sandstone walls, perched on the side of a volcanic mount and hidden deep in the mountains of the Iron Pinnacles. The enemy might seek this place for the precious crystals they mined from the fiery depths, but their location remained a closely guarded secret. Only the most trusted citizens were allowed to leave Elgoss, and only with the earl's permission.

Nor was there any crime to speak of. What little they possessed was shared among the community. To steal for personal gain contradicted everything her people believed; a violation of the precious unity that had held humanity together throughout a thousand years of war against their ceaseless enemy, the Elysian.

So when she heard the footsteps approaching, Kaila reacted as any upstanding citizen of Fresia would. She was already in motion as shouts echoed down the narrow street, a knife finding its place in her hand as she unsheathed it. She might be smaller than most of the men in Elgoss, but her father had prepared Kaila for this moment, training her to fight, to wield a blade and trust her instincts.

A figure staggered into view, face pale and smudged with ash. She recognised him; it was Leonardo, one of her father's men. Strange. The bell signalling the day's end had yet to ring; everyone was still in the mines or tending to the crops. Kaila only had the afternoon free to prepare for this evening, when she and her class-mates would sit the Trials of the Aegis, a final test that all children must complete to become full citizens. The Trials decided your future within the kingdom and served to root out any Elysian infil-trators among their ranks.

But Leonardo was a grown man. He should not have been here. She smelt treason.

The shadows were already long with the short winter day and the fleeing man didn't notice Kaila until she stepped into his path, knife glinting in the sunset. "Stop, Leo—" she began.

The man did not pause, launching himself at Kaila instead, a fist aimed squarely for her face. Her father's training saved her from the blow as she ducked, but not from his momentum. They crashed together, the impact hurling them both from their feet. She clung to him as they struck the ground.

"Get off!" he yelled, struggling to free himself.

Kaila refused, digging her fingers into his flesh and slashing at him with the knife. Desperate, he rolled, sending them tumbling down the steep street. Sharp stones tore her skin and her teeth rattled with each jolt of impact, but she endured, refusing to let go. She could hear the distant shouts of pursuers, the heavy thump of their boots approaching, and knew she just had to hold on a little longer…

They came to a halt with a *thump*. Still clutching her knife, Kaila found a well of extra strength and surged upright, pulling herself on top of the man. Pinning him, she raised her blade.

"No, please!" Leonardo gasped, his face red from exertion. He began to thrash. "No, I can't go back down there! Not again!"

She knew the truth then. Her stomach sank, jaw hardening. He was a deserter. His turn had obviously come for the deep shift, the newest tunnels in the volcanic depths, where the air boiled and harsh gases burned at men's flesh and lungs. It was the most perilous section of the mine, but it was also where agimet formed. The crystals were crucial to their soldiers on the frontlines, where they powered weapons against the Elysian. So each man did their duty, drawing lots and bearing the risk, knowing their sacrifice kept the kingdom safe.

Unless you were a filthy coward and fled.

Leonardo moaned and bucked, attempting to throw her off. Snarling, she pressed her blade against the soft flesh beneath his chin.

"One wrong move, coward, and you won't live to face my father's wrath."

With the mine down a man, someone else would have to step up. Her father, the overseer, would likely be the first to volunteer. Kaila's anger stirred at the thought of him risking his life because of this craven. She pressed down on the knife until Leonardo yelped and grew still.

His eyes watched her, dark in the dying light, black with hatred. It didn't touch her. What did she care about the hatred of a coward?

The thud of heavy boots announced the arrival of reinforcements. Kaila looked up to find Sareen standing over them. A muscular woman, she had once fought on the frontlines herself. Now she served as a guard for the mine.

"Kaila!" She gasped. "Bless the First Matron, we thought the spineless bastard had slipped away from us." She gave Leonardo a sharp kick in the ribs, making him double over in agony.

Another man in the scarlet uniform of the Fresian military arrived. Only then did Kaila release her grip and step back. Her heart was racing and as the moment passed, her scalp began to tingle with the shock of what she'd just done.

I stopped a deserter!

Duty to your fellow man was the first law of the Magisterium— the ancient association that had ruled humanity since their liberation. It was all that had kept humanity alive through centuries of slavery to their Elysian conquerors. And it had given them the strength to fight when T'iana, the greatest of their heroes, had risen against their masters—and called on them to do the same.

Pride swelled in Kaila's chest as Sareen dragged the moaning man up by his collar and shoved him into the hands of Tomas—another ex-soldier.

"Well done, kid," he grunted, locking shackles around Leonardo's wrists. Leonardo continued to shake his head and beg for mercy, but his captors steadfastly ignored him.

"It was an honour, sir," she said respectfully, offering a salute. "Do you need help escorting him to the pens?" The mine had several cages for deserters. They were always the first sent into the depths each morning.

Tomas chuckled. "I think we can handle it."

Kaila pursed her lips but ignored the mockery in his tone. The pair were veterans and she was no one. But one day soon, she hoped to wear their uniform, and not as a regular soldier. Her father had been preparing her for something more—to join the greatest order of heroes humanity had ever known.

The Wardens of Fresia.

Kaila's heart swelled. Her father had been a hero on the frontlines, beloved by his comrades. He had been awarded the medal of T'iana for saving his entire company. They'd been scouting in the mountains when the enemy had surprised them. Without the protection of a Warden, they should have been slaughtered—but her father had charged the enemy alone, buying his captain time to order the retreat. His company survived, but Gideon Dwyn was presumed dead—until, weeks later, he stumbled back into camp alive.

As for her mother, Kaila had never known her—only that she'd been a soldier as well, but had died shortly after Kaila's birth. Heartbroken, her father had resigned his commission the next day. Normally, such an action would have condemned Gideon as a coward, but since the captain owed his life to her father, a transfer was arranged instead.

"Don't you have the Trials today?" Sareen interrupted Kaila's daydreams.

She jumped. *"Oh!"*

Adrenaline had driven the Trials from her mind. Glancing at the sky, she swore. The sun had already set behind the curve of the mountain. She was late!

"*Sorry!*" she quickly apologised for the foul language. She would have to confess to Sister Eurador later, but if she wanted any chance of becoming a Warden, she needed to *move*.

Unfortunately, the end-of-day bell had already rung and a crowd had now gathered, drawn by the commotion. A pack of wide-eyed children had crept close, and as she turned to go, Kaila careened into one of them, knocking the boy to the ground, where he began to howl.

Kaila stumbled to a stop. She recognised him, of course. She knew every single one of the six hundred and twenty citizens of Elgoss. The boy was Jacob, the son of one of her father's miners. He was young, barely five years old, and curious—which meant he was always getting underfoot. Not unlike herself at that age. His lower lip trembled as he stared up at her, on the border of tears.

With a sigh, she offered him a hand.

"Is it one of *them?*" the little man asked quietly as he stood.

Kaila shook her head, eager to be on her way. "No, Jacob. It was just Leonardo. He turned coward. Don't let him worry you."

The boy's eyes widened. "He deserted?" he whispered, as though just speaking the word was sacrilege. "But what if he got away?" Tears finally spilt down his cheeks. "He could have *told*."

"But he didn't." She smiled, trying to reassure the child. It was a scary world beyond their walls, but there was no need to scare the boy.

"Thanks to you?"

Kaila, about to turn away, hissed in a breath between her teeth. "And Sareen and Tomas!" she said. "Remember, we're a community. Together, the enemy will never beat us."

The boy drew himself up, puckering his lips in what he likely thought was a look of determination. "Then I'll stop the next one!"

She was about to laugh when she remembered Tomas and his mockery. "Is that so?" she said instead, and then because it felt right, she unclipped the knife from her belt. "Here, take it," she said.

"That way if there are any other evildoers, you'll be here to stop them."

Jacob's eyes were as bright as the twin moons on a clear night as she pressed the dagger into his little hands.

"Really? I can have it?"

Kaila nodded. Jacob's fingers trembled as they closed around the hilt. She watched with satisfaction as his jaw hardened, his lips forming a little grimace. Now when he met her gaze, there was no sign of fear in their amber depths.

"Will you protect our home for me?" she asked.

"I will!"

"Then it's yours."

It would be useless to him—Kaila's father had been teaching her to wield a blade since she was old enough to walk. But courage wasn't always about the truth. Sometimes, it was about the lies you told yourself to confront the darkness. Or at least, that's what Sister Eurador said sometimes.

Besides, she had a spare knife tucked in her boot, if she needed it.

Patting the boy on the shoulder, Kaila rose. Her heart sank as she glanced at the sky. Darkness stretched across the distant mountains, the last glow of the setting sun turning their volcanic peak a violent red. Shadows filled the streets. Sister Eurador would have begun the Trials by now, and Kaila still had to cross half of Elgoss.

A weight settled in her gut as she pushed her way through the crowd. She was going to be late. Very late. Would there be enough time to finish? She had to try!

Emerging from the press of bodies, Kaila was about to start down the street when movement flickered in the corner of her eye. Turning, she found herself staring at an empty alleyway. Kaila frowned, a hint of unease tugging at her stomach. She could have sworn someone had been standing there, cloak swirling in the harsh wind funnelling through the narrow street.

Shaking her head, Kaila focused on the way ahead. The stone walls bore the scars of centuries, chipped and cracked by the harsh mountain climate. The ground sloped away steeply, winding down into the town centre where the black rooftop of the colonnade loomed above the three-storey flats of Elgoss.

There was nobody else around—the crowd had followed Sareen and Tomas uphill towards the mine and their homes.

Kaila hesitated, torn. People did not *run* in Elgoss.

But there was only one day in a young woman's life when she faced the Trials of the Aegis.

One day when she could actually, truly be *late*.

Cursing under her breath, Kaila Dwyn threw caution to the wind and ran.

EMERGING FROM THE SHADOWS WHERE HE'D HIDDEN, THERON studied the girl as she raced down the street and out of sight. She was handy with a knife, he would give her that, keeping her head as she fell and holding onto the weapon until an opening presented itself. Attractive too, in a rustic kind of way. Her raven-black hair had been brushed until it fell straight around her shoulders and there was still life in those emerald eyes. Duty to an ungrateful kingdom hadn't beaten her down yet. And she must have been hiding some muscle beneath her homespun tunic. The fugitive had stood a head taller than her and she'd taken him down by herself.

Poor bloke; he'd never stood a chance. Theron almost felt sorry for the man—if not for the fact he was human and on the other side. Whether he liked it or not, that was how the world worked. Humans and Elysian could never be friends.

The girl obviously understood as much. She was a zealot if ever he'd seen one. Most people were these days, to be fair. The Sisters of the Magisterium were nothing if not efficient, spreading their propaganda far and wide.

The crowd cleared as the guards departed, the prisoner held tightly between them. They were heading in the direction of the mine. Theron muttered a curse. That was inconvenient. He'd been hoping to have the place to himself for the night. He needed time to determine whether he had the right town, or if this was another dead end at the bottom of a long list of dead ends.

Instead, he would have company. Things could get messy. Honestly, how was a thief to make an honest living when the good citizens of Fresia were so eager to stick their noses where they didn't belong?

Ah, well. That's the job.

Detaching himself from the wall, Theron started up the narrow street. With his hood drawn around his face, the few stragglers in the streets didn't glance twice in his direction.

Unlike the girl. She had almost seen him. People didn't *see* Theron; he was a ghost, a shadow. He had perfected the art of going unnoticed long ago. People's eyes slid off the man in the grey trenchcoat. And yet there she'd been, just another peasant girl, staring into the shadows where he hid. There had been something perturbing about those emerald eyes, the way they shimmered in the dying light. Could she be Gifted? No, humans were annoyingly fastidious about weeding out his kind with their Trials.

He shook himself. She was no one, and he had a job to do. If this was really an agimet mine, he was about to be very, *very*, rich. Humanity and his kind had been fighting over the sacred crystals for centuries now. As far as Theron was concerned, they could go on doing so for another millennia, so long as he got his share. Raw crystals, uncut and fresh from the earth, went for a fortune on the black market back in Tah'raus. If the Trickster finally smiled on him tonight, he would be a rich man.

Theron snorted. Fat chance of that. The Elysian god wasn't exactly known for blessing his people with a life of joy and prosperity. He wasn't called the Trickster for nothing. But a good thief made his own luck.

The volcanic peak loomed above as he emerged from the buildings. An opening in the cliffs marked the entrance to the mine. His heart quickened. This was it. The last village on his list. The others had all been a bust—either they no longer existed, or they mined lesser minerals—coal and iron and copper. Theron cared for none of it. He'd borrowed from some powerful people to get the names on his list. If this was another dead end…

He pushed the thought from his mind. He couldn't afford another failure. This was it.

Tonight was the night.

"I'm here!"

Kaila's cry rang from the classroom walls as she burst through the front doors. Inside, a dozen of her classmates looked up from the papers on their desks, eyes wide in surprise. The room itself was small and windowless, cloistered in the basement of the colonnade along with many other of the town's governmental functions. The familiar odour of damp and mould greeted her as she stepped inside.

"Kaila Dwyn. You are late."

Sister Eurador stood at the front of the class, hands clasped before her, hidden in the sleeves of her garnet-red habit. A plain cloth belt cinched her overly long robes at the waist, while around her neck she wore the silver collar of a Sister. At that moment, her brow was creased in an expression usually reserved for troublemakers. Kaila cringed at the glint in her eyes.

"Half your time for the Trial of Knowledge has already passed," the sister continued. "You may wait outside for the Trial of Agimet."

For a second, Kaila stood fixed in place, frozen like a rabbit caught in the light. She struggled to formulate a response. If she didn't complete the first Trial, she could bid farewell to any chance of being a Warden.

"Please!" she managed to gasp. "Let me try! I can do it!"

The sister arched one silver eyebrow. "You believe you can pass with the time remaining?"

Kaila's confidence wilted beneath her iron glare. But she couldn't give up, not like this. She was a devoted citizen of Fresia, uncowed by a thousand years of war with their unrelenting enemy. She could stand up to the likes of Sister Eurador.

"I can do it."

An agonising second passed as Kaila stood alone in the doorway, impaled by the eyes of her classmates. Finally, the sister gave a single nod.

"Well then, are you going to just stand there, or are you going to take your seat?"

"Yes, Sister! Sorry, Sister!"

Kaila didn't need to be asked twice. Grateful, she darted to her desk. The rusty joints of the chair squealed as she sat, drawing glares from her classmates, who had already returned their attention to the exam. On the sister's desk, the candle used to mark the time was already burning low. Struggling not to let panic take hold, Kaila picked up her piece of graphite and set to work.

Question One: Who was T'iana before she became the First Matron?

Well, at least they started with the easy questions. It all went back to the Awakening. A thousand years ago, before humanity had won their freedom. The Elysian had been wily masters, often exploiting the abilities of their slaves to their own benefit. T'iana had been a poorly mechanist, until her master realised her genius and brought her to their hidden city of Iselador. There, she had slaved away on their machines, using her brilliance to make their arcane devices all the more powerful.

Ultimately though, her genius had become their downfall. T'iana had used her position to learn their secrets—and then steal their most precious artifact—a device known as the Aegis. With its power, she created the first Wardens and led humanity in a rebellion against their Elysian rulers. After the uprising, T'iana had ruled for many decades as First Matron, creating the laws and dictates that still governed Fresia to this day. The Aegis had been lost not long after her death, but the Wardens and their sacred armour remained to guard humanity from the enemy.

The next few questions were just as easy. They dealt with the value of societal roles and the hierarchical structures used by the Magisterium to maintain societal coherence. Easy. Her pencil flew across the page, even as her wrist began to ache. But there was still another side of the paper. Glancing at the candle, Kaila bit her lip. *Ten minutes!*

What function do the Daughters of the Magisterium play in Fresian society?

She glanced up at this question, her eyes drawn to another of her classmates. Eliza Wrenn sat primly in her chair, hands folded neatly on her desk. Her exam paper lay before her, filled margin to margin with tidy handwriting. As their eyes met, a smirk touched the other girl's lips.

They were not friends. At least, not now. A long time ago, maybe, before Eliza had apparently decided the daughter of an overseer was not a suitable friend for the daughter of the town's earl. Particularly one with ambitions to be a Daughter of the Magisterium.

Kaila had never understood why someone would *willingly* choose such a fate. Sure, it was an honour to be chosen. The Daughters of the Magisterium embodied the height of sophistication, selected for their beauty and intelligence, and then groomed in the etiquette of the nobility. If Eliza was chosen, she could look forward to a life of privilege, free from the physical toils and strict rations meted out to the rest of society.

But she would also surrender her autonomy. The Magisterium would decide what she ate and when she slept, how she behaved, who she associated with. And when the time came, they would choose her husband—a match decided not by desire, but who the Matron deemed of greatest benefit to the kingdom.

The Daughters were an important part of Fresian history. T'iana herself had created their order from the children of her closest allies, using their marriages to solidify the emerging kingdom. And so it had continued to this day.

It still sounded like *living hell* to Kaila.

She finished scratching the answer and glanced at the candle again. Her heart lurched in her chest. *It's almost gone!* The flame was guttering in the wax pooling at the bottom of the saucer. There wasn't enough time. Her future was slipping away with each drip of wax.

Cursing beneath her breath, she skipped to the last question on the page. If she couldn't finish the whole thing, she could at least answer the hardest question.

What is humanity's most important weapon against the Elysian?

Surprisingly easy. Her hand was beginning to cramp as she lowered it to write about the Wardens, before she paused. The Wardens *were* the obvious answer. Out of the corner of her eye, she could see the flame turning blue. The Wardens and their magical armour were a powerful symbol in the battle against the enemy. Their nobility, their sense of courage and heroism, they were all she ever wanted to be.

But ultimately, they were a tool. An important one, but it was not by their power alone that humanity had found the strength to discard their Elysian masters.

A smile spread across Kaila's lips as she realised what answer Sister Eurador was looking for.

Duty.

It was the central pillar of Fresian society. The war might still rage on, but the frontlines were now miles from their cities, beyond the vast wastelands to the west. How difficult it was to maintain your resolve against an enemy that could no longer be seen. How easy it would have been to forget their peril. Only duty kept them united.

"Pencils down!"

Kaila stifled a moan as she let the graphite fall. She'd left several answers empty, but she'd done all she could…hadn't she? Her hand twitched. She steeled herself to stop from picking up the paper and checking the answers. Sister Eurador was already moving through the classroom to collect the sheets. She grimaced as she took Kaila's—no doubt for the chicken scratches that were her handwriting.

Then returning to her desk, the sister took up her quill and ink pot. The class watched in silence as she picked up the first paper and peered at it through the thick lenses of her spectacles. For a few minutes, the scrape of her quill against paper was the only sound in the silence. Kaila could hardly breathe watching the woman, wondering if she'd done enough, which of the two dozen papers was her own, if her fate had already been decided…

"Psst, how'd you go?"

Kaila almost leapt out of her chair as the boy in the desk alongside hers leaned over and jabbed her in the shoulder with his pencil. It was Caellum, her only real friend in the village. His parents worked the maize field on the western slopes. The rocky soils and harsh mountain climate meant the crop was barely worth the effort, but 'barely' in the winter when the crown stipend ran out could mean the difference between starvation and survival.

The glare Kaila fixed him with had been known to rival Sister Eurador's when it came to silencing dissenters, but Caellum only replied with a wolfish grin. Of course, for him the stakes of this test were far less. Unless he suffered a calamitous failure, he would work the fields alongside his parents, just as his grandparents and great-grandparents had before them. That was the way of things in Fresia, except for those with aspirations to join the Magisterium.

However, by now others were beginning to chatter as well, the tension finally breaking as the pile of marked sheets outnumbered the unmarked. With a heavy exhale, Kaila relented.

"Terribly?" she muttered. "I had, what, twenty minutes?" She shook her head. Nothing more needed to be said.

Caellum snorted. "Even with half the time, I bet you *still* come out on top."

"Eliza seemed pretty confident."

"I think you're mistaking confidence with arrogance," Caellum replied, though he dropped his voice to a whisper as he said it.

Probably wise, given Eliza's parents had the power to make anyone's life in Elgoss miserable. Anyone but Sister Eurador, of course. Hers was the most important job in the village and even the earl couldn't touch her. She had taught three generations now the values of the Fresia and its Magisterium, and while her face was wrinkled and her vision fading, the old woman would teach another generation yet if she had any say in the matter.

"Whatever," Kaila muttered. "Even if I passed, no way my results are enough to get to the third Trial."

There were three Trials, though most only sat the first two. This one had been the easiest. After five years of schooling by the local Sister, every child in the kingdom was expected to have a basic knowledge of their duties and history. Failure meant being denied even their familial labour. Instead of following her father in the mines, for instance, if she failed Kaila would be consigned to cleaning chamber pots and beating laundry against rocks in the river for *at least* the next decade of her miserable life.

As for the third Trial, that was reserved for those the Sisters judged worthy. People with the potential to be Daughters, Sisters or Wardens. The Trial itself was a closely guarded secret. To Kaila's knowledge, in their class only she and Eliza harboured such high ambitions.

"What made you so late anyway?" Caellum asked, interrupting her thoughts.

"Oh!" Kaila's heart pulsed. "I didn't tell you. There was a deserter, from the mine. Leonardo. I stopped him up on High Street."

"*What?*" Caelum's eyes grew wide. Several heads swung around at the shout, but at her desk, the sister didn't look up from the papers. "You're not serious?"

"Yeah," Kaila said quickly. "Tomas and Sareen arrived a little after and took him to the pens."

Caellum nodded, his eyes still wide, but a knock came from the door before he could respond. All eyes in the class swung around, the silence returning. Kaila's scalp prickled. In her anxiety for the third Trial, she'd completely forgotten about the second and most perilous of the three.

The Trial of Agimet.

"Enter," Sister Eurador called.

The door swung open, admitting a pair of unfamiliar soldiers. They wore uniforms of the finest satin, the golden threads embroidering their cuffs marking them as active combatants. Between them they carried a chest of polished lead. Golden wires had been welded into the heavy metal in a pattern of swirls and twists, forming ancient runes against the magics of the enemy.

Kaila shivered, her hands suddenly clammy. Locked inside that box was the most dangerous substance known to humanity—a piece of agimet. But this would be different from the crystals her father and the other miners dug from the caverns beneath their volcanic mount. Those were still inert, useless to the Elysian. To be used in the enemies magics, the crystals had to be charged in a nexus—areas where energy known as *atar* gathered naturally.

There was no nexus in Elgoss, thankfully. The nearest was meant to be several weeks' journey away, somewhere high in the Iron Pinnacles. Even so, as a precaution, none of the agimet crystals they mined were stored in the village.

Kaila had never seen one of the crystals charged. That would change today. In the second Trial, each of the young men and women in this room would hold the glowing crystal, to prove they were not one of the enemy.

It made Kaila's stomach clench thinking about it. But, well, the risk was too great to ignore. Just last year, a girl in an older class had been found out. Because of the Trial, she had been caught before she could do any damage. But there were stories about other villages that were lax in their security. About the monsters that came to live amongst them. They always came to a gruesome end.

The chest made a dull *thud* as it was placed on the table at the front of the room. The soldiers took up positions on either side, standing to attention. Whispers spread around the room as her class-mates exchanged glances.

Then from outside came the heavy *thump* of iron footsteps on stone.

A vice closed around Kaila's chest as a shadow appeared in the doorway. Blue metal shimmered as a tall man wearing a suit of scale armour entered. The armour was a masterpiece of craftsmanship, a thousand steel scales rippling like water as the man moved, catching the flickering light of the oil lanterns.

The Warden had arrived.

His face was hidden behind a full-faced visor, but there was no mistaking the power of this man as he advanced down the rows of desks. Kaila watched him, breath held, hardly able to believe she was in the presence of one of *them*. Finally, after all these years.

Reaching the front of the class, the Warden laid a hand on the chest the soldiers had carried. It seemed to Kaila that he muttered a few words, but whatever he said was lost within the iron helmet. At last, though, he turned to face them.

"Children," he said, his voice soft, almost metallic. "Today you become true citizens of Fresia."

And then a new light appeared. Like six tiny suns, agimet crystals welded into his armour burst to life, casting back the shadows and catching them all in their brilliant glow. In that light, there was nowhere left to run, nowhere to hide. Kaila and the other students could only sit, transfixed, as the dark eyes behind the visor studied them.

Agimet, used not for the vile magics of the enemy, but to guard and protect.

As quickly as it had appeared, the light died away.

"I am called Elric Chain," the Warden continued, "and today you need not fear the enemy and their magics, for I am here to protect you. If any hide themselves amongst your people, it is my job to extinguish their dark magics." With that, he turned to Sister Eurador and nodded. "I am ready. You may proceed."

Stepping out from behind her desk, Sister Eurador produced a key, which she placed into the lock on the chest. There was a sharp *click* as it popped open.

Kaila leaned forward in her chair, curiosity momentarily overcoming caution. This Trial would reveal those twisted souls who put their own desires above the survival of their species. Those who had *bred* with the enemy, who sought to contaminate humanity with their filthy offspring. *That* was the Trial of Agimet. No one of Elysian blood could resist the call of the crystals, the desire to consume the *atar* inside.

And when they did, the traitors would reveal themselves.

There was a deadly silence now as Sister Eurador stepped back from the chest and turned to face the class.

"Well," the old woman said, folding her age-spotted hands in front of her. "Who would like to go first?"

A trickle of cold sweat ran down Kaila's back. She cast her eyes around the room. Were any of her classmates traitors? She had known each of them her entire life, since she'd been a little girl helping carry water from the well to the workers in the mine. She knew their parents, *their grandparents*, some of them. Some worked almost as hard as her father, while others like Eliza preferred to slack.

Not once had she ever suspected any of them of serving the enemy.

But no one had suspected Amelie either. She had been the one caught last year. The other kids said she'd tried to run when they brought out the agimet. But the Trials weren't optional—not since King Francis and Matron Anya had declared them mandatory three hundred years ago. All citizens of Fresia must go through this rite of passage.

So, the soldiers had caught Amelie and dragged her back. Sure enough, the moment she laid her hands on the shining crystal, her eyes had burned with a devil's light.

She had been marked as one of *them.*

The silence stretched out almost a minute before, to no one's particular surprise, Eliza was the first to rise. By virtue of her parents, her loyalty was practically unimpeachable. Yet even Eliza was uncharacteristically nervous as she approached the lead container. A soft glow seeped from inside, flickering on the golden wires on the lid. For a second, she hesitated, staring down at the source of the light. Her face was pale, her usual confidence leached away by the deadly substance that lay before her.

Then Eliza seemed to overcome whatever fear had taken hold of her, and reaching down, she plucked the crystal from the box.

The soldiers were instantly alert, hands going to their weapons, while the Warden only folded his arms and watched.

Kaila barely noticed. The instant the crystal had been drawn from the box, it had captivated her. It was…beautiful. For some reason, that surprised her. She had expected the charged agimet to be an ugly thing, corrupted by *atar* and the enemy's magic. But it was nothing of the sort.

The crystal was uncut, exactly as it had been when the miners had dug it from the fiery chambers beneath the earth. Yet there was a natural kind of beauty to that, the way the murky, uneven surfaces emitted the light within. And that light…it wasn't just a white glow like the polished crystals in the Warden's armour, but violet and sapphire and scarlet and indigo, and a hundred other colours Kaila could not put a name to.

Shivering, she looked away, her mouth dry. It scared her, how beautiful it could be, the forbidden power of *atar*. Yet with that power, a single Elysian could tear each and every one of them in the room to pieces.

No wonder the soldiers were on alert. But that was why the Warden was there, of course. His power would be more than a match for any Elysian.

A minute passed and no light appeared in Eliza's hazel eyes. Finally, the sister nodded, and with a snort, Eliza let the stone fall back into the chest. Grinning, she flicked a lock of blonde hair out of her eyes and strutted back to her desk as though she hadn't been trembling with apprehension a few seconds ago.

"Next."

The silence returned as the students of Elgoss looked at one another, each waiting to see who had the courage to face the crystal next. Kaila waited too, looking from Caellum to Johnny to Lyssa while the minutes stretched out…

In the end, Kaila was as surprised as everyone else when she found herself on her feet. She hadn't realised she was going to do it until everyone's eyes were suddenly watching her. By then it was too late. She *would not* be chased down and forced to do this. She *was not* a traitor—she was a loyal citizen of Fresia. A warrior, and one day soon, a Warden.

Let this be her first step on that journey.

Her heart crashing against her ribs like an enemy battering ram, Kaila took one step, then another towards the light shining from the lead chest. She caught a glimpse of Caellum, smiling and holding up two thumbs, while behind him, Eliza rolled her eyes. The rest of the class was a mess of apprehension and fear.

Drawing in a breath, she continued to the front where the Warden waited. She could feel his iron gaze on her as she approached. Despite her dreams, her nerves came fluttering back. It took an effort to force them down this time. She had nothing to fear from this man. He was here to do his duty, to protect them. He was no threat to a loyal citizen like herself.

Then she was looking down into the lead box, and there it was. That beautiful, deadly stone. It lay on a cushion of velvet, the light of *atar* rippling strangely from the lead and golden wires. As far as humanity knew, agimet was the only substance that could contain its shimmering energy. How beautiful it was.

Beautiful, and deadly, she reminded herself.

"Go ahead, Kaila," Sister Eurador said softly. Her earlier scowl had been replaced by a kindly smile.

A ripple of nervous laughter followed, and Kaila realised she'd just been standing there, staring at the box. Her cheeks flushed, but she forced herself to ignore the mocking of her peers. Eliza and the rest of them be damned, she was Kaila Dwyn and she feared nothing!

Swallowing the last of her nerves, Kaila reached down and grasped the stone.

And everything went a brilliant, fluorescent blue.

3

"Kaila, you can let go now. Kaila, are you okay?"

Kaila blinked. The voice seemed to come from a great distance. Then a firm hand grasped her shoulder and shook her. She gasped, head whipping around. She was still in the classroom. For some reason, that surprised her. The world felt as though it had changed somehow, shifted on its axis, revealing…

…a frown formed on her lips as she looked over the class of familiar faces. It was the same, wasn't it? And yet, she felt as though something new was there, something that shouldn't have been.

Heart still racing, she looked at the hand on her shoulder. It belonged to Sister Eurador. She was staring at Kaila, her face wrinkled with concern. The soldiers remained at their posts, while the Warden lounged behind them, somehow managing to look bored, even in his full suit of armour.

Finally recalling the crystal, Kaila's head whipped down. It lay in her hand, still dancing with the unnatural glow of *atar*.

"I felt…" she trailed off.

"You had a panic attack, dear."

"What…"

The sister offered a kindly smile. "It happens sometimes."

Heat spread to Kaila's cheeks. At the back of the classroom, someone sniggered. Kaila could have *sworn* it was Eliza. Trembling, she let the cursed crystal fall into the chest and practically ran back to her desk. As she passed Caelum, he gave her a big thumbs up.

"Well done!" he said. Grinning, he levered himself out of the chair. "Guess it's my turn."

Kaila nodded absently, still too thunderstruck for a response. Caelum would be fine. Now the two girls had passed, the other students were starting to relax and chatter amongst themselves again. Slumping into her chair, Kaila tried to keep the disappointment from her face. Had that really just happened? *And in front of the Warden!*

"So much for becoming a Warden," a spiteful voice whispered from behind her. Eliza. "No one's going to want a warrior who freezes at the sight of agimet."

The hairs on Kaila's scalp prickled. She longed to swing on the girl and show her *exactly* what she could offer the Wardens—starting and ending with the point of the knife in her boot. But the words wouldn't come. Because Eliza was right. If that had really been a panic attack, then Kaila *didn't* deserve to be a Warden. On the battlefield, cowards were a liability to everyone around them. Squeezing her eyes shut, she struggled to keep the tears from flowing.

"And with a face like that, you *know* the Daughters will never want you," Eliza's snide comments continued. "Maybe the Sisters will take you. Lock you in one of their libraries for a decade or two —" She broke off so suddenly that Kaila lifted her head, wondering if Sister Eurador had noticed the girl and decided to intervene.

Instead, she saw Caellum standing where she had been moments ago, the agimet crystal clutched tightly in his fist.

And his eyes were glowing.

For one innocent second—perhaps the last innocent moment of her life—Kaila couldn't comprehend what she was seeing. Her mind tried to understand it, to explain what could not be explained. It must be a trick of the light, the lanterns reflecting in his eyes. Or maybe it was the crystal itself. Agimet was a treacherous material. And it was clearly acting strangely, burning brilliantly one second, dying the next to barely a spark. It hadn't done that with the others. Yes, that was it. Something was wrong with the crystal.

It couldn't be what it looked like. Not Caellum. Not her friend.

Then Kaila met Caellum's eyes and she saw the truth. The terror, the knowledge of what was happening. It shone as brightly as the *atar* in his brilliant blue eyes.

"Kaila…" In the silence of the classroom, he whispered her name, almost like a prayer.

Then the soldiers finally sprang into action. The first slammed into Caellum from behind; the second went for the agimet.

Light blazed, blinding in the previous gloom.

A pair of *thuds* followed as, blinking the stars from her eyes, Kaila saw the soldiers hit the walls. She stared, unable to move, as they slumped to the ground. She waited for them to get back up, but neither so much as twitched. With growing horror, her gaze slid back to Caellum.

He stared back at her with those terrible, burning eyes. He was trembling, clutching at the crystal in his hand like his life depended on it. She watched, detached, as a tear ran down his cheek.

He's Elysian.

The truth struck like an arrow through her heart. Her best friend was a half-breed monster, a traitor sent to infiltrate their town, to burrow his way into their hearts and minds. How could she have missed it? She had known Caellum practically her entire life, ever since their first meeting as five-year-olds when he'd come out to sweep the section of street shared by their flats. And all along he had been a traitor, hiding this unnatural power. Had he been waiting, biding his time until he got access to the mines? Was that why he'd befriended her? To get to her father? What would have happened if he'd gotten into the tunnels…

"Kaila…" He spoke her name again. "Kaila, I swear…" He took a step towards her and she flinched.

Her gaze darted to the soldiers. She expected them to get back up and draw their weapons, but they still hadn't moved. In horror, she saw that one's neck had twisted at a horrible angle. And the other…blood had appeared in a pool beneath him.

A rock settled in her stomach. Caellum had killed them both with a thought.

"Stay away," she croaked. The sound of movement came from all around as her classmates scrambled for safety.

"Kaila," Caellum rasped. Tears streaked his cheeks as he darted towards her, hand outstretched, *atar* still burning in his eyes. "Kaila, please, it's me…"

She reacted instinctively. This was no longer her friend, but a monster from the stories her father had told her as a child. Her hand went to her boot, coming up with the knife concealed there. It glinted in the flickering light of the crystal as she pointed it at Caellum. There were no words. She couldn't find them. But he froze, hands extended. There was a moment where they watched each other, where she thought he would try to span the gap between them…

…and then, finally, the Warden appeared.

He emerged from the shadows behind Caellum, his armour shining, hand extended. Liquid metal sprang from his palm, solidifying into a sword as black as the midnight sky. With a roar, he charged.

The light in Caellum's eyes flashed again, just as it had with the soldiers. Kaila found her voice and cried out a warning, but there was no need.

The crystals in the Warden's chest plate blazed.

And the black sword met flesh.

A scream ripped from Kaila's lips. The terrible blade had run her friend through, tearing into his back and emerging from his chest. Their eyes met as Caellum staggered, and his lips moved as though to speak her name again. But this time, all that emerged was a final exhalation as the light that had filled his eyes flickered out.

His knees gave out as the Warden withdrew his blade, sending him toppling to the ground. He struck with a *thud,* the deadly crystal slipping from his fingers and tumbling across the floor. It came to a rest at Kaila's feet. She barely noticed. Her whole being was with Caellum, her only friend in the entire world. She watched as the last glint of life faded from his eyes.

And then he was gone.

"Well," the Warden, Elric Chain, grunted. "Least there was a bit of excitement after all." He glanced at the fallen soldiers as he lowered his blade. The weapon shone, becoming liquid metal once more before vanishing back into his flesh. "Shame about the lads."

He looked at her, as though expecting a reply. But all Kaila could do was stare at the body on the floor, the empty thing that had been her friend. She heard him speak again, then Sister Eurador's voice, but the words didn't make it through the ringing in her ears. Her breath came in rapid gasps and stars danced in her eyes. There was a shaking in her legs she couldn't control.

The agimet lay at her feet. Shuddering, she took a quick step back and collided with her desk. Relieved to find something solid, she sank into her chair, not caring what anyone thought now. The knife was still in her hand. She tried to sheath it, but her hands were shaking too much. In the end, she slammed it down on the desk, frustration and…some other emotion bubbling in her chest.

It had been *Caellum.* She felt the treacherous tears threatening her eyes. There was an ache inside her, like she'd been caught by a blow to the solar plexus. *It hurt.*

Distantly, she heard others enter the classroom and carry out the bodies. Words were spoken, questions asked, and eventually, the other students returned to their chairs. Soon enough, the Trial resumed. It was too important to stop. Caellum had proved that much. Kaila distantly sensed her classmates walking forward for their turn with the agimet. She hardly noticed. Her eyes were fixed to the desk, the same one she had sat at every afternoon for the last five years. In the corner was a little pair of stick figures, a boy and a girl, etched into the soft wood. Caellum had carved it their first year in class.

She screwed her eyes closed, refusing to let the tears fall. He had betrayed her, betrayed them all. She wouldn't cry for a traitor. But even as she screamed the thought, she saw again the last look in the eyes of the boy who had been her friend. Terror, and then pain, before he slowly faded away.

What would happen now? His parents would be questioned. Mary and Brian, the lovely couple who lived in the flats across from the unit Kaila shared with her father. They often had her over for maize cookies and tea. Her lip quivered. Was one of them a traitor too?

"Kaila?"

Her head jerked up and she was surprised to find the classroom was almost empty. Only Eliza and Sister Eurador remained. Even the Warden had gone, along with the chest. The other students had completed their Trial of Agimet without incident. Which meant…

"Did I pass?" she rasped, clinging to something, *anything* but the thought of Caellum lying on the floor.

There were only two reasons she would be kept behind. Either she had passed and was about to sit the Third Trial, or she had failed so horribly that Eurador would consign her to latrine duty for the next decade. The way she felt right then, Kaila wasn't sure she cared which.

The sister stared down her nose at Kaila. "A most unusual final essay," she muttered. "I would have thought a potential Warden would have considered their importance to our kingdom."

No, no. Surely, she hadn't overthought that final question. It couldn't have been that simple, could it?

"I did!" she squawked, "but…but the Wardens…they're so few, and without fresh agimet, and food and water and supplies—" she broke off, realising she was ranting. Gathering her courage, she looked the sister in the eye. "I stand by what I wrote, Sister."

Eurador's lips tightened into a thin line. "Good. Because against all odds, you passed." She grunted. "*Just.*" Her eyes flicked to Eliza. "Everyone else in the class wrote about the Wardens."

Relief. Kaila could hardly believe it. She slumped against her desk, letting out a long sigh as the weight of potential failure fell away. *She had done it!* Tears threatened again, though this time of joy. She blinked rapidly, glad for the dim light inside the classroom.

"Thank you, Sister," Kaila said, her manners reasserting themselves. "Does this…does this mean I can sit the Third Trial?"

Sister Eurador grimaced. "After your Trial of Agimet, I feared you did not have the nerve to be a Warden. But…when Caellum revealed himself, you alone of the students stood against him, even though he was your friend." She turned to Eliza. "It is fortunate a Daughter does not require bravery in the fulfilment of her duties."

Eliza turned down her lip, but otherwise stood resolute in the face of the sister's scorn. After a moment, the old woman snorted.

"Regardless, Kaila, I would understand if you no longer wish to attempt the last Trial, after what happened with Caellum."

"No!" Kaila exclaimed. Of all the foul things to happen this day, she couldn't let her dream escape as well. She rose on unsteady feet, lifting her chin in defiance. "I'm ready. Let me try."

Behind the sister, Eliza rolled her eyes. The girl stood with her arms crossed, the same smug smile on her lips that she'd worn for most of the past ten years—ever since she'd decided hanging out with someone of Kaila's social status was beneath her.

Sister Eurador saw none of this, of course. Instead, she removed a ring from her finger. The girls leaned closer as she held it out for them. The golden band held a tiny crystal. Kaila frowned. Little was known about this Trial—afterwards, they would be sworn to silence.

"The crystal is agimet," the sister said calmly.

The breath caught in Kaila's throat and she only just caught herself before she flinched. *Agimet?* What was Sister Eurador doing with one of the cursed crystals? There was no hint of *atar* about the ring, thankfully, but even so…

"Take it," Sister Eurador said, offering it to Eliza.

The other girl looked as confused as Kaila as she accepted the ring. What kind of test was this? As perilous as agimet crystals were, they were useless without *atar*. And besides, both of them had already passed the Trial of Agimet.

"What now?" Eliza asked.

"Do you feel anything?" Sister Eurador questioned, only continuing when Eliza shook her head. "Look deeper. Agimet is a vessel, but *atar* is all around us."

Kaila frowned. "I thought *atar* was only found close to a nexus."

"Nexus points are where its concentration is greatest," the sister replied, turning her amber eyes on Kaila. "but even in a place like Elgoss, there is energy all around us. Not enough to power the enemy's infernal magics, but enough for our purpose today."

"And what exactly does any of this have to do with *me?*" Eliza asked primly.

"You feel nothing?" the sister pressed. "No pool of energy... beyond the crystal?"

Eliza wrinkled her nose and glared at the shard like it had spilt wine on her favourite dress, but finally, she let out a sigh. "Nothing," she admitted. "What...what does this mean?"

It surprised Kaila to hear the sharpness in her rival's voice. She hadn't seen a hint of self-doubt in her former friend since Eliza had introduced Kaila and Caellum to her parents. And that *must* have been a disaster, since shortly afterwards, Eliza had stopped spending time around them.

"It means," Sister Eurador said, plucking the shard from Eliza's palm, "that along with your *above average* written results, you have passed your Trials."

"What?" Eliza stared at the sister in obvious confusion. "Then what was the point of all that?"

The old woman offered a wrinkled smile. "That answer, I am afraid, will have to wait until you reach the capital and are inducted as a Daughter," she said. "Now, why don't you go carry the good news to your parents? I understand they have harboured hopes for some years that you would earn this honour."

Still looking bemused, Eliza rose and left the room, leaving Kaila alone with the old woman.

"Before we begin, Kaila," Eurador said quietly, "I wanted to say how proud of you I am." Kaila's head jerked up at the praise, but her teacher went on. "You did not hesitate when Caellum revealed what he truly was. I could count on one hand the students who have passed through this class that would have done the same. You are a true patriot."

Kaila sat a little straighter, and some of the empty feeling in her chest seemed to fade.

"I believe with all my heart you would make a fine Warden," the sister continued. "I understand your father has even invested considerable time preparing you for the challenges of their order." She drew a breath, and in that pause, Kaila sensed there was a *but* coming. "But this final Trial will be far more arduous for you than it was for Eliza."

"What do you mean?"

Eurador pursed her lips. "A Warden's armour is a heavy burden. You saw how Elric Chain was able to subdue the Elysian with its power. But he could only do so because of a rare ability possessed only by a few amongst us."

"What?" Kaila breathed. She had never heard of this.

The sister nodded. "The ability to charge agimet without the need for a nexus." She held out the ring for Kaila. "To pass, Kaila, you must demonstrate you possess this power."

Kaila swallowed, her gaze drawn inexorably to the ring resting in the sister's palm. So this was it. The secret Trial of the Warden. All of her dreams, everything she had spent her life working towards, it all came down to whether she could use the enemy's crystals against them. To her shame, her hand trembled as she reached for the agimet. Eurador said nothing, though, only watched Kaila through her overly large spectacles.

This time there was no darkness as her fingers closed around the crystal, much to her relief. The agimet seemed strangely empty as it settled in her palm, as if it was incomplete without the beautiful, perilous light of *atar*. Hopefully, she could fix it. *Would* fix it. Everything else had gone wrong today, but not this.

Please, in the name of the First Matron, let me pass this test.

Kaila focused on the sliver of crystal, lingering on what Eurador had said. *Atar*—the energy of the world—was all around them. Even in a place like Elgoss. Not concentrated like a nexus, but it was here. If only she understood *how* the crystals drew on that energy, maybe she could understand her part in the process.

She dug deeper into the mystery. Agimet charged naturally when in the area of a nexus. She didn't know many of the details, but she knew that *didn't* happen with the crystals they mined in Elgoss. They emerged from the ground inert. So the rate of charge was dependent on concentration. When water diffused over a permeable barrier, the greater the difference in concentration, the more rapid the rate of flow. But she couldn't change the concentration of ambient *atar* in Elgoss.

Think, Kaila, think!

She could sense the sister standing over her. Even with her eyes closed, Kaila could imagine the furrows deepening in the old woman's brow as the minutes ticked passed.

How to speed up the process? Somehow, *she* was important. Like…*a catalyst!* Yes, that had to be it. Diffusion could still take place at lower gradients with a catalyst. Could Wardens act as some kind of conduit for *atar?*

It was all she had. Kaila drew in a breath, focusing on the passage of air through her lungs, on her sense of self, then turned her inner gaze to the agimet. It was cold in her hands, lifeless. *Wrong.* The other crystal hadn't been warm, but it had also not been cold. It had felt *full*, as though the *atar* had its own weight. A tiny, secret piece of her longed to fix this stone—to restore it to life. Maybe a little piece of her would be enough?

Gritting her teeth, Kaila focused on her own body. Her anxious heart pounded hard in her chest, the blood surging through her veins. There was an ache in the base of her skull and a sharp pain in her shoulder from where Leonardo had struck her. Her feet were swollen in her heavy boots, and she knew her hair was slick with sweat and dirt from this terrible day. Worse, her allocated slot at the bathhouse wasn't for another two days.

This was her, Kaila Dwyn. A beating heart and swelling lungs, the pulsing of muscles and murmur of distant thoughts. Human, all of her. And from all of her, she took a little piece, a fragment of all she was, and channelled it into the crystal in her hands—

Everything went dark.

Kaila awoke on the floor with no idea how much time had passed—only that the ceiling was spinning and there was a banging in her head like she'd been run over by the daily agimet carriage and its team of four horses. A wizened face was staring down at her, concern etched into her ancient wrinkles.

"Kaila Dwyn, are you okay?"

It took several moments for Kaila's memory of *why* she was there to return.

"Did it work?" she croaked, surprised to find even her jaw aching.

The sister's lips creased into a frown. "Sit up," she said, pointedly ignoring the question.

Kaila obeyed and immediately regretted it. She felt as though someone had stabbed a thousand tiny needles into her flesh. Even her feet prickled with a deadening sensation of icy flame. She'd never experienced anything like it.

But a Warden needed to be made of tougher stuff, so gritting her teeth, Kaila kept the pain from her face—even as sunbursts filled her vision and she clung to consciousness.

When the dizziness finally cleared, she found herself sitting on the floor of the classroom. Sister Eurador sat across from her, a grim look on her face. With reluctance, Kaila turned her gaze to the ring, which the sister must have reclaimed when Kaila had fainted.

The crystal was empty.

If the pain had been bad before, now it became a red-hot poker taken from the coal stove and shoved through her gut. She stared at the crystal in despair. How could she have failed? She'd given everything she had, and *something* had happened. Why else was she in so much pain?

"I'm sorry, Kaila…"

"Let me try again," she interrupted. An unthinkable act of disrespect—but what did she have to lose at this point?

"That's…" Concern was etched across the sister's face. "Kaila, I don't know what that was, but I don't think you should."

"Please, Sister."

Eurador frowned, but finally she relented, handing over the ring. Kaila felt such a rush of appreciation that the sunbursts momentarily returned. As they faded, she reached out with trembling fingers to accept the precious ring.

The second the crystal touched her palm, she sensed it had changed. The agimet was no longer lifeless—not completely. Trembling, terrified, she held it up to her eyes, seeking some glint of *atar*.

There!

A tiny spark, deep within. Not enough to light up the many faces of the agimet, but it *was* there.

"Sister!" she exclaimed, offering the crystal back to Eurador. "It worked, see?"

The sister took it with a frown. A minute ticked by as she studied it, lips pursed, brow wrinkled, until finally she shook her head.

"I'm sorry, Kaila, it's a trick of the light. I've witnessed the anointing of a new Warden. There is no doubt when one possesses the talent. The agimet would glow as brightly as the one from your Trial."

Kaila's budding hope plunged into the void that had opened with Caellum's betrayal. "But…" She *knew* the crystal had changed. It was *right there!* "Maybe I just need practice?"

The sister let out a sigh, and her withered fingers closed around the ring. "No, Kaila. I'm sorry. I know what this meant to you. But sometimes we must sacrifice our dreams for the greater good."

To her great shame, Kaila couldn't keep the tears from falling this time. "I understand." Hanging her head, she rose on unsteady feet. "Thank you for this opportunity."

Sister Eurador nodded. "You are a good girl, Kaila. Intelligent. You understand our history and our duties to the Magisterium." She drew in a breath. "I know you have trained with your father in preparation for a more…active role in the war, but I believe your perseverance and devotion would be a great asset amongst the Sisters."

Goosebumps raised hackles on Kaila's neck, and she heard again Eliza's taunt from earlier that day.

Maybe the Sisters will take you. Lock you in one of their libraries for a decade or two…

She swallowed. The Sisters carried their knowledge to every corner of the kingdom, bringing the teachings of the First Matron to rich and poor alike. The invitation was an honour, to dedicate her life as Sister Eurador had done to the propagation of knowledge…

…but a Sister must forsake her home and family to spend years —if not decades—studying in the capital. And even after that, she would be sent wherever her talents were most needed. She might never see her father and Elgoss again. To say nothing of her dream of serving on the frontlines.

Instead, she would fight a different kind of war. Against ignorance and division, misinformation and sacrilege. A war, of that there was no doubt, but was that *all* she could offer her kingdom? Would it be enough?

"Thank you, Sister," she croaked at last. "I will think on it,"

"Think quickly, child," Eurador said, not unkindly. "Tomorrow at noon, Eliza's carriage will leave for the capital. It would be best if you are with her, lest this opportunity pass you by."

Kaila did her best not to cringe at the mention of her former friend. The thought of facing Eliza, the condescending smirk on her lips when she learnt that Kaila would indeed become a Sister…

"I will speak with my father," was all Kaila could manage before she fled the classroom.

4

Kaila gazed over the flattop roofs of her village, listening as the sounds of men and women retiring to their beds carried from below. Darkness had crept over her little town as she had sat her Trials, and now the stars stretched above, a thousand tiny pinpricks in the sky. The silver sliver of the first moon was just beginning to reveal itself, while the second would remain hidden for another few days before joining its twin in the sky.

There was still no sign of her father. He worked longer hours than anyone else, always the first to arrive at the mine to unlock the great steel gates, and the last to leave after seeing everyone safely out of the tunnels. She was proud of him for that, for the solemn diligence with which he did his duty.

Tonight, though, she had hoped he would return early. The sadness in her soul swelled as she watched the narrow streets, straining to pluck detail from shadow, to preserve Elgoss in her memories as it was this day.

Is this the last time I will see the sun set over my home?

Sister Eurador's offer hung over her head like a guillotine, set to cut the last strings of hope for a lost dream.

You will never be a Warden.

She closed her eyes, feeling the heat of tears threatening. Her heart battled against it, but this was a truth she must accept. Because she had a decision to make; stay in Elgoss and work in the mines alongside her father, or travel to Tah'raus and accept the position of Sister.

Most wouldn't have even hesitated. Sisterhood was a chance for a better life, if not of luxury, of comfort at least. There would be no heavy labour or winters spent half-freezing, half-starving. And she would be provided with the means to spread knowledge across the kingdom. Any loyal citizen of Fresia would have leapt at the chance.

All Kaila needed to do was give up on her dreams.

Despite the darkness, she could sense the shadow of the colonnade looming above the other buildings in Elgoss. Their town was an old one. Some of the flats like the one she and her father occupied dated back almost to the Awakening. But the colonnade was different. It had been built only fifty years ago, fabricated from a radical new procedure that took sand and turned it into a material almost as hard as granite. Concrete, they called it. It had none of the imposing beauty of granite and marble, but it was revolutionising the kingdom, allowing Fresia to build faster and higher than anyone could have imagined just a hundred years before.

So the Magisterium had built a colonnade in every Fresian settlement, however large or small. These became places for the children to gather for their classes, and where every seventh day people queued to receive their stipend of food and coal. They even housed the courts, so the local Sisters could sit in judgement of those who contravened the laws of their land.

In Tah'raus was the greatest of all these houses. The Sanctum it was called. It was said to be so large as to contain all of Elgoss and still have space for three more of their humble town. If she travelled to the capital, that would be her home for the next decade, her entire life reduced to a concrete labyrinth of endless grey corridors.

A cold breeze blew across the rooftop. A shiver ran down Kaila's spine and she hugged her knees to her chest. Temperatures changed quickly in the Iron Pinnacles. Normally when she came up here to the roof, it was to train with her father. Then she was never cold—even on the coldest winter nights, when the snow drifts piled high against the town walls and the cold seeped into your bones, they could always come up here to escape the chill.

A smile touched her lips as she recalled the first time her father had brought her here. She had been a toddler, barely out of nappies, and had stumbled upon a secret compartment behind their coal stove. Inside was an old sword. Any blade longer than a hunting knife was forbidden in the settlements, but she hadn't known that at the time. Thinking she had discovered a lost treasure, she'd taken it proudly to her father.

He'd smiled and taken it from the child, returning it to its place behind the oven before sitting her on his lap and telling her of his time in the army, of standing side by side with his fellow men and women against their unyielding enemy, and of Wardens in shining armour…

From that moment, the young Kaila had known what she wanted for herself. The world was a cruel place, but those with a noble heart could still make a difference. So in the rare times when she found herself without chores, she had taken to removing the blade from its hiding place. The sword itself was nothing special, an old iron thing, pitted with dents and scratches from a decade of use. But holding it, Kaila had imagined herself a hero like her father and mother before her.

Eventually, her father had discovered her. But rather than admonishing Kaila, he had only sighed and told her if she wished to be a soldier, she should at least learn to fight properly. And so had begun their nightly climb to the rooftop and the long hours of training.

Kaila clenched her fists, but there was no release for her anger tonight, nothing to lash out at. There wasn't even the shoulder of her best friend to cry on. All she could do was sit with the emotion, with the disappointment and the rage and the *hurt* of this terrible day.

Until, from somewhere below, came a squeal of hinges. Letting out a sigh, Kaila rose from the ledge. She knew that door—her father was home. A fresh weight settled on her shoulders. He had been almost as excited as Kaila that morning, tense with hope and expectation. She dreaded seeing the disappointment in his eyes, but this wasn't something she could avoid. There was a decision she must make, one that would decide the rest of her life.

Levering herself over the side, she felt with the toe of her boot for the first hold. The climb had been difficult when they'd first done it all those years ago. She'd needed a rope and more than a little help from her father. Nowadays, she managed it easily, her calloused fingers able to find even the smallest of holds between the ancient bricks. Within minutes, she had descended the two storeys to their flat on the first floor and was slipping through the window to find her father.

———

"You have to accept."

Of all the things her father might have said, those were the last words Kaila had been expecting.

"What?" she whispered, then with more force than she intended. *"How can you say that?"*

Her father sat across the table from her, his thick lips drawn in a line, wiry beard giving him the look more of a bear than a human. He was by far the largest man in the village, with massive arms, barrel chest and a face like someone had dropped a boulder on it when he was a boy. She hadn't inherited his size—or more fortunately, his looks—but she'd always been proud of his strength.

Just now, though, he was looking at her with the strangest look in his eyes. Earlier, the village baker had given her a little package as she'd passed on her way home and thanked her for her bravery, stopping the runaway. It had contained a few biscuits and a scone— which her father's massive fingers were slowly tearing into shreds. The rest remained untouched in the package between them.

"Kaila, you're a brave soul. You have your mother's fire. But don't you see, this is your chance to be something more! To get out of Elgoss and build a real life for yourself."

Kaila couldn't believe what she was hearing. "More than *what?* A miner? Dad, what you and the others do is *important.* You taught me that, how each of us has a part to play in the war."

"Ay," he grunted, "but that doesn't mean I want it for you, Kaila. Doesn't mean I want you down there in the dark with me."

"I've been down there plenty of times!"

Since she'd been old enough to carry water, she had ventured into the depths, bringing the men refreshment and later helping to carry waste rock to the surface.

"Not the deep tunnels, Kaila."

Kaila opened her mouth, ready with an argument, when she noticed her father's face. There was something in his tone, in the way his eyes grew distant and his lips twisted downwards.

"We lost Ralph today," he said at last.

Kaila's heart stilled. "What?" Ralph was the son of one of the older miners, barely older than her. He'd joined his father in the mine last year after passing his Trials.

Her father's eyes were locked to the table, as though there was something of great interest in the hardened grains of the wood. "After Leonardo ran…" he said softly. "I was going to lead the shift, but Ralph volunteered instead." He drew a deep, shuddering breath. "There was gas, the type you don't smell, that doesn't give you any warning. One moment the lads were drilling, the next…" he trailed off with a shrug. "Ralph was in the lead. He must have sensed something was wrong, cause he yelled a warning. Gave the others time to go back. But he couldn't follow. Sid tried to go back for him, but he said it was like someone was hammering nails into his skull. Almost didn't make it out himself."

Her father fell silent, eyes on the table. Kaila clenched her fists, mouth suddenly dry.

"Why are you telling me this?" The words came out as an accusation.

"Because you need to know!" Gideon all but bellowed. "You need to understand why grown men would rather cut and run than face those depths!"

"Because they're cowards!" she screamed back, the emotions she'd been bottling all day bursting forth.

Her father's dark eyes glowered at her across the table. "We all have our limits," he said, suddenly quiet again. "I have seen men torn apart on the battlefield, seen soldiers under the influence of the enemy walk off cliffs or into the flames and die horribly. But when we recovered Ralph's body, his eyes had boiled from his face. And so there are times, Kaila, when even I fear to walk into the darkness." He drew in a shuddering breath. "But do you know what gives me the courage to continue?"

"Duty?" she spat. "Responsibility to your people."

"You."

She had already opened her mouth to snarl at him, but found her words lost at his response. A strange sensation spread through her stomach, like a bubbling, burning warmth that pushed away the anger and emptiness that had been growing there. Wetness touched her cheek.

"It's the only way I can face it, some days," her father continued. "Knowing I do it for you. So you can have a chance at something better. And if that can't be a Warden." Kaila was horrified to see tears on her father's face. "To be a Sister?" He shook his head. "Sisters never go hungry or run short of coal in the depths of winter. They don't have to risk their lives in the mines or the frontlines or even out in the fields."

"Dad…" Kaila's voice broke and for a moment she couldn't say anything. She reached out and squeezed his hand.

Her hand was engulfed as he returned the gesture. "Would it really be so bad?"

"I might never see you again."

"Even so, it would be better, knowing you were out there somewhere, safe."

Kaila blinked back the tears. "But, Dad," she whispered, her turn to glue her eyes to the table. "What if I don't *want* to be safe? What if I want to *fight*?"

"Then fight with your mind. Accept the sister's offer. Use what the First Matron granted you. Who knows? Maybe amidst all those old books and lessons, you'll find a way to finally defeat the enemy. And even if you don't…at least I will not have to bury my own daughter one day."

The words settled in Kaila's gut like a lead weight. She looked across the table at the man who had protected and mentored her all her life. His hand was warm around her own, comforting, and yet those words…

"That's not what I want."

She rose suddenly to her feet, a quiet fury taking over. She slammed a fist down on the table, causing the baker's package, still sitting between them, to leap sideways.

"Kaila, you don't understand…" her father started, but she was done listening.

"No," she hissed. "It's *you* who doesn't understand." She clenched her fists, thinking of his words, how *cowardly* they were. Looking at the man seated across from her, she almost couldn't recognise him. "Dad, how could I *ever* be happy when I know others are out there suffering, *dying* so that I can sit tucked safely away in some library? How can I live a life of security when everyone I know is battling to keep our species alive?"

Her father sat quietly, staring up at her, before he too rose. "Because it *is* your duty," he rumbled. "That's what the Sisters preach, is it not? Of service to a greater good. Like it or not, Kaila Dwyn, in the mines you would just be another body, another pair of hands. But as a Sister, you could do more good in a single year than you could in a lifetime here in Elgoss."

His words, so close to her own thoughts, struck Kaila like an arrow to the chest. She stood there shuddering, jaw clenched so hard she heard her teeth creaking. There was a shrieking in her ears, a need to scream that he was wrong, that she *could* help, that she was needed…

…but the repudiation would not come. The truth, like shards of glass, had cut through her dreams, leaving the tattered remnants to slip through her fingers.

She couldn't be a Warden. But she could still make a difference. However she might loathe to accept it.

"I hate you," she whispered.

She saw the effect those words had on her father. A little piece of her exulted in the pain that appeared in his eyes. *Good*, it whispered. He *should* hurt, like she was hurting. Even if she didn't mean it. Even if she knew he was only trying to do what was best for her. In that moment, the only thing that mattered was getting even.

So, casting one final glare at her father, she turned and stomped across the little flat they shared and threw herself onto the cot that served as her bed. Her outburst might have been more effective if there'd been a door for her to slam. Kaila made do with pulling the coarse woollen blankets over her head. She knew it was juvenile. She didn't care.

Tomorrow, she would accept Eurador's offer and journey to Tah'raus to become a Sister. She would do her duty like a good citizen of Fresia.

Tonight, though, she would relish one final day without responsibility.

LANTERNS GLOWED IN THE ENTRANCE TO THE MINE. THERON couldn't resist a chuckle. This place was well hidden and well protected. *Too well protected.* The quiet had made the villagers complacent. There were no guards on the entrance—only a heavy steel door he'd watched the overseer lock himself. Someone intent on taking the mine wouldn't even need magic—any thief worth his picks could crack an unprotected lock.

Hidden in a patch of nearby shrubbery, Theron didn't have any lockpicks himself, but subtlety wasn't exactly his speciality.

What he *did* have was magic.

The last workers had taken their time clearing out, but now all he had to do was break down the door without sounding the alarm, and he would have all night to explore the mine—and hopefully, discover the precious crystals he needed to make his fortune.

His heart quickened. He had a few pieces of agimet to work his magic, but they were tiny, pebbles concealed about his person. The largest was no larger than his thumb—and even that had cost him a safe full of gold. It hadn't been *his* safe, but regardless, the stuff was *expensive.*

Anything larger cost a king's ransom—so long as the humans hadn't tainted it. Cutting and polishing the crystals, as humans were like to do, changed their nature. Even breaking them altered their power, making them unusable to anyone with the Gift. More than one of his kind had burned up their insides using cut agimet.

But none of that would be a problem if this was the right place. Though after passing through the village, Theron couldn't suppress a touch of doubt. He hadn't seen a single crystal anywhere in Elgoss, not even for light. It begged the question—if this was really an agimet mine, where were all the crystals they were digging from the ground?

Gritting his teeth, Theron forced the doubt from his mind. This was the place, he felt it in his gut. He would make his fortune. But first, he had to focus. An hour had passed since the overseer's departure. He wasn't coming back. Time to make his move.

Rising from the vegetation, Theron slipped through the shadows towards the iron doors. A cautious man might have waited for the lanterns in the town below to be shuttered and the villagers to retire to their beds. But Theron was not a cautious man.

Stones crunched beneath his boots as he climbed the path. If someone had been watching, they would have seen a stranger known to no one in the village. A shadow. A ghost. But the day had been a long one for the citizens of Elgoss, and on this night all were already in their homes, preparing for the morrow.

And even if Theron had been seen, what could a few humans do to stop one of his kind anyway?

As he approached the bolted doors, Theron slipped a hand into his pocket, seeking his largest piece of agimet. A sensation not unlike pins and needles tickled his palm as he closed his fingers around the crystal. It brought a smile to his lips. Some might have described it as unpleasant, like trying to grasp a rosebush by the thorns.

Those people had never experienced what came next. They couldn't do what Theron could do.

A new light appeared in the night. Not the flickering of a lantern or even the distant glimmer of the rising moon, but a thousand tiny stars, like someone had reached into the heavens and brought the night's sky to Elgoss. *Soullights.* The building blocks of the world. They blazed in every pebble, every boulder and tree, in the dogs and the horses, even the great inventions humanity used to make their living and their warring easier. There was even a *soullight* inside every man and woman and child in the village below.

Most importantly, there was a spark inside the door to the mine.

Like a cat with a mouse in its claws, Theron grasped it with his power.

And with a soft click, then the whisper of old hinges, the doors swung open before him.

5

Kaila woke to a pounding headache and an empty room. She might not understand what she'd done with the agimet yesterday, or how she'd failed Sister Eurador's test, but *something* had clearly happened with that damned crystal. Otherwise, she wouldn't have been this sore.

Well, if this was the kind of pain Wardens had to suffer, maybe she was better off after all. She snorted and levered her legs over the side of the bed, then moaned as the pain redoubled. It felt like someone had splintered her skull with a wood axe. Rubbing at her temples with her knuckles, it was a few minutes more before she gathered the strength to stand.

There was no sign of her father, but a pot of porridge had been left on the coal range. It was still hot to the touch, warmed by the dying coals inside the stove. She must have been really out of it to have slept through his cooking—she could see the burnt flecks amidst the curds. Still, citizens of Fresia didn't make a habit of wasting perfectly good food, to say nothing of the coal. Only three pieces remained in the basket beside the stove, and the jar of oats on the shelf was almost empty. There wasn't much else in the way of food either. She muttered a curse. They wouldn't receive their next rations for four days and the nights were already growing cool. They would have to go cold for at least one of them.

Or rather, her father would.

Her stomach gave a little rumble, so she took up the pot and a spoon and carried them to the table to break her fast. The porridge had little flavour, not even of salt, but the oats were nutritious and a growing young woman needed her strength.

There was still no sign of her father when she finished. Stinking man! It was just like him to vanish when she had to make the biggest decision of her life. He had probably headed into the mine early to set out the lanterns and make preparations for the workday. Kaila couldn't fault his dedication, but if she was really going to become a Sister, she would be gone before he returned.

Her vision blurred. She blinked angrily and scolded herself, but for some reason, once the tears started, they would not stop. Instead, a sob unexpectedly bubbled from her throat. Always, she and him had been a team, tackling the world together. The thought of leaving Elgoss behind, of leaving her father to face the world alone…

She'd always known this day would come. A Warden was also required to sacrifice. Those who wore the armour of T'iana swore vows to take no partner and bear no children. But at least she would have been living out her dream, fighting to defend her kingdom so that others could live in peace.

The void in her chest, the one that had opened when she'd seen that terrible light in Caellum's eyes, swelled until it filled her up. The walls of their flat closed in around her. She shot back to her feet, chair scraping against the floorboards. Choking in little gasps, Kaila struggled for some semblance of calm. She could do this, couldn't she?

Couldn't she?

She batted away the tears and crossed to the little window that looked out over the street, yanking open the shutters. Cold air swirled into the room. She welcomed it. It cut through the panic. She needed to think, yet all she could see was her father, stooped and weary, returning from the mines to find her gone.

She couldn't leave. Not without saying goodbye.

The realisation brought everything into focus. Lurching to her bed, she pulled clothes from the drawers underneath. Her father had an old canvas bag he used for carrying tools to and from the mine. She claimed it and filled it with her belongings, before dressing herself in a set of rough pants and a tunic—the ones she usually wore on laundry day—followed by her heavy coat. There would be no time to return to the flat—she would go straight to the colonnade from the mine. Finally, she tucked her knife into the sheath in her boot, heaved the bag over her shoulder, and marched down the stairs into the street.

The sun was creeping into the sky, but the hour was still early and the streets were filled with shadow, the other residents only now coming awake in their neighbouring flats. Her teeth chattered as she began the long march uphill to the entrance of the mine. The air tasted of ice, and the breeze was so sharp it cut through her coat and set the base of her skull to aching. The sulfuric tang of coal smoke hung in the air, as those fortunate enough to have a few lumps remaining struggled to warm their flats.

A knot twisted in Kaila's gut as she threaded her way through the narrow streets and thought of leaving this place. Elgoss was all she had ever known. Its people were hard workers who wanted for little, happy for the safety they had in a world of violence. A simple place, but honest. Tah'raus was not like that. The heart and soul of their kingdom, everything she had ever read nevertheless spoke of the city's soiled underbelly. Of enemy agents who evaded the Trials and human criminals who rejected the teachings of the First Matron. A place of great virtue, and unspeakable evil.

But she was nearing the mine and the time for second thoughts had passed. The streets gave way to a winding path up to a dark hole in the cliffs above the village. There was a wide courtyard outside, with several piles of waste rock still waiting to be disposed of, but otherwise, the place was empty.

As Kaila approached the entrance, she found the steel doors hanging open. She slowed as she neared, relieved to feel the hot air billowing from the dark. As she stepped inside, she was already unbuttoning her coat.

Within, the inner chamber was mostly natural rock, chipped away by the first miners so many generations ago, but in more recent decades concrete supports had been added to brace the heavy stone. It had reduced the number of cave-ins, though all efforts to secure the deep tunnels had failed. Concrete that would endure decades on the surface rotted away in the space of weeks when exposed to the fumes that bubbled through those passageways. Recalling her father's description from the night before, Kaila suppressed a shudder.

The pens were empty. Her father must have already taken the condemned down for the first shift. Kaila allowed herself a smile as she thought of Leonardo chained and collared, forced into the bubbling darkness. It was vindictive and beneath her, but it was still gratifying to know after his cowardice had cost the life of another man that he would not escape unpunished.

She lingered a while in the quiet, waiting to see whether her father would return, or if any of the other early risers would arrive to accompany her down. Finally, though, she could wait no longer. Sister Eurador had told her midday, but if she had to venture into the tunnels to find her father, there was no time to waste.

Drawing a breath, Kaila took one of the lanterns hanging from the brackets in the entrance. The swish of oil from within confirmed it was full. The wick flared to life on the second strike of the mechanical flint inside. Then she faced the opening leading into the depths and started down the iron tracks the miners used to roll their carts to and from the surface.

She had come this way many times before, normally with her father or another of the miners, but this time Kaila couldn't keep the tremors from crawling down her spine. She imagined the weight of the rock looming above, how tiny she was amongst all of it, how even a small tremor in the earth might bring it all crashing down—or open a pit beneath her feet and drop her into the volcanic flames below. Her fear rose, its cold fingers closing around her throat, whispering for her to flee, to run back to Elgoss and her future with the Sisters…

I am not a coward.

Kaila forced herself onwards into the darkness. Silence embraced her. Funny, how easy it was not to notice the little sounds of everyday life. The chatter of voices from a nearby building. The creaking of floorboards shifting beneath boots. The whistle of wind and the rumble of a cart on unpaved streets—even the groan of the front gates as they were opened to allow the field workers access to their crops. All were a part of daily life in Elgoss, always there, in the background.

But now Kaila was embraced by the silence of the earth, swallowed by its darkness, wrapped in the stillness of the world beneath theirs.

Further into the depths she went, surrounded by a tiny sphere of light, her only lifeline to the world above. Her mind was heavy and unfocused, lingering on a future that just a few days ago had been unimaginable.

A Sister, her, Kaila Dwyn.

She both dreaded and was excited by the prospect. Tah'raus might be a dark and dangerous place, but it was also filled with wonders. Their histories claimed the enemy had built the city long ago, as a sister to their secret fortress of Eurador, where T'iana had first raised the rebellion. But while Eurador had been lost to the mists of time, Tah'raus remained, claimed by humanity as the seat of their own kingdom. She would study there for a decade before she was allowed to leave. It weighed on her, that knowledge, the cost she must pay for this new future.

Clang!

Kaila came to a halt as the harsh sound echoed up the tunnel. It sounded like the banging of metal. She stood frozen in the middle of the track, staring into the dark. Had that been her father? All of a sudden, she realised she'd been walking for ten minutes and this was the first noise she had heard. There should have been others, if her father was really down here with the condemned. The rattle of chains. The rasp of picks against stone. The grunt and cursing of men.

But there had been only silence—until that crash.

Her skin prickled as something else occurred to her. The entrance. There had been something odd about it, but only now did the truth occur to her, the thing that had been out of place.

There were no guards.

Her lantern flickered, guttering as the oil swirled inside. There were no lights other than her own. Shouldn't there be others? Her father would have left lanterns on his way down.

Her mouth was suddenly dry. She tried to recall the entrance, if anything else had been out of place, but her memory was foggy.

Cursing, she hesitated in the dark, before plunging onwards down the tunnel. Her father must have forgotten the lanterns. Yes, that was it. And the guards…they would be helping her father with the prisoners, so there were no more incidents like yesterdays.

But now she'd noticed the silence, Kaila couldn't shake her sense of unease. Goosebumps raced across her skin and her scalp prickled. Could it be the enemy? But there had been nothing. No alarm, no sound of combat. The town had been peaceful as she walked through the streets.

She was overreacting. Nervous after the decision she had made—

Clang!

She froze again, staring into the darkness ahead. Except it wasn't dark any longer. There was light ahead. The flickering of a lantern. The hairs on the back of her neck were tingling. So, someone *was* down here.

Her father?

Or the enemy?

Kaila stood rooted to the spot, blood roaring in her ears, fingers twitching in the direction of her knife. What the hell was going on? Something was wrong—she could *feel* it. But there were no answers waiting to leap at her where she stood. She could only continue down the tunnel, or go back and report…what, exactly? Some strange noises?

She shuddered, her mind made up. If something was going on, she needed to find out what. She knelt carefully and set her bag and lantern on the ground. She didn't want to alert whoever was below to her presence, just in case. With her load lightened and hands freed, she slipped the dagger from her boot. Then licking her lips, she summoned her courage and set off again. If there really were Elysian in the tunnels, she knew she couldn't fight them, but she *could* alert the rest of the town.

The air grew thicker as she continued, spoiled by dust and

burning with an acrid tang that had her eyes tearing up and her nose dripping. She placed her shirt across her mouth, but it did little to help. It was hot too, enough that she could feel it through the soles of her boots. Each breath grew more laborious, like a weight was pressed against her chest, forcing the air from her lungs. And these were not the *deep* tunnels. Fear fluttered in her stomach.

Fear is a great teacher, but you must never allow it to be master.

A favourite saying of her father. Easy advice to follow in the light. Down in the dark, she struggled to keep the beast in check.

Her eyes strained to pierce the black. The light source had grown brighter—she could make out the silhouette of the tunnel walls and uneven ground. She crept forward with deliberate care. If it was the enemy, even a whisper in this place might alert them. That could not happen. If something was wrong, Kaila was the only one able to raise the alarm.

"…all you can find?"

A voice echoed up the tunnel and Kaila froze. Distorted as it was, she couldn't identify the speaker, and she missed fragments of the reply that followed.

"Please…chains…help you…"

Holding her breath by instinct, Kaila crept closer. That voice had been thin and reedy. Familiar. Neither had been her fathers. The tunnel curved ahead of her, slowly brightening, until at last the scene came into view.

There were half a dozen people in the tunnel. Several men dressed in the grey overalls of miners were on their knees, hands bound behind their backs and mouths gagged. She spotted her father immediately, a purple bruise swelling on his cheek and blackening his eye. There were two other miners who appeared untouched, plus Tomas and Sareen, who were in worse condition even than her father, barely able to keep themselves upright.

And then there were the prisoners. Leonardo plus three others— the criminals from the pens, she assumed. They still wore iron manacles on their ankles, connecting them so they couldn't run anywhere quickly. Leonardo was holding out a bucket towards a man.

A man Kaila did not recognise.

He was young, maybe a year or two older than her, with stubble on his cheeks and scruffy blonde hair that hung around his shoulders. His eyes were strange, blue flecked with gold, and a little too large for his narrow face. He stood with his hands tucked casually into the pockets of a tattered trench coat, oozing a calm confidence that set every hair on Kaila's head on end. The way he stood between her father and the prisoners without a hint of fear, everything suggested this man was in control. And that smile, the casual smirk on his lips…

Kaila's heart gave a little thump.

"Is this all?" His voice was rough like gravel as he craned his head to study the contents of the bucket, before turning those gold-flecked eyes on his prisoners.

Chains rattled, then snapped taut as Leonardo tried to take a step towards the stranger. "The vein is almost empty," he rasped. "Please, maybe without the chains—"

The stranger interrupted with a short, barking laugh. "What's this?" he asked. "I thought we had a deal, Leonardo. You bring me a bucket of agimet, and I remove your chains." He raised the bucket, waving it in his face. "This isn't even half full. Now, what about other veins?"

Kaila's blood ran cold at the words. He was after the agimet!

Leonardo wrung his fingers. "Please, we can't go back down there," he rasped. "It could take days to uncover a fresh vein."

The stranger grunted. "I don't have days," he muttered, eyes flicking to her father and the other miners. He let out a sigh. "Well, I guess you won't be getting your freedom after all."

"Traitor!" Leonardo tried to hurl himself at the stranger, but the chain around his ankle snapped taut and all he ended up achieving was pitching face first to the ground.

The stranger chuckled as he scooped up the bucket before the thrashing man could knock it over.

"Sorry, mate. A deal's a deal."

Shaking his head, the man turned to the miners and placed his hand on his hips. "So," he said lightly, "it was most inconvenient of you lot showing up, but now you're here, maybe you'd like to tell me where you store all the agimet from this here mine?"

Her father and the others said nothing. Kaila swelled in pride for their bravery, but the stranger only tisked and walked down their line. Her father didn't flinch when he came to a stop in front of him. Kaila wondered how the stranger had gotten the better of him in the first place. All of them, even Sareen, were larger than the newcomer, and her father largest of all. Kaila had never seen him bested with blade or fists. How had the intruder overcome them by himself?

"Well?" the man asked her father. "Where is it?"

Looking up from his knees, Gideon Dwyn drew back his head and spat on the stranger's shoes. The intruder did not react immediately. His frown only deepened, lips curling into a frown.

"Charming," he muttered, wiping his shoe on a rock with a look of disdain.

Then reaching into his pocket, he drew out a piece of crystal.

And his eyes began to glow.

Kaila stiffened as light spilled across the cavern. Not the warm glow of a lantern, but with the burning white of *atar* trapped inside the facets of agimet. She stared at the crystal in abject horror, a cold sweat dripping down her neck. Bathed in that light, time seemed to slow, as she was gripped by the terror every child in Elgoss was taught from the cradle.

Agimet. He had agimet.

Now she knew why the others didn't resist, why they knelt, beaten and subjugated. This was no ordinary man they were dealing with, but one of the enemy. An Elysian. He might only be one man, but with that crystal, he could do terrible magics.

The *thump* of a body hitting stone snapped Kaila's attention back to her father. She stifled a gasp as she saw him pinned to the wall of the tunnel. The stranger hadn't laid a hand on him, yet he hung a foot off the ground, squirming against some unseen force. His mouth opened and closed, but no sound came out. To Kaila's horror, she realised he was choking.

"You have seen what I can do," the intruder said softly. His hand was stretched towards her father, eyes burning.

With a flick of his fingers, her father crashed to the ground, wheezing for breath. Whistling a tune to himself, the stranger turned to the next man in the line.

"Where."

He spread his hands.

"Is."

Rocks clattered against one another as they lifted into the air.

"The."

The light of *atar* burned brighter as the stones circled the hapless man.

"*AGIMET!*"

The last word came out as a roar, followed by a *crack* as a stone slammed into the miner's shoulder. He screamed as he was thrown to the ground. Moaning, he tried to scramble away from the Elysian, but the intruders boot came down on his ankle.

"I'm waiting," he hissed, those terrible eyes burning.

"Please!" the miner cried. His face now lit by *atar*, Kaila saw it was Everett Macy. He'd never been a soldier, but he was dutiful—one of the only men who would arrive each morning before her father. He looked terrified now, staring up into the face of evil. "Please, no—"

He screamed as another stone struck, this time square in the chest. There was force behind the blow, for Everett doubled over, clutching at his stomach.

Kaila's heart was in her throat. She had to do something to help them. But what? The Elysian had already defeated her father and four others. What chance did she stand alone? She could go for help, but the intruder would be gone long before reinforcements arrived. It was unlikely the vile creature would leave any witnesses alive when he was done. There had to be something she could do.

She slunk closer, keeping to the shadows, taking care only to step on firm rock rather than gravel.

"It's gone," Everett sobbed as he recovered his breath. "Please, it's gone. All gone!"

That brought a frown to the stranger's face. "Gone?" he quizzed. "I know it was here. How can it be *gone?*"

"We don't keep it in the village," Everett whispered. "They take it every night! Pack it up with the waste rock and wagon it out of here."

Traitor!

Rage, unexpected, boiled through Kaila's veins. Everett had just revealed vital information to the enemy.

"Interesting." Scratching his stubble with a dirty fingernail, the stranger seemed to consider this new information. "But quite unhelpful. You, *overseer!*" He swung back to her father. "Is this true?"

Her father leered back. "Those scraps are the only agimet you'll be stealing today, mongrel."

"Are you sure about that?" the stranger asked, his voice dropping a pitch, suddenly dangerous.

The air *hissed* as the stones shot towards her father, only to halt an inch from his face. Several yards up the tunnel, Kaila flinched and cracked her elbow against a protrusion in the wall. She had to slap her hands over her mouth to keep quiet.

"I'll give you one last chance. Tell me where it is—or die."

Muttering a silent curse, Kaila wiped away the tears that had sprung to her eyes and took a firmer grip of her dagger. This was it. The risk be damned, she wasn't going to watch while this monster murdered her father. His back was turned to her. And was it her imagination, or was his agimet dimmer than before? Yes! It made sense. The *atar* was the source of his magic. He was burning up its power with these little displays of strength.

"Burn in hell." His hands still bound, her father could only glare back at his attacker, defiant.

Stuffing her fears and uncertainty deep down inside of her, Kaila crept closer. It was a foolish, terrible plan, but it was all she had. She didn't have to fight the monster or his magic—only deny him *atar*. If she could knock the stone from his hand, her father and the others would have a chance of taking him.

"Trickster's Balls," the stranger muttered. Hands clenched behind his back, he began to stalk back and forth across the tunnel. "Sneaky Fresians. And I bet none of you have any idea where they take it. Maybe someone else in thrice damned village knows…"

By now, Kaila was close enough to see the bucket the stranger had set aside. She caught the glint of several crystals inside—maybe half a dozen. If he escaped, it wouldn't be empty-handed. Thankfully, the stones were dim, lacking the shimmer of *atar* that meant they'd been charged in a nexus. Only the one the stranger held was charged. If she could separate him from it…

"I could follow the wagons." The Elysian seemed to be brainstorming to himself. He snapped his fingers. "Yes, that's it. They can't have gotten far!"

Kaila was close now, her only concealment the faint shadows cast by the mix of lantern and *atarlight*. With his back turned, the stranger still hadn't noticed her. Nor had anyone else, thankfully. Every eye in the tunnel was on the man holding the magic—and all their lives—in his hands. Kaila was but a silhouette amidst the twisted shadows of the earth.

Her eyes never left the crystal. Nothing else mattered but separating the man from the source of his power. Ten yards and she paused, sucking in a lungful of air. Eight yards. She was almost inside the shroud cast by his agimet. Six. No one looked in her direction, but if they did now, they would see her. Her eyes flickered to the condemned. Their attention remained on the Elysian man.

Until Leonardo looked in her direction.

"Hey what are you doing—" he began.

Kaila didn't wait for him to finish. Screaming at the top of her voice in the hope of confusing her foe, she hurled herself at the intruder. He held the piece of agimet at his side. There was no time to think—she went for the stone with everything she had.

But warned by Leonardo's cry, the man was already turning. His eyes grew wide in the fraction of a second it took for him to realise his danger. He froze. Probably, the image of a halfway wild young woman hurtling at him from the darkness was enough to momentarily disarm him. Unfortunately, the moment didn't last. His hand snapped out, catching her dagger-wielding right hand—just as her other hand closed around the crystal and tore it from his fingers.

Then they crashed together and went down in a tangle of bodies. Light flashed from the agimet, brilliant in the darkness. As the magic failed, the flying rocks reverted to the normal rules of gravity and crashed to the ground.

Blessedly, this time the darkness didn't come for Kaila when she held the crystal. She scrambled across the ground, the agimet clutched desperately in her hand, trying to escape her foe. No luck. A weight slammed into her back, driving her face first into the gravel. Air hissed between her teeth as it was forced from her lungs. Choking, she curled into a ball. But even as stars filled her vision, she clenched the agimet tight in both hands.

Then another pair of hands closed around her own. Firm, yet soft, as though their owner had never done a day of honest labour in his life. Her vision cleared in time to see the grim face of the stranger crouched atop her. His hands were wrapped around hers, but she refused to release the agimet. To her surprise, he was smiling.

"I don't believe we've been introduced," he said casually. "They call me Theron. And who might you be?"

"*Lemmego!*" Kaila choked back, still struggling for breath.

Theron sighed. "So hard to have a proper conversation these days." To her horror, his eyes began to glow. He was drawing power from the crystal even though she was still holding it. "Would you care to let go, or are we going to have a *firm discussion* about property rights?"

Terror prickled Kaila's skull, warning her of peril, but she bared her teeth instead. "*Never!*"

"Very well."

Around them, the ground began to vibrate as a hundred tiny pieces of gravel rose into the air.

And Kaila *saw*.

The world changed. She was no longer in the dark, but in a cavern lit by a thousand pinpricks of light. They were all around, shining like the glow worms she had read about in Sister Eurador's books. Beautiful, shimmering, each slightly different from the last; this one a verdant emerald, the next ruby red, one as large as her fist, another as tiny as a grain of sand.

There was even a light inside of *her*, she realised with a start. And in her attacker as well. His burned brightly, swelling suddenly like a fire fed a fresh piece of coal. A dozen threads of gold spun away from his light, extending to the other stars, connecting them all in a fiery net. Slowly at first, then faster, the lights began to shift.

And the world moved with them.

A tingle spread down Kaila's spine as she realised what this was. *Magic.* This was how it worked. *And she understood.* The lights were a spectral representation of their physical world. The intruder had used *atar* to connect and bend them to his will. He could make the fabric of the universe dance to his tune…

…and Kaila realized she could do the same.

She didn't pause to think. The enemy was before her. He would kill her and her father and everyone else in this tunnel if she didn't stop him. She had to deny him the agimet. Clutching the crystal tight in her fists, Kaila reached for the golden power inside, and pulled on it.

Fire flooded her chest, a heat unlike anything she had ever felt. The Elysian thief flinched as though he sensed what she'd done, but Kaila couldn't allow herself to be distracted. Taking the power of the agimet, she touched the light inside the intruder.

Move.

And just like that, her assailant went hurtling backwards as though she had struck him a powerful blow. He crashed to the ground a few yards away, unharmed, but with a look of such stunned surprise on his face that one of the miners probably could have taken him right then without a fight, if they hadn't also been staring at her with utter bewilderment.

Still holding the agimet in both hands, Kaila scrambled to her feet. Theron rose as well, his manner unhurried. He made a show of brushing off his coat, the smile still on his lips.

"My, my, aren't you full of surprises," he said with a smile. "Where did you come from, girl?"

Kaila found a smile of her own. "I am Kaila Dwyn of Elgoss," she said defiantly, "and I will protect my home against your kind to my dying breath, *Elysian scum.*"

"Ah, Elysian scum?" Theron said, raising an eyebrow. "Bit of the pot calling the kettle black there, isn't it?" He took a step towards her.

Her hand came up, flashing the glowing stone. "Don't move," she snarled. Why hadn't her father and the others sprung on him already? She felt strangely weak, as though whatever she had done with the stone had drained her as well as the crystal. "Surrender, and I promise you will be given a fair trial."

Theron snorted. "Yes, with the executioner waiting outside with a sharp blade, no doubt."

"You have nowhere to run."

"My dear girl, you have no idea who you're dealing with."

Kaila bared her teeth. "I am dealing with a thief."

"The *prince* of thieves," the stranger corrected. "I *always* have a way out."

With his words, the glint of *atar* appeared in his eyes. Too late, Kaila realised one of his hands had reached into the pockets of his overcoat. He must have another crystal hidden there. With a jolt, the agimet was torn from her fingers by an invisible force. It shot across the tunnel to land gently in Theron's outstretched hand.

The moment it left her possession, the strange lights in Kaila's vision flickered and died away.

"Well, thank you for the bit of entertainment," Theron said briskly. He stepped over to the bucket of crystals and swept it into his hand, "but I'm afraid I have overstayed my welcome." Still eying her, he backed his way up the tunnel. "So, if you don't mind, I'll be going."

"Wait!" One of the prisoners, Leonardo, cried. "You're meant to free us!"

"Oh. Right." Theron hesitated, glanced at the dimming glow of his agimet, then looked back at the man. "Sorry, I'm a little short on *atar*, especially after this last part."

"What last part—"

Even without the crystal, Kaila *felt* the magic as Theron's eyes grew bright again. It didn't help. Even as she raised a hand as though to stay him, there was a roaring sound from above, before the ceiling came crashing down in an avalanche of stone and earth.

And everything went dark.

6

"...**A** *thief*..."
"...one of *them*..."
"Impossible..."
"How...the Trials..."
"*Wake her.*"

The voices fell silent. In that pause, Kaila's mind finally pieced itself back together. Her head ached like someone had hit her with a sack of coal. The rest of her didn't feel much better off, but at least she was lying in what she assumed to be her bed.

The dull plod of boots on stone approached. Strange. Their flat didn't have stone floors. There was only one building in Elgoss with—

All thoughts fled from her mind as icy water cascaded over her head. She tried to scream, but only a gurgle came out. Water filled her throat, and choking, drowning, she thrashed—only to find her wrists and ankles restrained by chains.

When the deluge ceased, she cursed the enemy between gasps for breath. Who else could be behind such foul torture? Blinking water from her eyes, she strained against her bindings. The manacles rattled against steel railings lining the bed. Definitely not home. She squinted against the blazing light in the room, trying to figure out where she was and what was going on. The last thing she remembered…she'd been heading into the mine, hadn't she? And there was that strange man…

…the room slowly came into focus, and Kaila found herself looking up at a familiar face.

It only added to her confusion.

"Sister Eurador?" she croaked. "What's going on?"

Her memories were hazy, but more of what had happened in the tunnels was returning now. A shiver ran down her spine. The enemy had infiltrated Elgoss. The thief had been after agimet. He'd had her father and the others bound, but she'd stopped him, hadn't she? In the end…

Kaila's skin crawled as she recalled the roar of collapsing stone, the flash of red followed by sudden darkness. The bastard had brought the ceiling down on them. How was she alive? Was anyone else…

"My father," she gasped, struggling against her restraints to sit up. What the hell was happening? Why was she bound? She recognised the room now—this was the infirmary in the colonnade. "Is he okay—"

Leaning over the bed, Sister Eurador struck her across the face. *Hard.*

"You will not speak." The sister's voice dripped venom. "Unless it is to answer my questions, you treacherous cur."

Kaila was so stunned by the blow that she could only stare at the woman, mouth hanging open. The blood drained from her face as shock replaced mortification. What…what had she done? She had never seen such a shade of purple on her teacher's face, nor that glint in her eyes. She struggled to understand. What had the sister said? Something about treason? Surely, she had misheard!

"Please, Sister, there was a thief—"

Sister Eurador struck her again, harder this time. Red burst across Kaila's vision and her ears began to ring. Tears sprang to her eyes and she had to bite her lip to keep from crying out.

"You. Will. Not. Speak," Eurador ground out through clenched teeth. Gone was her smile and warm words. There was no hint of the woman who had been the closest thing Kaila had ever had to a mother. In her place was a hard, unyielding woman.

Kaila wanted to scream, to beg her to explain why she was being treated like the enemy. She was *Kaila*, Kaila Dwyn, the most loyal servant the kingdom had ever seen. She would never betray Fresia…

…but one glimpse of those hate-filled eyes and she swallowed the words.

A terrible silence hung over the infirmary. There were others present. Kaila sensed them in the edges of her vision. The village doctor and his attendant. They lingered in the shadows, clearly eager to remain removed from the situation. This was between her and the sister.

"Good," Sister Eurador said when it became obvious Kaila would not try to speak again. "Now, perhaps we can get to the heart of your treason. How did you fool our Trials?"

"What?" Kaila croaked.

"The Trial of Agimet," Eurador snapped. "How did your filthy, contaminated blood slip past the crystal?"

Tears blurred Kaila's vision. "Please, I didn't—"

Kaila shrieked as the sister struck her again. For an old woman, she had a wicked swing. This time, she felt something tear in her jaw. She slumped into the sheets, breath rasping in her throat, a great sob building within. The cold iron of the shackles dug at her flesh. A trickle of blood ran down her wrist where they cut her skin.

"How. Did. You. Fool. Us?"

"*I don't know!*" Kaila screamed, rearing up as far as her bonds would allow to look her teacher in the eyes, blinking angrily as tears gathered.

She remembered what had happened down there in the dark, but she didn't want to face it. Face what it might mean, what Eurador was accusing her of. Because she had seen it. The magic of the enemy. And there at the end, she had used it.

But that didn't mean…it couldn't…

"I don't know," she repeated, voice falling to a whisper. "That man, he was going to kill my father. I stopped him. I don't know how…"

Words failed her then and she slumped onto the bed. The scene played out again and again in her mind, the man who called himself the prince of thieves, standing over the miners, and Kaila tackling him, wrestling him for possession of the agimet. Then the stars, the swirling lights of some other realm. And the energy that had sizzled through her, how she'd reached for the stars, for the intruder's light.

How she had moved him.

Looking into Sister Eurador's eyes, she saw the hatred there, and the pain. She recognised it, had lived it herself just yesterday, when Caellum had looked at her with *atar* burning in his eyes.

Betrayal.

"I didn't know," she whispered. "Please, you have to believe me, Sister. *I am not a traitor.*"

But Eurador only shook her head. "I have sent word after Warden Chain. With the blessing of the First Matron, he will be here by morning. Lie to me all you wish, devil. The Warden will have the truth from your deceitful lips."

With that she turned and stalked from the room. The doctor and his assistant hesitated, before following. Behind the open door, Kaila glimpsed a pair of guards standing outside. Tomas and Sareen. Her heart throbbed. They were okay. But what about her father? She wanted to call out to them. They had seen her fight the Elysian thief, hadn't they? They would speak for her.

But then Sareen stepped into the doorway and took hold of the handle, and their eyes met. Kaila saw the same rage in the woman's gaze as in Sister Eurador's. The same look of loathing, and hatred, and hurt. She was still searching for the right words when Sareen slammed the door shut.

The darkness swallowed her up. And the silence. Not of the terrible silence of the earth, this time, but the familiar quiet of Elgoss. The concrete walls groaned, and outside, the mountain winds whistled through metal awnings. Somewhere outside, a dog was barking.

Home. Yet never in her life had Kaila felt like such an outsider. Minutes crept into hours and no one came. Not even the doctor, or a guard with food. The void in her chest grew deeper, darker, fed by the loneliness, by the pain of seeing that look in her mentor's eyes, in the faces of her friends. In the agony of still not knowing her father's fate.

Finally though, not pain or sorrow or fear could hold out against the exhaustion creeping through her body, from the aching in her muscles or the pulsing in her skull. And so, at last, Kaila drifted off to sleep, not sure what tomorrow would bring—only knowing it could not be any worse than today.

She woke hours later to a hand pressed across her mouth. She opened her mouth to scream, but it died when Kaila felt the cold touch of steel at her throat.

"Ah, ah, ah," a voice spoke in the darkness, "let's not go waking the neighbourhood, shall we?"

Heart pounding and a cold sweat upon her brow, Kaila gave a careful nod. She recognised that voice—she would know it anywhere. The thief from the mine. Theron.

The hand left her mouth. The knife, however, remained, and her lips stayed carefully closed. She strained to pick out the vile Elysian thief from the shadows. As the glimmers of sleep faded from her eyes, he shifted into focus. He was wearing the same trench coat from before, though he looked to have added an extra layer of dust since the mine.

"Good girl," he said with a familiar smile.

The words stirred something in Kaila's gut. Rage. She had to bite down on her tongue to keep herself from screaming. The sharp sting of pain returned her to her senses and she settled for a glare. It wasn't like she could do anything with her hands chained to the bed anyway. He seemed to realise that, as still smiling, he pulled a nearby stool over to the bed and sat himself down, the blade never leaving her throat.

"How about we have a little chat? Starting with names. Is yours really Kaila? Theron isn't mine, but it's the one I go by."

Kaila glowered at him. She didn't know what the bastard was doing here, but whatever it was, she wanted nothing to do with it. Especially while his knife remained pressed to her carotid artery.

He seemed to realise that, as he let out a sigh. "Okay, look," he muttered, gesturing at the knife, "I'm going to remove this. When I do, I want your promise you won't scream. It wouldn't achieve anything anyway. Trust me when I say there are a dozen ways I can kill you and slip out the window before the guards outside can even find the key to your door."

If Kaila's eyes could have shot fire, she was quite sure Theron would have been crisper than a piece of her father's toast. As it was, she had to settle for the slightest of nods. Anything to get the cold steel away from her flesh.

"How about we skip the chat and you just leave," she said as he removed the blade.

The Elysian's eyebrows rose into his mop of golden hair. "My, my, what's got you so cranky, girl?"

"*You!*" she hissed. She almost choked trying to keep her voice in check. Her chains rattled as she shook them. "This is all your fault! *What did you do to me?*"

"Me? *I* didn't do anything to you. *You* were the one who went and showed off your powers in front of half a dozen humans. Don't tell me you didn't think at least *one* of them would go running to a Sister and report you?"

"*Liar*," Kaila snapped.

Theron pursed his lips. "Usually, I would agree," he remarked, with no hint of remorse. "However, in this case, I'm struggling to see how you think I have lied, Kaila."

Kaila had already opened her mouth to reply, but something about his tone gave her pause. There was a softness to his words, as though he was genuinely remorseful.

She swallowed. "You tried to kill me."

Her unwanted visitor chuckled. "Nonsense," he said, flashing a handsome smile that had Kaila grinding her teeth in anger. "If I wanted you dead, you would be dead. I just brought down a section of the tunnel between us. Couldn't have another Mover chasing me around and causing problems, could I?"

"You could have…wait, Mover? What are you talking about?"

"Oh, wow, you really are green, aren't you? Was that the first time you used your powers?"

"I don't have powers! I was tested!"

Theron arched an eyebrow. "Oh, yeah? Could have fooled me when you *moved me with your mind*."

"I didn't..." Kaila frowned. "Is that why you called me a Mover?"

"Why else?"

"Bit dumb, isn't it?" she sneered. "Come up with that one yourself?"

"It's not dumb!" Theron objected, the smile slipping from his face. "And no, I didn't make up the name." The way he said it, Kaila suspected he very well may have been involved.

"Doesn't make it any less stupid," she muttered, before remembering who she was talking to. She shook her head violently. "It doesn't matter. I'm not like you! I must have been contaminated by your magic! That's it, isn't it? Your foul magic is infectious somehow!"

"Well, that's a new one," Theron muttered. He toyed with the knife in his hands, making it spin between his fingers. "But I think even you know that's not true. If it was that simple, everyone would have magic by now, wouldn't they?"

Her heart sank. He was right. If magic really could pass between people like a disease, well, the war would have gone very differently.

"But I'm not like you," she whispered. "I'm not a traitor."

To her surprise, Theron sighed. Rising from his stool, he sat himself on the edge of her bed. "They don't care."

"I'll...I'll explain it to them."

"They don't seem like they're in the mood for listening."

"Sister Eurador was in shock. Maybe in the morning..."

"It won't work."

"What would *you* know?" Kaila retorted, maddened by the bastard of a man. He loomed over her, all dark and mysterious and self-assured. By the First Matron, if she had one of her daggers, she would wipe that smile off his lips. "You're a murderous Elysian thief! What would someone like you understand about duty?"

"What would I understand indeed." His voice was strangely sad as he rose. "Be that as it may, I *do* know a few things about being Elysian—which is what you are."

"Liar!"

Theron crossed his arms. It was a petulant argument and they both knew it. She bit her lip to keep from snapping again, and he went on: "As I was saying. I know a few things about your situation, and I know that if you stay here, they will kill you."

His words sent a chill down Kaila's spine. Fear. She shivered, wanting to say something, to refute his claim, but Theron was already speaking again.

"Look," he went on, a strange twist crossing his lips as he scratched his stubble. "I've got to catch that last load of agimet your village sent out before it disappears. I could use another Mover. I could take you with me—"

"Never!"

Kaila couldn't believe what she was hearing. He actually thought she would go with him! That she would betray her own kind to the enemy. And for what? Some crystals and coin?

"Seriously—"

"I would never betray my kind," she sneered.

A heavy silence fell between them. Kaila thought she glimpsed hurt in Theron's eyes, but surely that was only her treacherous imagination. This monster cared nothing for her—only about filling his own pockets. A part of her wanted to scream out now, to call for Tomas and Sareen outside, but the knife in his hand glinted in the moonlight, still perilously close. He was right; she would be dead long before anyone arrived to help. Yet the temptation remained. She might die choking on her own blood, but at least she would die *loyal*, would perish while proving to everyone that she wasn't a traitor. That she hadn't been working with the enemy against her people.

But the moment stretched out and Kaila did nothing, and finally, the strange man shook his head.

"Okay then," he said softly. "It's your life, Kaila. I just hope you live to regret the decision."

He slipped the knife back into the sheath on his belt and turned away.

The breath caught in her throat. This was it, her chance to alert the guards to his presence. Yet, as she opened her mouth to cry out, she saw again that glint in Sister Eurador's eyes, and in Sareen's, and the doctor's, and…

…and the words died in her throat.

Theron was already at the window. With a last glance over his shoulder, he disappeared into the night.

Then he was gone, and Kaila's only chance to prove her innocence and loyalty was gone with him.

———

THERON DIDN'T LINGER IN ELGOSS AFTER BIDDING THE GIRL goodnight. The *atar* in his crystals was burning low after their encounter in the mine and the closest nexus was several days away, high in the mountains near the old ruins. Too far for a detour. If they caught him skulking about the village, he would be hard-pressed to escape with the few resources he had left. So he used a whisper of power to silently open the gates and slip out into the night unseen.

It had been a little infuriating, actually, how much *atar* this village had cost him. Normally, all it took was a glimpse of his *atar*-filled eyes and humans would fall over themselves to do his bidding. But, oh no, not in Elgoss. The prisoners in the mine had been cooperative enough, but the miners when they'd turned up! The prisoners had been digging all night and still hadn't returned, so at the break of dawn, he'd gone up to deal with any early risers. He hadn't expected an actual *fight*. By the Trickster, the sister of this village had really done a number on them, wrapping them up in so many ideas of honour and duty that it was a wonder they didn't need her permission to take a dump. If the Magisterium was any sort of meritocracy, she had earned herself a goddamn medal.

Though, as far as Theron was concerned, the witch's reward should be delivered a great deal faster than capital bureaucracy, and with a much sharper point. Still, no wonder the town's location had remained secret so long. The entire populace was a giant cult to the teachings of the Magisterium.

Thankfully, there was always a weak link. One had spilled the beans about what they did with the agimet, and now he was hot on the heels of the wagon caravan. There was only one road in and out of the village, a pitted track that ran around the side of the volcano for a day before joining several others from villages deeper inside the

Iron Pinnacles. If he travelled quickly, he could still overtake them and recover his fortune.

Even if it meant abandoning the girl to her fate.

His stomach gave a pang. Kaila Dwyn. What a peculiar discovery she'd been. An Elysian who thought she was human. There must be some story there. Shame he couldn't stick around. If she was lucky, she would be imprisoned and sent to a labour camp, where she would serve the rest of her life alongside others unfortunate enough to have found themselves on the wrong side of Fresian law. An appropriate fate, some say, considering her high and mighty attitude towards him earlier.

But Theron couldn't find his smile. There was also the alternative. Execution. He'd tried to scare her with its promise, but…what if they condemned her for *his* crime? The theft of agimet was a capital offence.

A rumble of thunder jolted Theron back to the present. He cursed beneath his breath as a jagged trail of lightning sliced the sky. It was followed shortly by another *boom*. Great, just his luck. A storm was approaching. Maybe it would bring only rain, though with the cold breeze that cut the air, snow seemed more likely.

You should have left her a piece of agimet.

The ache in his gut grew stronger. He'd thought about it. But… the wagons were likely to be guarded. He would need every scrap of *atar* he had left if the waggoneers were as loyal as their compatriots in Elgoss. And there was no time for any detours. Every passing minute, the wagons grew closer to an intersection where they could turn off the road and vanish into the mountains, lost forever from his grasp.

He picked up the pace. He needed that agimet. The half a dozen crystals he'd taken from the mine were worth a fortune, but only a *small* fortune. They might not even cover the debt he'd racked up with Ambrose, assembling his list of potential villages. The man wasn't exactly someone you crossed.

Lost in his thoughts, Theron didn't notice the rumble of hooves from the road ahead until they were almost upon him. Immediately, he took cover, darting for an outcrop of rocks just off the trail. A few seconds later, the rider appeared, charging around a bend and urging his horse uphill at a pace most would consider reckless in the dark.

But this was no ordinary rider. As lightning lit the silhouette of the man on his horse, Theron caught the glimmer of the scale armour and shrank deeper into the shadows. Polished agimet blazed in the man's breastplate, lighting the path ahead as he charged past Theron's hiding place.

A Warden.

He was gone within seconds, making with all haste for Elgoss. A lump lodged in Theron's throat. He had thought they might send soldiers, or another Sister. He hadn't expected a godsdamn *Warden.* He must have been close to have responded so quickly. But even then, with Kaila already secured, what need was there for one of his kind?

I passed a test.

His blood chilled as he recalled the girl's words. He'd dismissed them as some fancy of her mad indoctrination. But what if she'd been telling the truth? What if she really had managed to fool the Trial of Agimet?

Well, that would certainly justify the attention of a Warden.

Theron watched the light of the storm rippling across the cliffs he'd spent the last couple of hours traversing. Somewhere back there was Elgoss and a young woman who had just discovered her powers. She was alone, and now a killer of Elysian came for her. She didn't stand a chance.

His fingers tightened around the shard of agimet in his pocket. With it, Theron could do incredible things.

Don't even think about it!

He swallowed. He only had five minutes left of *atar*, if he was lucky. And a Warden's armour protected them from the Gift. Plus, they had magic of their own. Powers only the Wardens themselves understood. He would be utterly outmatched in this fight.

And he would have to give up on the caravan.

She didn't want anything to do with you.

Theron saw the young woman again. Even lying helpless in that bed, she had been unflinching in his presence. He recalled how she had appeared in the mine, how she'd stolen his crystal, the blaze of *atar* in her eyes. In that moment, she had reminded him of someone he hadn't thought of in a long time. Only a memory now, and yet...

...Theron muttered a curse as he returned to the road and began to run. Not in the direction of the wagons and his fortune, but back the way he had come.

Towards Elgoss and a young woman, and a deadly Warden of Fresia.

7

Morning arrived and Kaila found herself still living a nightmare. Until then, a piece of her had still hoped it was all a kind of dream. That her real body lay someplace else, maybe in her bed with a fever or even slowly dying, trapped in the depths of the mine.

But no, it seemed she could not escape her fate so easily.

The chains rattled as she struggled to sit up. It was difficult. The pillow was scrunched beneath her and the guards hadn't left any give in her chains to adjust it. She'd also kicked off the thin sheet that was all she had for warmth. Thankfully they'd left her clothes, but by the time the glow of dawn filtered through the drapes, she'd started to shiver.

For a while, she just lay there, staring at nothing in particular while every so often her body trembled. As the sun grew brighter outside, she tried not to think about what came next, when the Warden arrived…

If you stay here, they will kill you.

She forced the words away. Who did Theron think he was, telling *her* what the Magisterium would do. They were *her* people, not his. They would listen, once she explained herself. Even if she somehow had powers, she'd used them to try and stop a thief. She was *not* a traitor.

Then why didn't you call out last night?

She bit her lip as the doubtful thought crept in. There had been a moment she could have alerted the guards. Why hadn't she called out?

He came back for you.

A shiver shot down her spine that had nothing to do with the cold. She recalled Theron looming over the bed. He was not a large man, this supposed prince of thieves, but he had an undeniable presence about him. The confidence of a man who had looked at the world the way it was and decided he wanted nothing to do with it. A tiny, treacherous part of Kaila wondered what that would be like. To forsake duty and responsibility and do whatever you wanted…

She forced that thought away as well. Left to fester, those beliefs could undermine the unity Fresia had been built upon. They were dangerous. *Theron* was dangerous.

That was why she hadn't gone with him. Why she had resisted his temptations. She was a good and loyal servant to her people. And if Sister Eurador and the others couldn't see that, well, Kaila would *make* them…wouldn't she?

All they see is a dangerous Elysian, a deceitful voice whispered in her mind.

Kaila was blinking back tears as the door swung open. Sareen entered, Tomas a step behind. This time, Kaila was ready with her story, but when she opened her mouth, the woman raised a leather-gloved hand.

"Not a word, *Elysian*," she said. "I have orders to gag you if necessary."

Her vision blurring again, Kaila carefully shut her mouth. By the First Matron, she'd never cried this much in her life. How could no one *see?* She was still the same Kaila she had always been; loyal, studious, dutiful Kaila, who had never put a foot wrong in her life. But how could she remind them of that if they wouldn't even let her speak?

But she complied, saying nothing as her restraints were removed from her bed and her wrists bound in front of her. Another chain was run from the cuffs to the shackles around her ankles. They were taking no chances. The weight of all that metal dragged on her arms and shoulders, but she didn't complain. If they gagged her, Kaila would lose her only chance to convince the Warden that she wasn't a traitor. She needed to pick her moment. He would believe her. He had been there for her Trial!

Tomas grasped her firmly by the shoulders while Sareen took the lead, pushing her to follow. She shuffled awkwardly out the door into a narrow corridor, then onto a winding staircase and up several flights. This was definitely the colonnade. They had already been on the second floor from what she could tell from her window, and there was only one building in Elgoss taller than three storeys.

Reaching the fifth and highest floor, she was led along another corridor and directed into a tiny room. Inside, there were no windows or other exits but the door she'd entered through, and only a single table and chair for furnishing. Sister Eurador was already there. She stood rigid behind the little chair, arms clasped before her, hands hidden in the sleeves of her robe. Her face betrayed no reaction, but Kaila could *sense* the anger permeating the room. It struck her like a tangible force and she wavered in the doorway—before a shove from Tomas sent her stumbling forwards.

The guards pushed her even more roughly into the chair, where her chains were locked through heavy metal loops in the table. The table itself was fixed to the concrete floor by iron bolts. The chair, however, was not. It shifted as she sat.

With the last lock in place, Sareen handed the key to Sister Eurador, and then both guards left without so much as a spiteful goodbye. Kaila sagged as she found herself alone with the sister. She twitched, a piece of her wanting to try one last time to explain herself. In the end, though, she said nothing. Her face still ached from the sister's blows, and she wasn't sure her soul could take one more cruel comment from her mentor. She would wait for the Warden.

She did not have long to wait.

Within minutes, the wooden door creaked open again, revealing a towering figure in his blue-scale armour. Despite his presence at her Trial just two days ago, the breath still caught in Kaila's throat. That day, the Warden had barely spared her a glance, but now she experienced the full weight of his attention as he stepped into the room. The agimet set in his armour blazed, lighting up the tiny chamber, setting the shadows to dancing.

Kaila shrank in her seat, courage abandoning her entirely. Here was one of her idols made flesh, a man who had dedicated his life to the ideals of the Magisterium, protecting humanity from their relentless enemy. How could she possibly explain herself to someone like that? An inexplicable dread sank its hooks into her soul. She felt his power poised above her like a naked blade, ready to strike down the tiny, irrelevant girl for her blasphemy.

Unless Kaila could somehow convince him that she was innocent.

"Good…good morning, sir," she stammered, unable to keep the quiver from her voice. "Please…I am afraid there has been a…a terrible mistake. I am…am a loyal servant of Fresia."

No response came from the shadow behind the visor. At least he had let her speak. She shuddered, suddenly cold in the windowless room. The chair creaked as she squirmed, unable to sit still beneath that unseen gaze. The eerie glow of *atar* outshone the single lantern, filling the little interrogation room with its harsh and unnatural white.

"Where is the stolen agimet?" The words came out metallic, as though it was the armour that spoke, not the man within.

Kaila quelled. "I swear, I don't know!" she gasped. This couldn't be happening. The Wardens were her *heroes*. He had to believe her. "It was a thief. Theron, he called himself!"

If the Warden heard her reply, he didn't show it. "What is the agimet to be used for?"

Tears stung Kaila's eyes. She shook her head. "I tried to stop him. Ask my father. Ask the other miners. Please, they'll tell you!"

Finally, something she said registered with the man within the metal, for his head turned slightly. Towards Sister Eurador.

"The father has been retested?"

"Of course, Warden Chain," she replied. "He's clean."

Kaila slumped in her chair, relieved at least to learn her father was alive. Her fingers closed around the arms of the chair, squeezing hard as she sucked in one harsh breath after another. Thank the

First Matron. Whatever else had happened, at least she knew he was okay.

"And the mother?" the Warden pressed.

"Dead. But there are discrepancies in the story. We are holding him for further questioning."

Her heart pulsed at that, her relief short-lived. They couldn't blame him for what had happened as well.

"I see." There was a pause as the Warden straightened. "Take your guards and bring him then. I want to know if he was involved in this."

Eurador wavered, seeming ready to question the man, before apparently deciding better of it and departing with a nod.

Leaving Kaila alone with the man in iron.

"Do you know who I am, Kaila Dwyn?"

Her head snapped up at the mention of her name. The Warden leaned over her, his visor barely inches from her face, yet still all she saw inside was darkness. She tried to answer the question, but tendrils of fear constricted so tightly around her throat that she couldn't squeeze out a single word. Trapped in that black gaze, she found herself wilting, all her rage and passion and *life* draining away, until only despair remained.

Suddenly, she was trembling. She was alone. *Alone.* No one was coming to save her. This man didn't know her. Why would he listen when everyone Kaila had ever loved had turned against her? The only person who had treated her like an actual human being since she'd woken was the bastard Elysian. Theron-whatever-he-called-himself. Kaila found herself wishing she had gone with him when she could.

Fool, fool, fool!

"I am called Elric Chain. I am a Warden of the Order."

"I…I know, sir," she managed to rasp, though she was no longer able to look at that terrible helmet. "You were there…for my Trial… two days ago."

Her heart twisted at the memory. Not just for all that had passed since, but for the look she had seen in Caellum's eyes. The fear. The betrayal. Betrayal Kaila now experienced for herself. For the first time, she began to wonder. Had he really been a traitor, an Elysian intent on stealing their secrets? Or had he been like her, ignorant to the power inside of him until the moment the crystal touched his hand?

The Warden grunted. "Ay. And that is why we are here. Because you passed the Trial of Agimet." Straightening, Elric clasped his hands behind his back. Steel scraped against concrete as he moved behind her. With the chains binding Kaila to the desk, she couldn't follow him. "And yet, last night, I received word from your Sister that you used the profane magics of the enemy." The footsteps came to a stop. She sensed Elric looming behind her. "I have come to find out how that is possible."

Cold hands settled on her shoulders and squeezed. "Any ideas?"

She shook her head vigorously.

"You will tell me the truth, one way or another."

"Please—"

The pain struck Kaila before she could get the words out. It struck like a landslide, sudden and overwhelming, crushing her resistance before she even knew what it was. She gasped, a single intake of breath all she managed before her lungs locked in agony. Red fire flashed across her vision, and she was screaming, shrieking until…

…she saw the lights. Those burning, otherworldly stars. And she saw her own fire, thrashing, *hurting* as another light lashed at it…

She moaned as the agony vanished. The sudden absence was almost as bad as the pain itself, like the blood had ceased to flow in her body, only for it to go rushing back to her limbs all at once.

But the Warden allowed Kaila no time to recover. A metallic fist grabbed her by the hair and yanked her upright. Fear returned as she found herself staring again into the black behind the man's visor.

"Well?" Elric growled. "How did you do it? How did you fool the Trial?"

"I don't know, I swear!" Kaila cried, desperation giving her voice. "I didn't do anything! It was only when I was wrestling with *him* that I saw the lights!"

Snorting his derision, the Warden tossed her back from him. The chair rocked on its flimsy wooden legs and only the chains bolted to the table kept her from toppling over.

"Ah, yes, *him.* And how does this *Theron* figure into all of this?"

He loomed over her again. Kaila quailed, helpless as an iron hand took her by the chin, forcing her gaze up into the empty slit of his helmet.

"Please, stop. I don't know his plans," she rasped, her voice cracking.

"A likely story." His fingers dug into her cheeks. "Who is he, this accomplice? Where did he come from? What does he want with the agimet?"

A scream tore from Kaila's throat as pain jammed into her skull like a bolt hammered by a clumsy blacksmith. This time, though, the pain lasted only a second, as a woman's voice cut through the red haze. Sister Eurador…

"Warden Chains…"

Kaila sagged against the table as the steel hand released her. Through the stars dancing across her vision, she saw the Warden turn away. A great shape filled the doorway, too big to be the sister. For a second, she didn't understand. Her mind was in turmoil, her thoughts scattered as the emotions that had fled came crashing back. Anger, pain, betrayal. Their heat filled her, pushing back the despair.

Blinking, she looked up to find the last person in the world she had been expecting to see.

Her father.

Kaila hadn't really registered what the Warden had said when he'd ordered Sister Eurador to bring him. Now she realised in a rush of horror that she couldn't face him. She had already seen hatred in the eyes of so many friends and mentors today. It would be too much to see it in her own father. They might have disagreed and argued at times, but it had been the pair of them against the world her entire life.

But in the end, she had to know. If this might be the last time she saw him…she lifted her head.

Gideon Dwyn stood in the doorway, dark eyes fixed on her with an intensity Kaila had never seen before. Her heart gave a little pulse as he stepped into the interrogation room, Sister Eurador gliding in after him.

"Gideon Dwyn," the Warden greeted. "Thank you for coming. I have some questions…"

"A thousand pardons, Warden." Her father's voice was taut, rough. "But I wondered if I might…" His voice cracked, seeming to tremble. At his side, his enormous fists were clenched tight. "If I might speak with the Elysian a moment. Alone."

Kaila flinched. Hearing those words from her father's mouth was worse than any torture Elric Chain could have inflicted. With them, the last remnants of her old life broke into a thousand pieces. Theron had been right. She should have fled. The second she'd touched that piece of agimet and unlocked whatever power was inside of her, she had condemned herself in the eyes of every man and woman in Elgoss.

Even her father.

Silence followed as the Warden considered her father's words.

"Overseer Dwyn." To Kaila's surprise, it was Sister Eurador who responded. "Your dismay is understandable. But this creature has proven exceedingly dangerous. She infiltrated our town, betrayed our secrets to the enemy. Who knows what else she might be capable of?"

"I understand, Sister," her father growled, bowing his head. "More, perhaps, than even yourself." He turned to the Warden. "There are questions you want answered, no? I can help. She may have played me for a fool all these years, but she still lived beneath my roof, and ate at my table." There was a tremor in his voice, like a terrible rage desperately contained. "Please, Warden Chain. A moment only."

The Warden regarded him before offering a nod. "Afterwards, we must speak of the mother."

"I will tell you everything you wish to know."

"Then you have five minutes. Sister, come. We will wait outside. She is restrained, but beware their tricks. Shout if you should require our assistance."

He strode through the doorway, gesturing for the sister to follow. Eurador's gaze lingered on Kaila, and she looked like she might argue, but a glance from Chains seemed to convince her otherwise.

She left, the door swinging closed behind her with a *bang*. A screech followed as the bolt was drawn into place.

And then Kaila was alone with her father.

A strange, choking noise came from his throat. A strangled gasp.

Then his strong arms were enveloping her, drawing her close, hugging her.

Kaila had never known relief in her life until that moment. Not like this. She tried to hug him back, but the chains made it hard. It didn't matter. The moment he wrapped her in those familiar arms, the horrible feeling in her stomach, the one that screamed the world was wrong, fled. She sobbed, hot tears burning down her cheeks to soak her father's shirt. She could feel his tears on her shoulder.

"I'm sorry." The words tumbled from her lips. *"Imsorryimsorry-imsorry!"*

She was blubbering now, choking on her tears, struggling to breathe as snot gummed up her nose. Her father squeezed tighter and then drew back, using one of his massive fingers to wipe away her tears.

"Nonsense, girl," he croaked. "You saved us. Fool on those idiots if they can't see it." His voice cracked. He drew a shuddering breath and glanced at the door. "Time's almost up. Here, I know those chains. They're the ones we use in the pen. This should unlock them, when the time comes."

He slipped a piece of iron into her fingers. Kaila stared in disbelief at the key in her hand. "Dad…you can't."

"You're my daughter," he said, straightening. He hesitated then, his face twisting with some unspoken pain before resuming a grimace. "Kaila, there's something you must know. About your mother."

Sniffing, Kaila looked up at him with a frown.

"She wasn't Elysian, whatever they claim," he whispered, "but…I fear I have been a fool. I should have told you the truth long ago. That day in the mountains, when the enemy had me trapped…" His voice cracked. "I only survived because of your mother."

"What?" It didn't make any sense. Her father had been alone that day, sacrificing himself so the rest of his company could retreat.

"She saved me, though I never saw how. I caught a blow in the head from an enemy mace and did not wake until hours later. She nursed me, until I was well enough to return to camp." He hesitated. "I never thought I would see her again, until she found me one night, almost a year later, and presented me with you."

A tingling spread across Kaila's scalp. "How…"

"My captain helped me cover it up. It's why I retired—"

He broke off as the sound of the bolt being drawn back came from the door. "Quickly," he hissed. "Get those chains off. And when I give the sign, *run!*"

And then it was too late for questions. The door swung open and Sister Eurador entered, eyes narrowed in suspicion as they flicked between the pair of them. Warden Chain followed.

"Now, Overseer Dwyn. About the mother."

"Of course. I only knew her a short time." Something in her father's voice made Kaila's head snap up. He hadn't shifted from her side, but that look…his eyes were glowering, glinting with a madness that made her tremble. He drew in a breath, shoulders straightening, and all sign of subservience left him. "But she was the love of my life."

With those words, Gideon Dwyn hurled himself at the Warden.

Sister Eurador screamed, and even the armoured soldier seemed taken aback as three hundred pounds of hardened muscle collided with him. With a crash of metal and stone, the Warden and Gideon toppled through the doorway into the corridor.

Her father came up first, his fists battering at the Warden's helmet, slamming his skull into the floor again and again. Shrieking, Sister Eurador tried to tackle him, but the old woman was half Gideon's size and he shrugged her off like a hound would an excited puppy. Snarling, his fists closed around the Warden's throat and began to squeeze.

But this was no ordinary soldier, and the shock of her father's assault had already worn off.

An iron hand caught one of her father's. Light flashed, brilliant, blinding, and suddenly there was an energy in the air, crackling like the moments before lightning struck. Kaila's ears went *pop* as her father reared back, hands clasped at his temples. Crying out, he staggered, clenching his eyes closed, teeth bared.

The sight snapped Kaila into action. She surged from her chair, the chains falling empty from her unbound wrists. Heart pounding, she sprang for the doorway. But she had forgotten Sister Eurador, who had recovered from her father's battering. She tackled Kaila and they went down in a tangle of limbs, the older woman shrieking and clawing at her eyes. Eurador's elderly face was demented, twisted with such hatred that Kaila flinched.

But thankfully, the sister was still an old woman and Kaila a young one. She would not be stopped from helping her father, whatever it took. She struck out, fist connecting with the woman's shoulder, and something went *crack*. The woman fell, moaning and clutching her arm.

A *crash* came from the doorway. Tomas and Sareen had joined the fray and were wrestling with her father while the Warden gained his feet. Kaila was about to go to his aid, when a groan from Eurador drew her attention. The sight of her mentor on the ground, gasping and clutching at her shoulder, tore shreds in Kaila's soul. Then she glimpsed the ring on her finger—and its little agimet crystal from her third Trial. The one she swore she'd charged with a little bit of *atar*.

She dove and tore it from the woman's finger. A hiss came from Kaila's throat as she did so. She *felt* it, a little jolt from the energy inside. She had been right. But could she do something with it?

The world shone bright with a thousand pinpricks of light as she drew on the *atar*. The fight outside had moved away from the interrogation room. She stumbled into the hall and watched the battle between her father and the others. Each man and woman shone with that otherworldly glow—the Warden brightest of all, though there was a twisted, distorted shimmer to his power. The five crystals in his armour, charged with a thousand times the power she held in her hand, were blinding to look at.

Her courage wilted. She was just a young woman from a nowhere town. What did she know about any of this?

A thread ran from Elric to her father, but whatever the Warden was doing, it didn't seem to slow him as he grasped Tomas by the neck and slammed his head into the concrete wall. The guard slumped to the ground with a groan, where Sareen had already fallen.

Roaring, her father faced the Warden. The thread connecting him to Elric Chain suddenly blazed and Gideon's bellow turned into a scream. He sank to one knee, struggling for breath.

"It seems we have found the source of corruption in this town," Elric growled as he advanced. Kaila's skin crawled as he extended his hand and liquid metal emerged from his palm, extending and solidifying into a shining sword. "Clearly, Sister Eurador has been negligent in her duties. That must be corrected, once I have cleansed the bad blood."

"You. Will. Not. Touch. My. *Daughter!*"

Screaming, her father surged to his feet and launched himself at the Warden. The blade came up, but he battered it aside with a powerful arm and smashed a right hook into the Warden's helmet. The armoured man rocked back, but before her father could strike again, the Warden recovered. This time, when the sword slashed at Gideon, he could not evade the silver blade as it slashed across his chest.

Blood dripping through his shirt, Gideon grunted and retreated a step. The Warden advanced.

"I'll admit, you are a bold man," Elric chuckled. "I didn't expect to find any real sport in these backwater villages. But your heart betrays you. Though, maybe I can fix that, and you can die serving your kingdom one last time."

In Kaila's vision, the line connecting the Warden to her father thickened. Now she sensed a difference in the light, one she couldn't quite decipher. It coiled around her father's light, binding it tight and then sinking barbs into its fiery glow. And the pure white of her father's soul changed, darkening to an angry red.

He stiffened, not from pain this time, but something else. A tremor seemed to ripple across his face as he bared his teeth, a moan rattling up from the depths of his chest.

And then a sudden stillness came over him. A strange sort of peace. Kaila stood frozen, staring at him, trying to understand what was happening.

"Dad?" she said hesitantly.

At her voice, he turned abruptly towards her, and she gasped. His eyes were empty, showing no hint of the man who moments ago had sobbed as he hugged her. His face was twisted, his lips drawn back in a sneer. Fists clenched, he took a step towards her, then another.

"Dad?" she said again, fear clogging her throat. "Dad, it's me. *Dad!*"

She screamed the last word as he lunged, his massive fist swinging as though to crack open her skull. But he flinched at her scream, jerking as though stung.

"You know the truth now." Elric Chain's voice came from behind them, mocking. "You cannot resist it."

Gideon shuddered, his eyes squeezing closed. Veins bulged on his forehead as he trembled. She could almost feel his agony as he fought whatever compulsion the Warden's magic had placed over him. Kaila ached to help him, to use her power and sever the magic that bound her father to the Warden, but she didn't know how.

"Bring me the girl." Elric's words were like steel. Hard, unyielding.

And yet with them, her father's eyes snapped open. They were shot with red, and blood dripped from his nose, as though the Warden's magic had broken something inside him. But he did not move towards her.

"No."

And Kaila saw recognition in his gaze. That was her father. He might only be a man, but his was an inner strength that didn't care about magic or *atar* or whatever arcane powers the Wardens could wield. And so he bared bloody teeth and faced the Warden.

"Daughter," he panted. "Remember what I said."

Kaila didn't have a chance to respond before he charged. The Warden's sword came up. There was no way he could miss this time. No time for her father to react. The magical blade glittered as it plunged down, piercing her father's chest.

"*No!*" Kaila screamed.

Fingers clenched around the stolen ring. She sucked in the drop of *atar* inside and its strength filled her. Not enough, but she didn't care. Her father was the only person left who still cared about her. She couldn't let him die.

Shrieking her rage, Kaila hurled everything she had at the Warden, trying to move him like she had with Theron. If she could get him away from her father, knock him down, disable him and that terrible suit of armour, maybe she could still save him…

But rather than moving the Warden, there came instead a *pulling* in her gut—then all the energy she'd used seemed to *ricochet* back on her. In an instant, Kaila was picked up and hurled backwards. She threw out a desperate hand to try and stop herself, but there was nothing to grasp before she slammed into the only object behind her —a window.

The *crash* of breaking glass followed. She had one final glimpse of her father falling to the ground, blood pumping from the ruin of his chest left by the Warden's sword.

And then she was falling, plummeting towards the ground seven storeys below.

THE FIRST RULE OF MAGIC THAT ANYONE LEARNED—MOVERS LIKE Theron especially—was that their power had limitations. One of the greatest of which was that the greater the magnitude of an action, the greater the cost. This was both in terms of *atar*, and on the vessels which channelled it—in most cases, this being your body and the crystal you were drawing from.

As far as Movers were concerned, costs were contingent on mass, distance and the change in velocity of whatever object you were attempting to control.

A pebble was easier to lift than a person.

Deflecting a pebble shot towards you at great speed was harder.

Most difficult of all, catching a *person* falling towards you at terminal velocity.

Which was to say that Theron's day did not begin in an ideal manner. His rescue plan was still in the draft stages as he wandered into the ugly concrete complex that was the colonnade of Elgoss. A stablehand was grooming an enormous, black Fresian charger—the horse the Warden had ridden, Theron assumed. Behind the man, a door had been left open. That was his way in.

Theron was about to slip past the villager when it happened.

A *crash* came from above, followed by the tinkling of breaking glass. A shadow flitted across the courtyard as all eyes turned upwards. And there, eyes wide with horror as she fell, was the girl he had come to rescue.

Theron was so stunned that she plummeted several storeys before he could react, by which point, the aforementioned laws of mass and motion were rapidly coming into effect.

So much for your brilliant plan.

Gritting his teeth, he unleashed his power and immediately felt the strain of *atar* in his veins. Kaila was already moving with significant velocity and she lurched as he attempted to arrest her fall, her headlong plunge towards the courtyard barely slowing. If she struck at that speed, she would be cracked open like an egg.

But stopping her abruptly would risk tearing her apart from the inside anyway. Delicacy was required, but Theron was worthy of the challenge. Hopefully.

People screamed and scattered as glass crashed down around them. Theron was grateful for the chaos. His hood was up, shielding the light of *atar* in his eyes, but it wouldn't take more than a curious glance to notice his presence.

By the time she passed the third floor, Kaila's velocity had halved. Unfortunately, she wasn't exactly helping. She screamed and thrashed, apparently unaware of his efforts. The movement made Theron's task all the more difficult.

Still, he held his concentration, and by the time she passed the final landing, Kaila's fall had slowed to practically a hover. Tempted as Theron was to let her drop the last few feet, he set her gently on the concrete beside him.

"Well, fancy you dropping by like this," he said with a grin.

Hazel eyes that looked surprised to be alive widened. *"You!"*

"Me!" Theron beamed.

"I...I thought you left."

"And I thought you were going to 'talk' to them."

Boom!

Their heads snapped up as, overhead, the remnants of the window were torn from its brackets by a force somewhere inside the building. A shadow darkened the twisted hole that was left. The Warden.

"Look, I'd love to stick around and chat," Theron said quickly, eyes never leaving the man. What powers did this one have at his disposal? Could he reach them down here somehow? "But if you don't mind, maybe the questions could wait for later."

"My father…" Kaila rasped.

Theron pursed his lips, still watching the Warden. A second later, the man vanished back inside and Theron breathed a sigh of relief. They had a few minutes if the monster had to take the stairs. He turned to Kaila with a grimace.

"If your father is somewhere up there, then there's nothing either of us can do for him now."

Kaila looked like she would argue, but Theron was already turning away. The stablehand stood beside the Fresian charger, his mouth was agape and eyes bulging as he stared at them—or rather Kaila. Theron supposed it must seem as though she'd just flown down seven storeys to land on the ground before him. The poor lad seemed to be wavering between guarding the horse or trying to apprehend them.

Theron made it easy by lifting a piece of rubble with his Gift and smashing it over the lad's head. As he crumpled to the ground, Theron lunged for the reins of the horse before it could bolt.

"We should go," he said to Kaila, already swinging himself into the saddle.

But when he glanced back, the girl was still frozen, fists clenched, eyes scrunched closed. He was about to shout at her to move, when another *crash* came from above. His head snapped up, but the Warden did not reappear. Yet.

Grimacing, Theron offered Kaila his hand. Face pale, lips pursed tight, she took it and he pulled her into the saddle behind him. Somewhere outside, a bell began to toll. Cries of alarm rained down from the walls of the colonnade. Elsewhere, he heard the shouts of angry voices approaching. The good citizens of Elgoss were coming to stop the enemy.

"The gates?" she gasped.

"Leave them to me," Theron replied. "Hold on."

When he felt her hands clasp around his waist, he spurred the horse into movement. A little cry came from Kaila as the charger surged forward, but then they were away, racing from the courtyard out into the streets of the settlement.

***

Glass crunched beneath Elric Chain's boots as he crossed the courtyard. The attendant he'd left with his horse lay on the ground, groaning softly as he tried to lift himself from the rubble. There was no sign of his mount.

Steel creaked as Elric clenched his fists, the *atar* in his veins pulsating. So much power, and yet the girl had slipped through their fingers. How?

His gaze shifted to the building looming above. The father had been unexpected. He had resisted Elric's psionic pulse—and then thrown off the control he'd attempted. That should not have been possible for these weak-minded villagers.

Perhaps that was the problem. He had underestimated the man. An error on his part.

When facing the enemy, one must always stand vigilant, mind sharp and heart steadfast.

The words of the Nameless, the lost god of the Magisterium. His identity, like so much else, had been lost during humanity's centuries of servitude, but his teachings remained for the faithful to follow.

The first mistake had been his own, but not without cause. He had already been on his way to the next village when the messenger found him. Each year, four Wardens were chosen to oversee the Trials—one for each of the three Dominions, plus the capital region. Unfortunately, Elric's pilgrimage to the Iron Pinnacles had been long and mostly uneventful. Weeks had turned to months and the most excitement he'd had was cutting down a few snot-nosed brats that had slithered like worms into the kingdom's flock.

So when he'd received the message, he'd been over-eager,

rushing headlong back to the town without pausing to consider it might be a trap, or that the conspiracy might extend beyond the two suspects the sister had identified. Now Elric had to reconsider his assumptions. There were questions to be asked. The sister better have the answers, for her sake.

He found her crouched in the ruin of the interrogation room, sitting in the dirt and blood while a woman attended to her shoulder. It was one of the guards who had stood outside the room. The other had not gotten back up after the father crushed his skull against the wall. A shame. The pair had proven their worth, and it seemed like loyalist were going to be difficult to find in Elgoss.

The soldier looked up at his approach and rose sharply. "Sir," she said smartly, "what happened? Is she…"

"Escaped," he grunted. "With the aid of the second Elysian." He considered her a moment. "What is your name, soldier?"

"Sareen, sir. And I'm just a guard nowadays. Completed my commission a couple of years ago."

Elric nodded, shifting his gaze to the father of the Elysian. The man lay where he had fallen, his tainted blood pooling on the concrete, slowly spreading along the fine cracks in the grey material. "He was the overseer of the mine?"

The woman nodded and he grimaced. "Poor tidings indeed." It meant the entire facility was compromised.

Sareen's eyes widened. "You think others could be involved?"

Elric nodded. His iron boots grated on stone as he approached the sister. "How could you allow the enemy to infiltrate your congregation?" he growled. "To taint one of our most valuable assets."

Pain shone from the woman's eyes as she lifted her chin to meet his iron gaze. "I have failed my post," she said simply. "I offer my life in reparation."

Elric grunted. "The Magisterium will require more than the life of an old woman after this disaster." He stepped into the interrogation room. The chains that had held the girl lay discarded amidst the debris. They showed no sign of breakage. Someone had unlocked them.

"The father slipped her the key," he surmised.

Sareen nodded. "When she was knocked unconscious in the

cave-in, we used the chains from the other prisoners to bind her." She bowed her head. "I'm sorry, sir. We never thought to switch them for something more secure."

"It was not your place to make such considerations, soldier," Elric rumbled. "A Sister is responsible for matters of security when it comes to the enemy."

Sister Eurador bowed her head. "Yes, sir."

"That's all you have to say for yourself?" he growled. Returning to the corridor, he surveyed the ruins of the window. "The girl had a piece of charged agimet. How?"

That provoked a response from the sister. Her head jerked up. "Impossible."

"The girl tried to move me," Elric said, stepping toward her. "I'll decide what's impossible."

"My ring," she whispered. "Kaila...the Elysian, she attempted the third Trial after you left. She claimed to have charged its crystal."

"*She what?*"

"She was mistaken!" the sister exclaimed. Finding her courage, she glared at Elric. "I am no fool, *sir*. That crystal was empty. I swear it."

Elric pursed his lips beneath his helm, considering her words. The Third Trial established whether a candidate could draw ambient *atar* into an empty crystal. All Wardens possessed this ability, though their strength varied. It took Elric hours to charge a piece of agimet when he was far from a nexus.

Could this Elysian fugitive also possess the ability? The thought made his blood run cold. That should not be possible. The ability was a blessing from the Nameless, passed down to his many children. If the enemy had found a way to copy their ability…

He grimaced. So there were *two* mysteries here. How the girl had passed the Trial of Agimet, and whether she possessed the powers of a Warden. The Sanctum in Tah'raus needed to hear of this.

"Sareen," he said, turning to the woman. "I need you to travel to the capital. I will prepare a writ of passage, and a message to bring to the Sanctum."

"Why…why me?" Sareen stuttered, forgetting his rank in a moment of shock.

"I do not know who else is involved in this conspiracy. But I saw you fight. I know I can trust you." He eyed her from beneath his iron visor. "Can you do it, soldier?"

She stiffened at the question, her lips drawing into a tight line. "I can, sir."

"Good. Then fetch me a quill and paper while I speak further with the sister."

The woman saluted and raced off to complete his order. Elric turned to regard the woman. She was a sorry sight, arm still hanging limp at her side, face crumpled with pain.

"You have failed your kingdom, Sister Eurador," he said quietly.

To her credit, the woman did not try to defend herself, only bowed her head in supplication. "I understand."

He nodded, considering her. He did not believe she had deliberately misled the Magisterium, but her failures here were unforgiveable. She should have tested her ring for *atar* residue. And not one, not two, but *three* Elysian had been discovered in this village in as many days. One had even fooled the Trial of Agimet. Her negligence was unquestionable.

His blow fell before the woman could see it coming, the blade forming silently in his hand. She crumpled to the ground, pale eyes staring up at him, empty. They were still watching him when Sareen returned. She staggered when she saw the body, gaping.

"What…what happened?"

Elric turned to her, face calm beneath his helmet. "The girl's father went on a rampage," he said softly. "The Elysian witch clearly left a spell in his mind. Sister Eurador was killed trying to stop their escape. Understood?"

Word of this failure could not be allowed to spread. Fresia relied on the stability of their political systems. From the lowliest miner to the Daughters and Sisters and Wardens, all the way to the king and his Matron, everyone knew their place in the system. It did not —*could not*—fail. Whatever internal battles took place between factions of the Magisterium, outwardly, they must maintain their infallibility, or else everything would crumble.

Trembling slightly, the woman met his eyes and gave a nod.

"Good. Now come. I have a letter to write for you."

"Yes, sir." She hesitated. "What about you?"

He glanced out the ruined window. "First, I will see that this village is locked down. No one but you may leave until all trace of the enemy has been cleansed from inside its walls."

"And Kai…the Elysian?"

Elric grunted. "Our enemy think they have escaped, but they have only delayed the inevitable. I will hunt them down and discover how they tricked our Trials." He turned his iron gaze on the woman. "And then I will send them both screaming to their maker."

Kaila's mind was the void. Nothing remained. Not her love or her passion or her hope. Someone had taken a knife and carved them from her in great, bloody chunks. The world seemed blurred, the mountains and the path and the storm clouds merging into a watercolour of darkness and shadow. Empty. It was all empty.

At least there were no more tears. She would never cry again. How could any day ever hurt as much as this one? Seeing the people she loved turn against her, her heroes try to kill her. Watching her father die for her.

She hadn't even gotten to say goodbye.

The rhythm of the horse was Kaila's only constant, her anchor to this awful world. Without the beast's weight between her legs, she might have just faded away. Laid down in a ditch and waited for the Warden to find her. What was the point in going on anyway? They had already taken everything.

Thunder rumbled and a heavy rain began to fall. The horse shied at the flashing in the sky, but Theron called out something and it steadied. The thief had set a terrible pace since they'd bolted through the gates of Elgoss, leaving her village and everyone she had ever known behind. Kaila hadn't ridden a horse in years—not since the pony kept by Caellum's family to work their fields had died in the four-year drought—and certainly never anything as large as a

Fresian charger. Fortunately, the stallion had a smooth gait and she had managed to cling to Theron so far.

Within seconds, the rain had soaked through her tunic and breaches. A few minutes after that she was trembling uncontrollably. Water rushed across their path, turning red with the heavy iron deposits that gave their Dominance its name. In this harsh land, rain was rare. In a good year, they might have one day where the heavens opened. In the bad ones, years could pass before the rains returned. Then even the deep wells of Elgoss turned scarlet with the promise of death.

Kaila had only seen rains like this once in her life, ten years ago, when half the mountain had given way in the deluge. It had taken weeks to clear the landslides and open the roads again.

Eventually, even Theron couldn't continue in the torrent. Cursing, he drew back on the reins, slowing them to a walk. By then even the mighty charger was panting and Kaila was swaying in her saddle. The roar of the storm was all around them. It was still late in the afternoon, but darkness had come early to the mountains, the clouds so black only flashes of lightning remained for light.

The respite was brief. There was no shelter to be found on the exposed side of the mountain. They pressed on at a trot and Kaila's void was soon joined by a fresh sensation—pain. Her aching thighs could barely cling to the saddle and where they *did* manage to hold on, the wet fabric rubbed at her flesh and the harsh bouncing of the beast jarred her spine.

Lightning turned the sky white and thunder boomed, so loud it had to be right overhead. The horse reared and Kaila clung to Theron with everything she had. She actually *smelt* the burning in the air. As her vision cleared, the stallion settled. Cursing, Theron urged the beast on through the night.

Body aching, Kaila gritted her teeth. This was nothing. Less than nothing. Soldiers of Fresia rode for days without complaint when the need arose. Her stomach panged. Those same soldiers would hunt her now. All because of a stupid mistake…

Mistake, mistake, mistake.

The word chased itself through her mind. She kept trying to reconcile everything that had happened with what she *knew*. To make sense of it all. Because it *had* to make sense, right? The Elysian were the great enemy. Their spies were everywhere, using their magic and cunning to infiltrate human society. Only the eyes of the enemy glowed with *atar*. Except…

Her eyes glowed.

She had power.

But she wasn't a traitor. She loved her people, her duty. If they had asked, Kaila would have used that power against the enemy without hesitation—just as she had in the mines.

Instead, she had been branded a traitor like all the rest.

She closed her eyes. Her head was spinning. No matter how hard she tried, Kaila couldn't put the two together. She was missing something.

By the time Theron led them off the road and into the shelter of a cave—a fissure in the cliffs barely large enough for a horse to fit—Kaila was trembling so badly she couldn't even move her legs. She sat there shaking after Theron dismounted, jaw clenched, trying to will herself to rise, even as the void whispered that there was no point, that there was nothing left for her anyway—

"Need a hand?"

She flinched at the gentle tone of Theron's voice. Blinking, she found him at her side. His hand was extended in an offering of help and there was a strange look on his face.

Pity.

Somewhere in Kaila's core, in the depths of the void, something stirred.

Anger.

"I don't need anything from you," she said, slapping away his hand.

Kaila would never know where she found the strength to swing herself out of that saddle, nor to clamber down from the enormous beast. She *would* remember, though, how her knees shook and trembled as her feet touched the ground.

"You could have fooled me back there," Theron remarked, arms crossed and one eyebrow raised. "You know, when I was rescuing you."

"I...saved...myself!" she tried to say, but the effect of her words was somewhat ruined by her chattering teeth.

Wrapping her arms around her chest, she settled for flashing him a look that, had it been an arrow, would have pierced the bastard right through the heart.

"Oh, yes." The thief snorted. "You *definitely* looked in control of things when you came tumbling out of the seventh-floor window."

Kaila was shaking again, though she wasn't sure if it was the cold this time, or her pure, unadulterated *rage*.

"I never would have been there if it wasn't for you!" She actually managed to get the words out. "This is all *your* fault! *You* did this to me!"

For a few heartbeats, Theron said nothing. A crash of lightning shook the mountain and the rain roared louder. Gusts of wind still sent it swirling into the cave on occasion. Kaila doubted there was a single dry patch left on the mountain tonight. It didn't matter. Turning away from Theron, she staggered as far into the cave as the narrow walls allowed and slumped to the ground. Squeezing her eyes closed, she pulled her knees up to her chest and willed the vile man to go away.

And Theron did, for a time. He returned to the stallion and began rummaging through its saddlebags, removing a brush and several rags. He then set about removing the saddle and other tack, setting them nearby before returning with the rags, which he used to rub down the charger. The horse twitched and trembled as he worked, nickering occasionally to make its displeasure at being ridden in such conditions clear.

When he was done with the rags, the Elysian thief brushed down the stallion's fine black pelt and then led it to the rear of the cave, as far from the elements as possible.

Outside, the pounding of the rain was replaced by a soft crunching noise. Kaila rose with a frown and made her way to the cavemouth. Peering out into the darkness, her heart fell. The rain had stopped, but now swirling specks of white came hissing down from above.

It was snowing.

She shivered as the breeze sliced through her rain-soaked tunic, an ache beginning in the base of her skull. She quickly turned away. She had removed her jacket back in the mine and the clothes she was wearing weren't made for this weather.

Back inside the cave, Theron was rummaging in the saddlebags again. He looked up as she approached, holding a heavy leather jacket. Her heart leapt.

"Give it to me!" she gasped.

The thief raised an eyebrow as he passed it over. "It won't do you any good soaked to the skin like that."

She was already slipping her arms into the leather sleeves and ignored him. What would an Elysian know about human frailties? With his magic, the man had probably never had to work a day in his life. Theron shrugged and returned to his search of the saddlebags. A few moments later, he drew out a bundle of kindling and a small cloth sack stained black by the coal inside. He eyed it a moment, lips twisted in a frown.

"A few hours' worth," he muttered, glancing at the snow. "Enough to dry us, maybe."

Kaila swallowed. Her bones ached from the cold. The jacket wasn't helping. She rubbed her hands together and hopped from foot to foot, hoping the exercise would warm her. Outside, the whisper of snow and howling of the wind continued.

Theron set about preparing a fire.

"Can't you just light it with your magic?" she muttered as another tremor shook her.

He raised an eyebrow. "Only Binders can do that, and they're generally a bit noisy for campfires."

"What do they do?"

"They can change the physical state of matter," Theron grunted.

Kaila wanted to ask more, but her teeth were chattering so badly it made conversation difficult. Theron continued his work, stacking the kindling into a kind of tower before piling the coal around it. It was painstaking, watching while the cold ate into her, feeling the numbness spreading from her toes and fingers to her hands and feet.

Finally, Theron appeared satisfied with his work. He took the piece of flint and struck sparks into the pile. Kaila hovered close, hands extended as little tongues of fire emerged from the kindling to lick the coal, only to die back again. For a second, it seemed the stones wouldn't catch, but Theron leaned in close and blew into the base of the fire. With a *whoosh*, the blaze came roaring back, the coal glowing bright with orange light. Kaila had never seen a more beautiful sight.

Apparently satisfied, Theron grunted and stepped back. Then he began removing his coat.

"*Whatareyoudoing?*" Kaila gasped, the words squeezed from her lungs by a particularly violent convulsion. The jacket hadn't helped at all.

"Trying not to freeze to death," Theron replied. "I suggest you do the same."

His shirt followed his coat, both of which he hung from protrusions in the cave wall. To Kaila's mortification, his boots and pants were next. Mercifully, he stopped short of removing his underpants. Only then did he crouch alongside the fire with a sigh, hands extended to the flames. He flicked a glance at her, one eyebrow raised.

"You know, I hear frostbite is pretty unpleasant."

Kaila scowled at him. Wrapping her arms stubbornly around her chest, she remained where she was. But the trembling continued to worsen, and her feet had gone from numb to aching. The flames warmed her hands, but otherwise, the heat did not seem to reach her.

Finally, with a curse, she shot to her feet. "Look away."

Chuckling, the Elysian complied and she quickly stripped off the jacket, followed by her shirt, face flushing as she did so. Her boots were a more difficult prospect. A cry slipped from her lips when she tried to remove them, pain shooting through her feet. Biting her lip against any further weakness, she all but tore them off. Her pants followed last, the damp fabric clinging to her skin. Trembling, she hung each garment from the walls before finally settling down by the fire.

"Can I look now?" Theron asked, his voice rich with humour.

"*No,*" Kaila spat. "Keep your eyes to yourself, Elysian."

Theron laughed, though to his credit he did keep his eyes

averted. Sitting on the cold ground with only her underwear for protection, Kaila felt horribly vulnerable. Even the pebbles dug into her flesh. If anyone came upon them now, they would be helpless. Yet as she stretched her feet and arms towards the crackling flames, she finally felt the heat wash over her. She let out a little moan.

"The jacket will be great to keep the cold out tomorrow," Theron said softly, after they'd sat there in the dark a few minutes, "but it was also keeping out the warmth of the fire. Especially when wearing wet clothes."

Kaila muttered something unintelligible that could probably have been interpreted as a thank you.

The silence stretched out. Eventually, the last of Kaila's trembling ceased. It was beginning to feel quite warm in the cave. The wind had ceased and silence enfolded the darkness. Settling herself into a more comfortable position, Kaila stole a glimpse in Theron's direction. She'd been doing a good job of ignoring the thief up to that moment, but curiosity had always been her vice.

The Elysian sat absently shredding the bark from a piece of kindling. His back was to her and she swallowed when she saw it. He would have been small beside her father and she had expected a weak man, used to cheating with his magic. Instead, his back and shoulders were all corded muscle, and his skin was bronzed, probably after years spent beneath the hot sun. Several scars marked his arms, jagged and thick, probably the remains of old wounds collected in battle, while others criss-crossed his back. Those Kaila recognised as the kiss of a lash.

"What happened back there?" he asked softly.

She jerked at the question. "What?" she snapped, still not quite over her discomfort.

Gravel crunched as he twisted and nodded in the direction that might have been Elgoss.

"Back in town—how did you get away from the Warden?"

A vice closed around her heart. "My father," she whispered.

"Did he also have the Gift?"

"The what?"

"Magic," Theron replied. "Was he another Mover, like you? Or a Weaver? A Binder, maybe?" Doubt entered Theron's voice. "You really don't know any of these names, do you? Ah well, he had to have some kind of powerful magic to get out of there alive."

"He *didn't* get out alive." She drew in a shuddering breath. "He snuck me a key. And then…then he attacked the Warden. Distracted him so…so I could run." Her voice cracked as she remembered her father's final words, urging her to flee.

"Ah." Theron seemed to consider this. "Then he was a braver man than most. Few have the courage to reject the Magisterium."

"My father was a loyal citizen of Fresia…" Kaila began, before she realised what she was saying.

Her father *was* loyal…until his only daughter had been accused. Then he'd been the only one to stand up to them, to say they were wrong. The only one who saw the truth.

"You're beginning to understand?" Theron asked.

Kaila shook her head. "Sister Eurador is a good person," she whispered, the words catching in her throat. "She thought they were doing the right thing."

"Ah, yes, the *right thing*." Theron fell silent for a while, then continued. "I knew a man once. Good bloke. Or at least we thought he was, until he butchered his wife and children. Swore they were possessed by demons. Said he'd saved their lives, killing them. Spared their souls or something of the sort."

"What's your point?" Kaila asked through gritted teeth.

"My point is, just because you *believe* you are doing the right thing, doesn't mean your actions cannot be evil," Theron said softly.

Kaila suppressed a shudder. "He was clearly mad."

"Ay, sometimes I think this entire world went mad centuries ago. Doesn't change my point." His eyes found hers in the darkness. "You know I'm right. I can see it in your eyes."

Her head jerked up to find him watching her. Heat raced to her face. "Hey!"

"Sorry." Raising his hands in surrender, he turned his head back to the wall, though not before she caught a glimpse of that smile again. It set something more than just anger churning in her gut.

"Bastard," she muttered at his back. Then, because she needed to distract herself from that damned smile, she added, "Why do you care anyway? You were going to kill him."

There was a pause before the thief seemed to understand. "Your father was the overseer?"

"Yes!"

Theron fell silent. The mouth of the cave was dark, though whether that was because of the storm or night had fallen, it was impossible to tell. Nearby, the charger nickered and shifted on his feet.

"I wasn't going to kill him," Theron said at last, his tone strangely muted. "I just needed the threat to seem genuine, so he would tell me the truth. I don't kill slaves."

"My father was *not* a slave!" Then, realising what he was saying, added, "*We* are not slaves."

"No, of *course* not," Theron said, swinging on her with a wave of his hand. "I mean, *obviously* you're free to leave whenever you like."

"It's dangerous outside the walls!"

"And choose your own jobs."

"We have to put the best workers in the best positions."

"And *of course* you're paid well for your work."

"The Magisterium provides…" she trailed off with a glare.

She wanted to scream, to yell at him that it wasn't true, but the truth was, everything felt wrong. Like the world had tilted on its axis and now she didn't know what was up from down. Her entire life, she had never questioned Sister Eurador's teachings. She was Kaila Dwyn, daughter of a hero, loyal to her kingdom, ready to do her duty for her species, whatever the cost.

But now her kingdom called her a traitor and the Magisterium was hunting her. And maybe she wasn't even human—at least, not entirely.

Her mother. Who had she been? Her father said she wasn't Elysian, but what Kaila had done in the mine seemed to prove the lie in that. She had so many questions. Questions she feared she would never have the answers too.

Abruptly, she realised Theron had faced her again in the heat of their argument. She opened her mouth to yell at him some more, but somehow the energy wouldn't come. She was so tired, she wanted to close her eyes and sleep for a long, long time, and hope that when she woke, this would all turn out to be some horrible dream.

But she shouldn't sleep, not like this, alone with the strange man, so instead she asked the first thing that came to mind.

"Where did you get those scars?"

Theron glanced at his chest. The lines that crisscrossed his skin continued there. "Oh, so you're allowed to look?" he asked, raising an eyebrow.

Kaila tried and failed to keep the heat from her cheeks as she felt his eyes roving over her. "Bastard," she muttered, but this time she didn't tell him to look away. "Well," she continued when he didn't speak, "where did you get them?"

"Oh, here and there," he replied with a casual wave. "You know, the prince of thieves has many enemies."

She snorted. "I doubt you're even a prince of paupers. Besides, some of those are from a lash. The kind the Sisters like to use, if I'm not mistaken."

Theron was silent, his head bowed, so that his eyes were cast in shadow. "Not all fathers are as loyal to their children as your own."

"Oh." Kaila mumbled, struck mute by the admission. She looked away, recalling her father's final embrace, the relief that had filled her to bursting, that at least someone she loved had not turned against her.

A strained silence hung over the cave as they both sat, staring at nothing. Then with a grunt and a shrug, Theron rose. Placing his hands on his hip, he grinned down at her.

"Well, My Lady, are you ready for bedtime?"

"Scoundrel!" she snarled, leaping to her feet in outrage. "How dare—"

But Theron had already turned his back on her. Wandering over to the saddlebags, he rummaged inside before coming up with a heavy woollen blanket. He swirled it around his shoulders like it was the height of fashion, eyes dancing with amusement.

"Excellent. More blanket for me, then."

Kaila gaped at him as he carried the blanket to the fire and laid himself down beside it.

"You knew we had that all along?" she gasped, finally recovering her wits.

"Couldn't have you getting your wet clothes all over it now, could I?"

"I…you…*bastard!*" It was all she managed.

Then because the man was *infuriating*, she sat herself back down before the fire, crossed her arms, and stared out into the night. All was dark beyond the cavemouth now. She couldn't even see the snow slashing down to cover the ground, or the flashes of distant lightning, or even feel the wind…

A frown touched Kaila's brow. Rising slowly, she squinted, trying to figure out the strangeness. One step, and another, and then she saw. A tingling sensation spread down her spine. It was snow. All snow. The entrance had been buried.

"We're trapped!" she gasped, swinging on Theron.

"Oh relax, would you?" His muffled voice emerged from somewhere in the folds of the blanket. "I'm trying to sleep."

"We've been buried beneath the snow!"

"And what exactly do you expect me to do about it?"

"Use your magic!"

An exasperated sigh came from the folds. "And then what? Did you want to ride back out into that storm?"

Kaila hesitated. "No," she admitted.

Even so, she couldn't keep her heart from pounding at the thought of being trapped once more beneath the earth. Her eyes snapped to the fire and their already dwindling pile of coal. If it went out, they would be left in darkness. Entombed…

"Relax, Kaila," Theron said with a sigh. "When the storm passes, I'll use my power to get us out. That much I can do. In the meantime, that wall of snow is going to keep the wind and the cold from us, okay?"

She swallowed, trying to take comfort from his words. After a moment, she nodded and returned to her seat. But she couldn't keep from thinking about it. The stone above. The darkness. The voices that whispered to her…

"So," this time, Theron's intrusion on her thoughts was welcome. The Elysian hadn't retreated into his blanket, but remained sitting up. "What happened after your father got you out of the chains?"

Instinctively, Kaila's hand went to the ring she had taken from Sister Eurador. It was empty again. Hugging her knees to her chest, she studied the ground, wondering how much she could trust this man. Sure, he had come back for her, helped her escape, but…he was still Elysian. And a thief. His kind were the enemy.

And yet, she also had questions. About how the magic worked. She thought she had understood it back in the mine, but when she'd used it against the Wardens…

"I stole a piece of agimet from Sister Eurador," she said quietly, deciding she would tell him a part of the truth and see what he revealed. "I thought I could use it against the Warden, but…"

"Ahhh." Theron chuckled. "Now it all makes sense."

"Ha?" Kaila asked, a frown coming to her lips. "I don't understand."

"The Gift doesn't work on Wardens—at least not while they're manifesting their armour. Whatever you do to them will recoil back on you. Thus, your backflip out the seventh-storey window." He seemed to consider that for a moment. "Though it still leaves me with one question: what was a Sister doing with a piece of charged agimet?"

Kaila shrugged. "I don't know," she lied.

She sensed the thief's eyes on her. This time she just scowled back at him. He wanted to embarrass her, she was sure. Otherwise, he would have been a gentleman and offered her the blanket instead of hogging it for himself.

"Ah well," he said, "guess that secret will die with the sister."

With a shrug, he lay down again and rolled over, drawing the blanket tight around him. She watched him for a while, a scowl on her lips. A part of her wanted to stomp over and kick him until he gave up the blanket, but she resisted. He was Elysian, after all, with untold magic at his command. Who knew how long his patience would last.

Though, she wasn't sure that was the entire reason.

Shaking herself, she noticed the fire burning low. She reached into the sack for another chunk of coal, but her handed closed around cloth. Her heart stilled as she lifted the bag and found it empty. The fire flickered lower. Soon it would be reduced to the orange glow of its coals. Then the cool would creep back in, however thick the wall of ice that sealed them inside.

"You know, I don't bite," Theron's muffled voice came from the blanket.

Her face flushed, but this time she didn't immediately reject the offer. She glared at the empty sack, as though if she scared it enough it might replenish itself. But it was no use. A *pop* came from the fire as the last piece of coal crumbled to ash. It was no use. Muttering a curse beneath her breath, she stood.

"Just keep your damned hands to yourself," she muttered.

* * *

THERON WOKE AN HOUR BEFORE DAWN TO THE RUMBLING OF THE storm—or at least, that was his first impression, until he realised the source was a great deal closer. Cracking open his eyes, he glared at the young woman sharing the blanket with him. Despite her protests, sometime in the night, she had snuggled up close to him and now her arm was draped across his chest.

Another snort came from Kaila, followed by several grunts and a high-pitched wheezing. Deciding he wasn't going to be getting any further sleep, Theron carefully disentangled himself from the blanket and rose.

His stomach rumbled as he moved to the saddlebags. There was no fuel left for a cooked meal, but he found plenty of beef jerky in the Warden's supplies. As he tore into a strip, he sat himself near the horse and considered his situation.

The rest of the agimet was lost now. There was a chance the wagons had been delayed by the storm, but more likely they'd already travelled far enough into the valley to escape below the snowline. By the time he and Kaila dug themselves out and tried to find the trail beneath several inches of snow, the caravan would be long gone.

He allowed himself a little sigh of self-pity. At least he hadn't come away empty handed. If he was lucky, the agimet he'd stolen would cover his debts with Ambrose. Maybe. An earlship in a frontier town was definitely now out of reach.

Ah well, he would figure it out. He always did. That was, if he survived his current predicament. Theron grimaced. He was under no delusion about their escape. Wardens were nothing if not persistent once they got a whiff of their prey. He'd hoped to vanish into the winding trails of the Iron Pinnacles, but the storm now made that impossible.

He slipped a hand into his pocket, bringing out his tiny collection of agimet. Three crystals. Two still had the glint of *atar* about them, though the largest was dwindling. The third was dead, its contents drained when he'd used it to disarm Kaila back in the mine.

Not much, when a Warden was on your trail.

His gut tightened. There was always the old ruins. They had been built on a powerful nexus. On foot, the climb would have taken two days, but with the stallion they might make it by nightfall. Maybe a little more in the snow.

Except no one went near that place nowadays—and for good reason. Too many Elysian had disappeared in recent times, seeking refuge in the ruins to charge their crystals. The few who'd passed that way and returned spoke of a presence. Even his friend Quintin, an old Psionic who wasn't taken to superstition, had sworn off the place after his last journey.

But this part of Fresia was sparse in the way of nexus points. Something about its volcanic nature, scholars had postulated a long time ago. It might very well be true, unlike most of the garbage humanity came up with these days. All Theron knew for sure was that the only other nexus was more than a week's travel from them, even with the stolen mount.

The world turned to stars as Theron tapped into his remaining *atar*. Despite his words to the girl, part of him twitched at the thought of being cornered in this cave, trapped with nowhere to run. But looking through the snow blocking the entrance, he was reassured to see all was still.

A snort drew his attention back to the girl. She was wedged in the corner now, arms wrapped around the woollen blanket for warmth, a rock serving as her pillow. She was older than he'd thought when he'd first seen her. Eighteen or nineteen? Not much younger than him, though you wouldn't think it from the lines under his eyes. Life on the streets of Tah'raus would do that to you.

Yet life hadn't been easy for Kaila Dwyn either, had it? They had made her a servant to duty, a soldier in a war that had already claimed ten thousand others exactly like her.

Well, not exactly like her. An enigma wrapped up in a mystery, this one. There weren't many Elysian that grew up in human society these days—and even fewer that survived their Trials. He studied her, watching the gentle rise and fall of her chest. Her face was harsh, even in sleep, as though unused to joy or happiness. Yes, she was well acquainted with the harshness of life. But she had prevailed anyway, propped up by her belief in the higher powers of the Magisterium and her kingdom.

What would she become now those had been stripped away? She had a lot to learn, and more than a few terrible truths yet to uncover. Theron was loath to be the one to tell her. Would she give up, crumble beneath the truth of a new world—or would she do as she had always done?

Fight.

Probably. There were things she was hiding from him, he was sure, but it was clear as day she was telling the truth when it came to her power. Her expression when she'd used his agimet had been almost as surprised as his own.

Too many questions. But the answers could wait until they were safe.

Not that the world was ever truly safe for their kind.

9

K aila woke to a rock digging into her spine and a large tongue licking her face.

"*Yicckkk!*" she groaned, pushing the horse away.

The creature nickered like it found her disgust amusing. Gravel crunched beneath its hooves as the beast backed away. She grumbled a few choice words, her mind still sluggish. She was surprised at how deeply she had slept. Despite her protests, it had been warm beneath the blanket, Theron's body practically a furnace.

It was cold now though, and blinking sleep from her eyes, Kaila pushed herself up. It remained gloomy inside the cave, but now trails of light had filtered in from the entrance, where the wall of snow trapped them inside.

"Rise and shine, sunshine!" Theron wore a broad smile as he held out a stick of what appeared to be jerky. "Slept well I trust? Gods alone know no one else in this cave could with that thunder of yours."

The horse whinnied as though it agreed. Kaila glared daggers at the man, but a rumble from her stomach sucked the heat from her fury. She snatched the jerky from his fingers and shoved the entire thing into her mouth. Then aware she still did not have her clothes, she pulled the blanket around herself and rose.

Her muscles immediately screamed their protest as blood rushed to limbs that had been denied by her awkward sleeping position. As she staggered, a firm hand caught her beneath the arm, steadying her.

"Easy," Theron said.

For a second she leaned into the hand, drawing reassurance from his presence—before she remembered who he was, and her distinct lack of clothing beneath the blanket. Jerking away, she glared at him.

Chuckling, Theron shrugged as though to say, *well, I tried to help you,* before turning to their horse. He gave its pelt another quick brush while she dressed, and then saddled it.

"Where are we going anyway?" Kaila ventured the question as she did the buttons of her tunic. She was relieved to find her clothes had mostly dried from their drenching in the night.

"As far from that Warden as we can get."

"That's not a destination."

"And I'm not a cartographer," Theron snapped. He drew a breath, sinching the strap around the horse's belly before turning to her with calmer eyes. "Have you ever been hunted by a Warden, Kaila?"

"Of course not."

He nodded. "But you know a bit about them, right?"

"I wanted to *be* one until you came along and ruined my life," she snapped. "They're our mightiest heroes, men and women worthy of wielding the power of T'iana's armour."

Theron snorted. "The only truth in all that hogwash is the part about their power." He ran a hand down the neck of the stallion as the beast stamped a hoof. "No one really understands the things they can do. Some of their powers are like the Gift. Reliant on *atar.* But others…" He shrugged. "That's not important right now. What's important is that I am almost out of *atar.* Without it, we don't stand a chance against one of his kind."

Kaila frowned. As Theron spoke, his eyes were fixed on the wall of ice. There was a glint there, as though at any moment, he expected an armoured man to come smashing his way into their sanctuary.

"You're afraid of them, aren't you?"

She should have been satisfied by the realisation. Instead, she found herself surprised. Theron had seemed unflappable in the brief time she'd known him, immune to the chaos in the mine or the discord of her escape. Even amidst the storm, he'd remained unshakeable. Yet now she saw the glint of fear in his eyes.

It had her stomach tied in knots.

"Only a fool would not fear those things."

"You speak of them like they're not human."

Theron's emerald gaze bore into her own. "Aren't they?"

The silence stretched out—until with a snort and a squelch, the stallion emptied its bowels between them.

"Arg!" Kaila exclaimed, the stench burning in her nostrils.

"I think our companion is politely suggesting it's time for us to get moving." Theron chuckled, reaching into his pocket.

As he drew out a piece of crystal, the glow of *atar* touched his eyes. He held out a hand towards the snow—

"Wait!"

Blinking, Theron glanced at her, one eyebrow raised. Pinching her nose, she nodded at the agimet. "Can I watch…" she left the question hanging, not even sure herself what she meant.

But Theron seemed to understand. A grimace touched his lips as he weighed the request. His fingers clenched around the crystal before, with an exhale, the fire in his eyes died away.

"Catch," he said, tossing her a crystal.

Caught off-guard, Kaila squawked and fumbled the thing. Her heart lurched in her chest as the precious stone slipped through her fingers. It tumbled towards the ground, but at the last second she recovered, snatching it from the air. Gasping in relief, she cradled it to her chest.

"Well, remind me never to do *that* again."

"I wasn't ready!" she snapped, drawing in a calming breath. "What would have happened if it had broken?"

"Nothing immediate," Theron replied, "but let that be your first lesson in the ways of us Elysian. Never draw *atar* from a crystal that has been broken or cut."

"Why?"

He hesitated, studying her. "Broken crystals become attuned. They charge in seconds while inside a nexus."

"Isn't that a good thing if they're the source of your power?"

"Too much of a good thing," Theron said. "If you're lucky, the power of all that *atar* will burn your insides to a crisp."

"Lucky?"

Theron nodded. "The unlucky are those who survive." He fell silent a moment, before grunting and gesturing to the wall of ice. "Anyway, we were escaping from this cave before our mighty steed gases us to death. Care to do the honours?"

"Me?"

Kaila looked from him to the agimet in her hand. She could feel the *atar* tingling in her veins—had sensed it from the moment her hand had closed around the crystal.

"You wanted me to show you, right? Well, I'm a big believer in doing instead of watching."

She swallowed. "I thought you said you were almost out of *atar*?"

"I am." He shrugged, hands deep in the pockets of his trench coat. "But this needs to be done. And if that Warden *does* catch us, well, better odds with two Movers than one."

"Still sticking with that name?"

Theron scowled. "I don't see you coming up with anything better."

Twisting her lips, Kaila thought for a moment. "What about a psychic?"

"Too similar to Psionic."

"And what exactly do they do?"

"They manipulate emotion," Theron replied before waving a hand at the ice. "Look, do you want to learn or not?"

Kaila sighed. She was stalling and she knew it. Her eyes fell to the stone in her hand. Despite their imminent danger, a part of her still resisted this power. Magic, or the Gift as Theron called it, wasn't who she was. She was *human*. Her strength came from their collective might, a legion working together as one—not some corruptive power that raised one above the rest...

...and yet, there was a part of her that yearned for these crystals and the energy inside, a desire to see those lights again, the unseen forces that made up their world.

Clenching the crystal tighter, she searched for the *atar* inside, just as she had done in the mine. She inhaled sharply as it touched her, her skin crawling as electricity danced beneath.

"That's it," Theron said. "Now, *look.*"

She obeyed, and a world of stars revealed itself. Everything, from the jagged rocks to the coals of the fire to the wall of ice, it all contained that ethereal glow. Some pulsed brightly from a single point, like Theron and the stallion, while others were softer, more… dissident. The snow blocking their exit was like that; not a single light but a wall of shimmering stars, as though each flake contained a light of its own.

"Can all Elysian see this?" she wondered out loud.

"With *atar*, yes," Theron replied, though his voice was grim. "It's how they find us, remember. While holding a crystal, those with the Gift gain our *atarsight*, but it also betrays us."

Their eyes, Kaila thought, but only nodded, returning her attention to the snow. "What are they? The lights?"

"*Soullights*, we call them," Theron replied. "Everything has one. Each Elysian is different in how we interact with them, but as Movers…"

"We can move them, yes, I get it. But the snow…it's like there's a thousand different lights."

"That's because there are. But they're tiny, so they aren't so hard to bind. You remember how you moved me in the mine?"

Kaila thought back. "It was like I used the *atar* to connect my light to yours."

"Exactly. You only touched one light, but you can link to many with the same thread, so long as you plan to move them all in the same direction. And you have enough *atar*, of course. As I said, the snow is light. Why don't you give it a try."

Kaila grimaced. The *atar* bubbled beneath the surface of her flesh, tugging at her, as though eager to be used. When she finally complied, it leapt to her command, spinning itself into a thread which she directed at the wall of icy light. It struck like an arrow loosed from a bow, piercing a dozen stars on its first pass. With each one, Kaila felt a tingling of connection. Satisfied she was on the right path, she painstakingly reversed the thread of *atar*, weaving it through the wall of snow again and again, each pass collecting a dozen more of the glowing stars.

At first, it was easy, but as the connections grew, she began to feel a weight upon her mind, a strain like she had set herself to one of Sister Eurador's math problems. She tried to ignore it, gritting her teeth and pressing on. Eventually though, it became so great even her body was trembling and there was a pulsing in her head, like she had too much blood in her skull.

"I think you've got enough," Theron said at last. "Why don't you try giving them a push?"

Kaila nodded. The pressure was so great now, she couldn't even form the words of a reply. In her mind's eye, she grasped the thread of *atar*. It was threaded with hundreds of tiny stars by now, and when she tried to shift it, she found it no longer light and easy to manipulate. She drew more *atar* from the crystal and almost sighed as its power filled her, replenishing what she had spent. With a final effort, she hurled the thread forward and heard a soft *thump*.

Blinking, she let the *soullights* fade from her vision, and the connections with them. Sunlight streamed into the cave through the entrance, where a few seconds before had been a wall of snow. She stared at it in shock for a heartbeat.

A dim horror curled around the base of her spine and the stone slipped from her fingers. It struck the ground and luckily did not shatter. She stared at it, at the light flickering within, diminished, but still burning with a fierce internal glow.

Magic. She'd done magic. Deliberately. Somehow, that made it different.

Kaila jumped as a slow clapping came from nearby. Theron wandered over and slapped her on the shoulder. "Well done," he said, bending to scoop up the agimet. He made a show of brushing off the dust. "So, shall we get out of here? You know, before the man in the iron suit shows up to violently murder us."

The words were spoken in jest, but Kaila sensed the tension beneath them. She lingered as he mounted the stallion, still feeling the weariness in her body, and beneath that, deeper, the disgust and self-loathing. She had used the wicked magics of the enemy. Again. A part of her wanted to argue that she had not chosen this path, that she had been placed on it by Sister Eurador and the Warden. And yet…

…she might not have taken the first step, but she walked it now by choice. She didn't *have* to accept the unnatural magics of the enemy. Whether they were a part of her or not, she could spurn them, instead of embracing the light within.

For now, though, they needed to move. Because whether she became the monster Sister Eurador believed her to be or not, Theron was right. The Warden had not seemed the kind of man to leave a loose end flapping in the wind.

Glaring at Theron's offered hand, she scrambled up behind him and reluctantly placed her hands on his hips for balance. The presence of his body, even with the musty scent of his mostly dried coat, sent her back to the night and the heat of him alongside her. Some of that heat seemed to have taken root in her gut. Thankfully, she didn't have long to linger on the sensation, as Theron kicked his heels into the stirrups and the charger surged from the cave.

They emerged into a world of white. With the storm passed, the sky was an almost violent blue, while the mountains shone bright with freshly fallen snow. The air was crisp, the jolt of cold as Kaila inhaled beginning an ache at her temples. Her eyes watered as Theron led the charger onto what she hoped was the trail, the glare from the ice almost blinding. A thick silence hung over the world, broken only by the soft crunch of the stallion's hooves as they broke the icy ground.

Theron glanced over his shoulder with a grimace. "Suppose we can't help but leave a trail in this."

Kaila pursed her lips. They were still winding their way down the trail from the volcanic mount, about two hundred feet above the valley floor.

"You really think he'll follow us in this?" Kaila asked, hopeful.

"I'd be surprised if he wasn't already on the road. We're a little early in the year for a snowstorm." He nodded at the cliffs from which they'd emerged. Water dripped over the scarlet stone. "Look, it's already starting to melt." He hesitated. "Not that it matters. He would come anyway. They always do."

"Why are you so afraid of them?"

Theron said nothing for a time, concentrating on guiding the stallion down the narrow, snow-strewn path. The dirt beneath the ice began to appear as they neared the lower slopes of the mountain, the normally parched gravel turned to mud by the fresh precipitation.

"Did you ever hear about the Sutton Street Robbery?"

"Strangely, we don't hear much news from the capital in Elgoss," she said dryly.

He snorted. "Well, Sutton Street is where the jewellers of Tah'raus ply their trade. A few years back, half the merchants were robbed by a crew of Elysian thieves."

Kaila frowned. "There are Elysian in the capital?"

"Of course. Try as they might, humans haven't managed to wipe us out yet."

Us. She shivered. He spoke like she was already one of them, like because she'd used magic, she had joined his side. She swallowed and wondered if it was true.

"Anyway, I knew a couple of them. Old hands, some of the best in the business of separating the nobility from their ill-gotten gains. Though of course, they didn't have my style."

"So, what happened to them?"

"A Warden," he replied softly. "They had it all planned out so carefully. In and out. They fled Tah'raus that same night with enough gold and diamonds to make them all proper men and women of Fresia. They rode all day to make sure they were in the clear before stopping at an inn known to be friendly with our kind. They were going to wait out the heat there."

"But?"

"A Warden caught up with them. Walked into the inn calm as day, armour manifested, sword formed, and asked who wanted to die first. Now keep in mind, these were all Gifted folk, and there were five of them. No small challenge, even for one of *them*. At least, I assume they thought as much, since they decided to stand and fight."

He paused a moment, and Kaila felt cold fingers tickle her spine.

"He killed them all," he continued at last. "Not just the crew. The innkeeper. The other guests. Even a child. No one was spared —except one man."

Kaila swallowed, her mouth suddenly parched. A part of her wanted to ridicule the story, to tell him it was ridiculous. A Warden would never commit violence against the innocent.

Except now she knew better.

"How do you know it's true?" she rasped.

"I found him," Theron said softly. They had reached the valley now and Theron was leading the horse carefully around the banks of snow. There was no sign of the trail, but there was only one direction to go unless you wanted to climb the mountains on the other side of the valley, their dark slopes strangely absent of snow.

"Who?"

"The man he left alive. I thought the story might have been a rumour put about by the Magisterium, a lie to keep people from getting ideas. So I went looking for the truth." His shoulders swelled as he inhaled, before releasing a heavy breath. "I thought I'd find my old friends laid up on a beach in the Cascadelands somewhere, drinking whisky and playing backgammon. But all I found was silence. Not a trace of them anywhere. They were good at disappearing, but not *that good*."

"So I followed the rumours instead. Traced them down the grapevine of cutthroats and grifters and pickpockets, back to Tah'raus and a beggar on Soul Square. Oric Songbird. He was the Weaver who led the crew, planned the whole thing. But even illusion magic couldn't have hidden what they did to him." He fell silent, as though considering his next words. "They had put out his eyes and cut off his limbs below the joints. Every wound was cauterised with burning iron, so he didn't bleed out. They wanted him alive. His nose and his manhood were given the same treatment. They spared his tongue though—so he could tell his sorry tale to any soul kind enough to pass him a copper gint."

"That's…awful," Kaila whispered.

Theron nodded. "So, you can see why I'd rather that bastard Warden *didn't* catch us up. Speaking of…" He paused to rummage through the saddlebag at his side, coming up with a knife in a sheath. He passed it back to her. "Probably won't be much good against a Warden's armour, but I saw you back in Elgoss. Seemed pretty handy with one of these."

"My father taught me," Kaila said absently as she accepted the blade and turned it in her hand.

It was a hunting knife, the blade almost as long as her forearm—closer to a shortsword than one of her own easily concealed daggers.

"Just promise you won't stab me the first time my back is turned."

"Tempting," Kaila muttered. But she smiled to herself, glad Theron couldn't see, and clipped it to her belt.

Its weight was reassuring, a reminder that she didn't *need* to rely on the magic, that her father had imparted other skills on her. The entire world might have turned on its head, but she was still Kaila Dwyn, her father's daughter. If the Warden came for her again, he would not find her so defenceless this time.

As they made their way down the valley, the snow continued to melt, proving Theron's words correct. Despite the cold snap, it was still only late autumn and winter had yet to sink its teeth into the mountains. She glanced back occasionally, but clouds hid the volcanic mount that had loomed over her entire life. Soon, the curve of the valley hid even its lower slopes from view. Sparse vegetation appeared through the white, patches of thistle and ironwood scrub that dotted the red soils of the Iron Pinnacles.

It reminded her of spring, in a way. People thought these mountains were barren, but every year after the snow and ice melted away, the desert came to life. Flowers bloomed, yellow brittlebush and purple lupine, and a dozen other colours filling the scarlet hills. It had been her father's favourite time of year. Often after his shift in the mine, they would just sit on the rooftop instead of training, and look out over the valley as the sun set.

But today there were no flowers beneath the ice, only mud and broken earth. As the last of the snow faded, the trail appeared from the white. They took turns walking the horse, preserving its strength. Theron spent his first shift collecting scraps of wood as he moved through the scrub. Kaila did the same when her time came.

Eventually though, as the sun neared its apex and began the slow journey towards the far horizon, Theron drew them to a stop.

"We have a decision to make."

Kaila, who'd been taking a turn in the saddle, frowned down at him. "What decision would that be?"

"This is the only road from your village. If we stay on it, chances are the Warden will catch us sooner rather than later."

"I didn't hear a choice in there."

Theron gestured to the mountains. The trail had drawn them close to their dark slopes and now they loomed above, their peaks shrouded in mist. "You asked earlier where we're going," he replied, before hesitating. "Well, somewhere up there is a nexus. If we're to stand any chance against the Warden, we're going to need *atar*."

A stone settled in Kaila's gut as her eyes tracked the harsh slopes leading up to the icy peaks. "And how exactly do you propose we find this nexus?" Despite featuring occasionally in the sister's teachings, she didn't even know what one looked like—if they even looked like anything at all.

"There's a pass."

"Are you sure?"

"Sure enough to gamble our lives on it."

Kaila arched an eyebrow. "Why doesn't that inspire the confidence you seem to think it should?" She sat, studying the incline. The lower slopes started out gentle as they rose from the valley, before turning to a steep forty-five degrees. Even the horse would be struggling by then. And then at the top, if they couldn't find the pass...

She glanced at the rolling hills of the valley, straining her eyes for movement. Nothing yet. But that did not mean he wasn't out there, drawing nearer with each passing hour. Theron was right, they couldn't stay on the road. And if this little detour could recharge the agimet crystals and give them a chance...

...her heart panged at the thought of actually raising a weapon against a Warden of the Magisterium, but she nodded, and without further discussion, Theron led them off the trail.

"If Wardens are impervious to our magic, how do we fight them?" Kaila asked as they started up the hillside.

Theron chuckled. "Generally, you don't. Better to run."

"That's not very helpful when one's hunting us."

"Technically, I believe he is hunting *you*."

"You're the one who stole the agimet!"

"True," Theron said, raising a finger, "but I got away."

Kaila scowled. "By bringing the mine down on my head," she reminded him.

"Work smarter, not harder," he replied, knocking a knuckle against his skull. "As for fighting them, our power might not work on that armour of theirs, but it still works on everything else. You drop a boulder on our friend and he won't be getting back up." He paused. "Theoretically."

"You've never actually fought one, have you?" Kaila said. "And didn't you just tell me how one Warden killed, what, *four* of your friends?"

"Only *two* of them were actual friends," Theron replied. "And besides, they didn't have any Movers. We're special."

Kaila swallowed. For both their sakes, she hoped he was right. It disturbed her, this talk of killing Wardens. A part of her still railed against the thought. The Wardens were heroes, their first defence against the magics of the enemy. Their sacrifice had protected humanity for hundreds of years. The thought of killing one of them twisted in her stomach like a knife, carving out a fresh piece of her.

So she changed the subject. "How many types of magic are there?"

If Sister Eurador had been light on the details of *atar*, agimet, and the nexus, her teaching had been a vacuum when it came to the magics of the enemy—other than that they were a vile, unnatural perversion of the world. Something to be hated, destroyed, not understood.

"A dozen, we think."

"You *think?*"

"Well, some powers are more common than others. Psionics, for example. They're a gint a dozen--especially of the weaker variety—"

"Psionics are the ones that manipulate emotion, right?" Kaila interrupted.

"Right. I keep forgetting how green you are," Theron said. He'd climbed back into the saddle now and glanced over his shoulder at her. "The weak ones can only sense emotions. The most powerful can suck everything out of you, so you only feel what they want you to feel."

Kaila's skin crawled, remembering when she'd been alone in the interrogation room with the Warden. It had seemed that all of her anger and fear and hope had bled away, until all that remained was despair.

"He did that," she croaked. "Elric Chain, the Warden. He did that to me."

"Ah, so he's *Psionic*. Good to know."

"What does that mean?"

"It means we have a chance. Wardens are impervious, and you don't want them to *ever* touch you. They'll drain the *atar* and the life right out of you. But as far as their other magics go, they're like us. They only get one Gift."

"So, you think you can beat him?"

Theron did not reply to that and the silence stretched out. The wind whistled through the rocky outcrops above, carrying fresh promise of winter's chill. Finally, Kaila realised Theron wasn't going to answer.

"So," she said to break the awful quiet, "you were telling me about the other sorts of Elysian…"

"Yeah…" Theron said, clearing his throat. "Yes. So, you know us Movers can move things. Binders are similar, but instead of shifting things around, they change them. Add to make things go *boom* or subtract to freeze them. Weavers create illusions. Those are the more common varieties. Others, like Wraiths, are basically myth at this point."

"What can they do?"

"They were fast. Very, very fast. Rumours about one pops up here and there, but I've never met one. And I don't trust anything I haven't verified myself."

Kaila pursed her lips, considering everything he'd told her. About the Elysian, and the Warden they would have to face. Some of it made sense with what she already knew. Others…

"What about the Wardens?" she murmured. "How can they have your powers if they're not Elysian?"

"Their armour," Theron grunted. "At least, we assume it's the armour. Truth is, even after all these centuries, we don't fully understand how their powers work. The Magisterium guards its secrets closely."

Kaila swallowed, her hand falling to the crystal she'd stolen from Sister Eurador. The one she had charged.

He didn't know.

A shiver ran down her spine. Theron was right; the Magisterium *did* guard its secrets tightly. But no Elysian had ever passed their Trial of Agimet. She had. And then she'd attempted the Trial to become a Warden. She knew something about them he did not.

But could she reveal that to him? Theron was her only ally in this horrible new reality. But he was also Elysian, the ancient enemy of her species. Two days ago, she would have driven the dagger on her belt through his spine without a second thought.

Now, though, if humanity was her enemy…

She opened her mouth to speak, but found the words would not come. Seated in front, Theron didn't notice. The conversation petered out instead, silence falling between them as they continued the climb into the jagged peaks.

As the sun dropped towards the horizon, they made camp between a cluster of boulders. There, sheltered from the wind and sight of anyone below, they were able to make a small fire with the wood they'd collected and heat some broth taken from the supplies in the saddlebags. There looked to be enough for a few more days—which Kaila hoped was enough to see them through the peaks. Though, Theron ate altogether too much for a man half her father's size. It was a reminder of the sacrifice her kind were willing to make, while those like Theron lived only to indulge their selfish desires. It reassured her, that she hadn't shared her little truth about the Wardens—even if Theron had given his knowledge freely.

They settled down for the night early, and this time Kaila stubbornly refused to share the blanket, leaving it to Theron. The heavy jacket was enough now the storm had passed and her clothing had dried. Or at least, that's what she told herself as she lay with her knees drawn up to her chest, shivering in the dark. But after every other compromise she'd made, she clung to this one with every scrap of willpower that remained to her.

She was almost surprised when she woke to the morning. Feeling the blanket covering her, she glanced around and found Theron dozing nearby, arms wrapped around himself against the chill. A pang of regret stabbed at her chest. She'd spent so much of the night trembling, in the end, she'd given up on sleeping altogether. He must have given her the blanket at some point while she'd dozed.

Not that it seemed to have done her any good. Her body ached from the long day in the saddle and the hard ground. Lying in the dim light, she stared at the dark red sky, wondering what had woken her.

Crack.

She bolted upright as the sound of breaking rock echoed off the nearby cliffs. Staggering to her feet, she swung around, looking for the source, but the cluster of boulders blocked her view. The stallion snickered nearby and pawed the ground. Heart thumping, she slipped through the stones to the edge of the boulders and glanced down the trail they'd climbed yesterday afternoon.

At first, she saw nothing but scarlet dirt and churned mud. Then another *crack* of breaking stone rattled up the mountainside.

"There," Theron said softly, coming alongside her unnoticed and pointing.

She followed his direction, her blood growing cold. It was the shifting stones that gave the Warden away. He was still far below them, at least a few hours back, but moving at a prodigious pace. The blue scales of his armour rippled in the morning light as he charged up the slope, seemingly impervious to the shifting earth and slick mud.

"What do we do?" she whispered, heart pounding hard in her chest.

"*Run.*"

10

The stallion thundered up the twisted slope. Every few steps, the loose earth shifted beneath its iron hooves, threatening to twist an ankle and send Kaila and Theron crashing to the unforgiving ground. And each time, Kaila gasped and clung to Theron and prayed to the First Matron they would stay upright.

Each time, somehow, the mighty Fresian charger managed to right itself and continue.

They were nearing the pass now. She could *see* it, a dark slot in the stark cliffs, as though some giant of old had taken a mighty sword and carved his way through the mountains. The nexus lay beyond, its power promising them…

He killed them all.

A shiver ran down Kaila's spine. A *crash* came from somewhere below, like metal armour slamming into stone. Kaila didn't risk a look back. He was gaining on them; no point risking a fall to confirm what she already knew. And the stallion was fading, gasping in the thin air, its coat drenched with sweat. She gasped as it lurched, a hoof catching an outcrop of rock. For a second, she thought that was it and braced for impact—but Theron dragged on the reins and the beast lurched, somehow finding its footing. They continued, slower now, the poor beast limping, gasping, its whinnies echoing from the cliffs above.

Theron's face was grim, eyes fixed on their objective. Her vivacious ally didn't look so confident now, with the armoured monster closing on them. Short on *atar* and time, they were rapidly running out of options.

They raced onwards.

And then they were there.

The shadow of the pass swallowed them up, the heat of the midday sun giving way to the sudden chill of ancient stone. Theron didn't linger. The *clip-clop* of hooves echoed loudly in the narrow passage. The mountain swallowed them in its stony embrace. Kaila shivered as their breaths misted hot on the icy air.

The mountains opened again.

The breath caught in Kaila's throat with the return of the sunlight. Blue skies stretched overhead, the orange sun shining upon a landscape of verdant green. Long grasses waved in the mountain breeze, and leafy trees grew upon the steep slopes of the vale. She recognised some from Sister Eurador's books. Pine, fur, and beech. But books were one thing. Kaila had never seen so much green in her life. It was beautiful.

A lump lodged in her throat. To think, this had been only a few days' journey from their home. How was that possible?

But the luscious vegetation of the valley was not the most surprising of sights. For there, nestled against the cliffs below them, was a *city*. One unlike any Kaila had seen in her life or her books. Tah'raus and the other major cities of Fresia favoured architecture of the blunt, practical variety. Buildings were constructed for functionality, squat, plain, and often identical for speed. They also prioritised defence, meaning windows were narrow and high up on the walls, and every settlement was protected by fortifications at least twenty feet tall.

This place put the limited imagination of Fresian architects to shame. Its buildings were all unique; some built from granite, others the scarlet sandstone of her own Elgoss, yet more a strange greenstone or an even stranger jet-black, almost glassy material. Some stretched tall as stark towers, while others spiralled outwards like a kind of upside-down cone, with larger upper storeys held up by what Kaila could only assume was magic. Intricate archways leapt across streets, some connecting rooftops and balconies, while others seemed to provide no purpose at all, beginning and ending in solid walls.

But even the walls stood stark in contrast to their Fresian counterparts, the facades carved with complicated patterns or even what looked to be images, as though the inhabitants of this city had the luxury of time and safety to decorate their homes.

Yet amidst the individuality, there was something greater as well, a pattern formed from chaos. The streets spiralled inwards like smaller and smaller wheels laid over one another. The buildings on the edges of the city tended to be the smallest, while closer to the centre they grew taller, rising beyond five storeys, until they reached the soaring tower at the centre of the wheels. Mammoth beyond anything Kaila had ever seen, the tower, unlike the rest of the city, had been built only from that strange black material that shone like glass. Its height was terrifying, rivalling even the mountains themselves.

Kaila couldn't believe any human could have built something so tall. She sat stunned in the saddle as Theron swung the horse around, unable to take it all in. Such extravagance, the enormity of its presence…

"What is this place?" she whispered.

The city sat on a plateau below. There were no defensive walls, but this city of the heavens had no need for them. It was surrounded on three sides by sharp cliffs that plummeted into the green of the valley. The only approach was the pass through which they'd just emerged.

Theron hadn't said anything about a city. Suddenly, her chest was clenched, her body taut as she realised her foolishness, trusting this man, following him up here into the clouds. Could this be a secret fortress of the Elysian, a hidden base used to launch their vile attacks against Fresia?

"A ruin," Theron grunted. He swung his leg over the saddle and slipped from the horse.

"What are you doing?" Kaila gasped. They were still in the mouth of the pass. She glanced at the shadows, expecting the flickering glow of the Warden's agimet to appear at any moment. "Where's the nexus?"

"We're at the edge of it here, but it's centred on the Black Tower." As he spoke, his hands dug into the pockets of his trench coat, reappearing with three crystals. Two were dead, the last a dim spark. He grimaced. "Here," he continued, offering the first two crystals to Kaila. "Take these and hide as close to the tower as you can get." He hesitated. "It'll take twelve hours for them to charge."

"*What?*"

He nodded, grim-faced. "Don't worry," he said quietly, his eyes beginning to glow. "I'm going to slow him down."

Then he turned and walked back into the passage. Kaila stared, torn. Surely he didn't plan to face the Warden alone! The *atar* in his crystal already seemed to be fading. Whatever scraps of power he had left couldn't be enough to stop Elric Chain—not if the story Theron had told her was true. If the Warden caught him now…

She shuddered, recalling the man as he'd stalked towards her father, the quicksilver emerging from his hand to form the polished blade. She couldn't leave Theron to face that alone, could she? Her fingers crept to the hilt of the dagger he'd given her. There was only one Warden. Maybe together….

"Kaila, I said *go!*"

The words were guttural, spoken with an authority she hadn't heard from the man before. She reacted before she realised what she was doing, dragging on the reins to spin the stallion in the direction of the city. Putting heels to its thighs, she kicked the beast into a gallop.

There was a roaring in Theron's ears as he studied the stars. The rushing of blood from his panicked heart. He could feel the *atar* fading, the power slipping from him. Each second he held it inside was a little less power, a little less strength he could exert. Time was rapidly running out—but he couldn't act, not yet. Not until he found it. A fault in the stone, a piece of rotten rock, a broken vein of crystal, something, *anything* in the lights that would indicate a weak spot in the cliffs.

But this was no mine shaft, chipped and broken by a hundred

human tools. This was a *mountain.* These cliffs had stood for millennia, worn by time, unfazed by the elements. They had witnessed civilizations rise and fall, uncaring to the fleeting lives of those who lived in their shadow. They were eternal.

Until today.

Today, one of those fleeting mortals would find their weakness. Today, he would drive a nail through the immortality of the mountains.

Or a Warden was going to cut him in half.

Time ticked on. The *atarlight* flickered. He cursed. If only there'd been more time! He was within the influence of the nexus now, could feel its distant warmth at his back. But its power was useless to him! It needed to be channelled through agimet first to be compatible with the Gift. And that would take hours.

The pounding of hooves faded as Kaila disappeared over the rise…

His heart squeezed, but he forced himself to concentrate on the rock formations. Maybe that vein of crystal? It was softer than the surrounding stone, running halfway up the cliff face. But he couldn't tell how deep it went. If it was shallow, tearing it from the bedrock wouldn't shift a single pebble. He needed something *big.*

"I can smell your taint, Elysian."

The voice echoed through the passage, turning Theron's blood to ice. The distant *thud* of an iron boot on stone followed.

"You are weak, almost out of *atar.*" The Warden's voice grated metallically in his ears. "Surrender the girl, and I will grant you a quick death."

"Warden, you insult me!" Theron roared, redoubling his search for a flaw. "It was I who stole your precious agimet—just as I have stolen from so many of your noble houses. *I* am the prize you seek!"

Kaila again. Honestly, what was the Magisterium's interest in the girl?

"You are a bug, Elysian, like the rest of your kind," came the response. Amidst the stars, a sun appeared, still deep in the passage, but approaching one cautious step at a time. Now his prey was within his grasp, the Warden had no need for haste. "To be crushed beneath my boot and forgotten."

"Now, that's just hurtful," Theron grunted.

And then he spotted it. Higher up, right at the limits of his range, a void of darkness amidst the otherworldly light. *A crack!* And it ran deep too, a fissure forced open by the incessant freezing and melting of ice over the centuries. But would it be enough?

Only one way to find out.

He grasped it with his power as the Warden stepped into view of his mortal eyes. A shudder ran down his spine at the sight of the man's soul. Wardens didn't flicker and change like other people, not while they wore their armour. Instead, they blazed like a little sun trapped within a snow globe, cut off from the world. It made them seem more like inanimate objects than people. It was manifestly unnatural.

No time to linger on that now though. The last of the *atar* was slipping through his fingers.

Now or never.

The air *crackled* as he unleashed his Gift, simultaneously lifting part of the rock while pushing down on the other, creating a twisting movement. He threw everything he had into the crack, the last fizzling bits of *atar*, even the tiny piece he kept in the sleeve of his trench coat for desperate situations. If this didn't count as desperate, what did?

Somewhere above, stone shrieked as it warped under the unnatural pressure.

And fell silent.

It wasn't enough.

Theron swore.

Blue metal glinted as the Warden appeared. The shadows retreated before the burning glow of the agimet implanted in his chest plate. Theron tensed, hand going instinctively to his pocket, only to find it empty. He'd given his other crystals to Kaila. They were empty anyway. Just like the one clenched between his fingers.

He was out of magic.

Cursing some more, Theron reluctantly drew the blade on his belt. Steel whispered on leather as he settled into a fighting stance. It was a worthless gesture and even his adversary knew it.

Laughter rang loudly between the narrow walls as the Warden

raised a hand. Darkness coalesced in his palm, shimmering strangely in the glow of his agimet. Theron shuddered. The sword of a Warden was as unnatural as their armour, hungry, devouring things that *ate* some part of the world they touched. The rest of the world seemed to recoil from their very presence.

Theron's fingers tightened around the hilt of his blade. He knew from Oric that if the weapon connected with the Warden's sword, it would be corroded, that it could maybe withstand three or four hits before it crumbled to rust. And even if he could get within the man's guard, the chances of penetrating that armour…

Despite all his bold words, Theron's heart wilted and he found himself retreating a step. He felt blind without his *atarsight*. Helpless. Laughter chased after him as the Warden advanced.

"May the Nameless guide my hand," the man in iron growled. "I am sent to cleanse the world of your foul kind."

⁓

THE ROAR OF HOOVES AND THE SCREAMS OF THE STALLION FILLED Kaila's ears, yet she urged it on down the uneven slope, gasping, stumbling every few steps. They were almost there. Almost to the city. It rose before her. The combination of green and white and black-glass buildings stood like monoliths on the empty plateau. The streets were silent as she approached, still. It really was a ruin. She could hardly imagine it; a city so grand and opulent, abandoned to the world. It seemed impossible she had never heard of it, that the kingdom had not claimed it for themselves.

Yet here it stood, abandoned by time and memory. Until now.

She allowed the poor beast to slow as she neared the city, glancing over her shoulder. The mountain pass was silent. No sign of Theron. Something inside her twisted like a dagger. The void. Another piece of her she hadn't even realised was there teetered on the precipice.

Alone…

A trembling ran down her spine. She clenched the reins to keep the shakes from spreading to her hands. It didn't help. She could feel the chasm inside growing, threatening to swallow her up. She looked at the empty city. Closer now, she saw the signs of abandonment. Empty windows watched her, their wooden shutters long since worn away by the harsh mountain climate. Only stone remained, but even this revealed signs of wear. Chips broken off corners and cracks running through walls. Some were even crumbling, exposing holes large enough to fit her arm.

The stallion came to a stop at the limits of the ruins, trembling in the cold breeze. Kaila let the beast rest, looking back at the pass, searching for some sign of Theron. Damned man! Why had he stayed behind? He had said himself that he couldn't fight a Warden. She'd thought maybe he intended to cause a landslide to close the pass, like he had in the mine. But there was nothing.

Then the breeze swirled, howling down from the peaks, and with it came the ring of clashing weapons.

A horrible fear gripped Kaila around the chest and squeezed. Suddenly, she couldn't breathe, couldn't move. All she could do was sit in the saddle and watch the pass above and wait…

Run, Kaila!

Run. That was what her father had screamed as the Warden cut him down. That was what Theron had told her just a few minutes ago, as he turned to face their hunter. Run, run, run. Save herself. Live. Survive.

Alone.

She dragged on the reins, turning the stallion back towards the pass. The First Matron be damned, she was tired of running. The beast protested as she set it back up the slope, but she pressed her heels harder, urging one last effort from the exhausted beast. And despite all it had already given, the poor creature obeyed.

And then they were charging up the mountainside. Her mind was filled with the memory of her father facing down the Warden, and Theron standing in the pass as she had left him, solitary, yet defiant. And as she rode, something changed within her.

Warmth returned, pressing back the void. Not of hope or joy or even some vague hint of optimism. She was charging headlong towards an enemy she couldn't hope to defeat. It made no sense. But that wasn't the point. She could keep running, but what would that achieve? Even if she could escape the Warden's blade, she would be alone in the world, lost without a single hope for the future.

No, this wasn't a choice between life and death.

It was a choice to die a warrior, facing her enemies as her father had taught—or as a coward.

She was Kaila Dwyn of Elgoss.

And she would face her death with a weapon in her hand.

The stallion was slowing now, drained from the long journey and the race up the hillside. But the pass loomed ahead and Kaila could hear the grunt of voices now. Teeth clenched, she crouched in the saddle and urged the stallion up the last bend in the track. The hunting knife pressed against her side and she longed to draw it, but hesitated. Even with the weapon, she would struggle to aid Theron in the narrow confines of the pass. What could she do to make a difference?

You can do what they can, a voice whispered to her.

The hairs on Kaila's head stood on end. *The Third Trial!* Sister Eurador had revealed the one ability that separated Wardens from others, even before they received their armour. They could charge agimet, even without a nexus.

And so could she! Or at least, she *thought* she could. Couldn't she? Doubt touched her, but there was no time to second guess herself. She thrust her hand into her pocket and clasped one of the crystals Theron had given her. Immediately, she sensed its emptiness. It was wrong, that void, the stillness within the crystal. But it was more than that. There was a something about it, almost a longing of its own, a *need* for power, *to be full.*

Well, Kaila would like nothing better. She just had to remember what she'd done last time. The power had come from herself, hadn't it? She closed her eyes, struggling to concentrate. It was difficult, with everything around her, where she was. The stallion lurched and weapons clashed ahead. Overhead, an eagle screeched, and the chill wind howled as it emerged from the pass. Even the majesty of the broken city behind. How could she concentrate through all of that?

She had to try. Seeking to block all distraction, Kaila delved inwards, feeling the weight of her muscles and bones, the sharp sting of ice in her lungs as she inhaled, the pain in her spine and her exhausted heart. There was no calm this time, no quiet, but for a moment she knew only herself, a tiny scrap of flesh and bone clinging to the side of a vast mountain…

…and she knew her energy. Her power.

Trembling, she clasped it and pressed it into the piece of agimet.

Instantly, she felt the change in the stone. Warmth burst from her fingers and spread through her flesh, while the world filled with light as she opened her eyes. *Atarsight.*

It worked!

She saw Theron, the swirling glow of his *soullight* alongside the twisted, frozen glare of the Warden's. A surge of hatred swept over Kaila. This was the man who had slain her father. Righteous rage burned in her, screaming for her to attack, to grasp that strange light in the man's core and hurl him off the side of the mountain.

Then the exhaustion struck. Like in Elgoss with Sister Eurador, but worse this time. Stars burst across her vision—and not the *atar* kind—and the world spun. Suddenly she couldn't tell up from down. She swayed in the saddle—and then she was falling. The ground rushed up to meet her with a heavy *thump.*

Groaning, Kaila pushed herself to her hands and knees. Her bones scraped and grated, like her joints were filled with sand. A gasp tore from her throat as fire burned down her spine. Red filled her vision and unconsciousness beckoned.

Then energy trickled from her hand. Digging her fingers into the soil, Kaila forced herself to focus. The crystal. She still had it. Her joints *screamed* as she lifted her head. To her surprise, she lay not a few yards from the mouth of the pass. The stallion had disappeared —no doubt taking its opportunity to flee their abusive company while it had the chance—but Kaila didn't need the beast anymore. She would likely die here anyway, whatever happened next…

…she would not die on her knees.

Her every muscle was screaming, but Kaila pushed through the pain like her father had taught her. There was no room for weakness on the battlefield. Their enemy knew no mercy, so you fought on, or you died. Nothing in between.

Drawing the blade from her belt, Kaila jammed the point into the hillside and used it to push herself up. The screech of steel on rock echoed harshly from the pass. Her head jerked up. Theron fought in the narrow gap between the rocks, but he had lost his sword. Now he fought with bare hands, using his mobility and the narrow confines to dodge and deflect the Warden's black greatsword.

It seemed to be working—insomuch as he was alive—though without a weapon or agimet, he had no way to threaten the armoured man. So bit by bit, he was being forced back, almost to the mouth of the pass. Once the Warden had room to swing that awesome blade, it would all be over.

Teeth bared, Kaila stumbled towards the passage. Even that was almost beyond her screaming muscles, but she drew a tiny bit of *atar* back from the crystal. Johnson's *law of conservation* rang in her ears; whatever energy she had given could not be greater than she took back now. If she took it all, it might restore her strength, but nothing would remain to use against the Warden…

Theron stood his ground in the mouth of the pass, using fists and boots to hold his ground, but one more step and the Warden would be free.

Unless she could help him.

Her fingers tightened around the crystal. Then, drawing back her hand, she screamed out a warning.

"Theron!" she called. "Catch!"

And hurled the shining piece of agimet.

The second the crystal left her hand, though, Kaila realised her mistake. Cut off from the energy within, her body hit a wall. Agony lanced through her, and with it, a terrible, horrible lethargy. Her knees collapsed and she crashed to the ground. Her heart throbbed in her chest. Once, twice, and then…silence.

Everything went black.

"Theron, *catch*!"

Without a single drop of *atar* and his blade long since crumbled to dust, Theron was at the point of surrender when he heard the shout. Twisting to avoid being skewered on his foe's blade, he caught a glint of light from behind him. His heart almost tore itself out of his chest. It couldn't be…

But he had to hope. Taking a final step back to put some space between himself and the Warden, he spun. A crystal flew towards him. Quick as a tomcat, he snatched it from the air. The breath caught in his throat as *atar* flooded his weary limbs.

Where…

There was no time. His veins thrummed with fresh power, setting his eyes aglow, for a moment matching the brilliance of his enemy. The Warden did not falter though. Why would he? He was impervious to the Gift. Roaring, he charged, blade raised high to split Theron in two.

Despite his exhaustion, Theron found his smile. A thread of *atar* spun from his soul, gathering a rock the size of his head. Energy surged and the projectile shot past him to crash against the Warden's breastplate. The man rocked back on his heels, staggered by the blow.

Theron didn't hesitate. He tapped another rock, then a third. They followed the first, slamming against the iron defences of his enemy. The Warden raised an arm to fend off the assault, but the sheer ferocity of Theron's attack forced him back one step, then another. His heart leapt. For the first time in the fight, he was on the front foot, but wherever Kaila had found the *atar* in this stone, there wasn't much—nowhere near a full charge. He could already feel it dwindling. And despite forcing Elric Chain to retreat, there wasn't a scratch on that shining armour.

He clenched his teeth, and as the Warden backed off yet another step, he abruptly cut off the flow of power to his projectiles. Even as the rocks crashed to the ground, Theron gathered everything he had and hurled it at the crack in the cliff-face again, twisting and yanking and pushing at that line of emptiness, praying all the while to the Trickster it would work.

Somewhere above, rock groaned. Breath hissing through gritted teeth, Theron pulled harder. The *atar* in the crystal guttered, flickering like a dying lantern in the depths beneath the earth. He could feel it slipping from him. He threw the rest into the fissure anyway.

Crack!

As the last drops of *atar* faded, Theron finally felt the rocks give way. The sound of stone splintering *thundered* through the passage. Then a sudden silence. His heart pulsed. *Damnit, no!* Laughter came from the shadows as the Warden took a step towards him.

Then something moved. From high above came the sound of crumbling stone—followed by a grinding noise, as of something large beginning to shift. Theron stared at the cliffs, praying, hoping.

Crack, crack, crack!

With a rending, roaring, *boom*, the entire cliff face peeled away. He had only a second to spin and hurl himself through the entrance to the pass before it all came crashing down. The earth shook as he landed, shards of rock *hissing* as they slashed the air above him. He grunted as a few struck him, tearing through his overcoat and lodging in his flesh.

Groaning, he crawled away from the rumbling earth, even as the ground rolled in waves beneath him. A boulder slammed down a few feet away. Another followed, then another, striking with enough force to send great fountains of stone and soil raining down around him. It was like the mountain itself was collapsing.

He struggled on and glimpsed a figure lying unmoving nearby. Kaila! As he reached her, the world finally grew still, the mountain apparently settling back into place. Theron sucked in a great lungful of air as he glanced back and saw the result of his work. Earth and stone filled the place where moments before there had been a passage.

The breath rattled from his chest as he exhaled. He could hardly believe it. Somehow, impossibly, they had done it!

Grinning, he burst into laughter. "By the Trickster, Kaila, you're a wonder!" he exclaimed. "Where in the hell did you find that piece of agimet?"

He turned from the mountain to where Kaila lay, so swept away with relief that for a moment he didn't care about anything else. He laughed again. By the gods, it was a good day to be alive! A Warden defeated, a bag full of agimet in his pack, and now they had a nexus nearby to charge it all…

He frowned, glancing at Kaila. She hadn't responded at all to his celebration.

"Kaila?"

Nothing. Suddenly concerned, he pulled himself to his hands and knees and crawled to where she lay. Had she been struck by a falling rock? He saw no marks or bruises. Exhaustion? She had come back for him, found a piece of agimet charged with enough *atar* to turn the battle.

Grasping her shoulder, he turned her onto her back. Her eyes were closed, her face pale. His heart pulsed.

"Kaila, you all right?" he asked, giving her a little shake.

She still didn't respond. Not even a flicker from her eyelids. His frown deepening, Theron leaned closer. Was she breathing? He placed a finger to her throat, searching for a pulse.

Nothing.

"Kaila!"

11

High in the Black Tower, a woman sat with her legs crossed on the wooden floor. Eyes closed, her breath came only every minute or so, and even then, it was only the slightest of inhalations. A ring lay in her upturned palms, its single piece of agimet glowing slightly in the afternoon light. To the casual observer, she might have appeared dead from the stillness.

She was not, however.

And as the distant rumbling of breaking stone and crashing earth broke the Reaper's trance, her eyes fluttered open. A glint of *atar* shone in their icy depths, already fading as the light in the crystal flickered and died. Its sudden absence caused the woman to draw a sharp breath. Her eyes shimmered as withdrawal sank its terrible hooks into her flesh. She swayed where she sat, a groan building in her chest.

The intrusion was decidedly…unpleasant.

Eventually, she regained control. It was not that the pain had faded, more that she became one with the sharp bite of its presence. But the agony itself would never fade. *Atar* provided some scant relief, like a soothing balm on the burns from a fire. But it could never heal the terrible rents in her soul, the scars left by her one foolish, selfless act.

Do you still live, my sweet Jenna?

A face appeared in her mind, so young and full of life. She forced it aside with a grimace and rose. Four grand windows stood at each point of the compass, looking out over the ancient ruins that had been her domain these past…

How long has it been?

She couldn't say. Years, certainly. Decades? Perhaps. She had spent so long hidden away from the world, what did such measures matter now? Time passed, but the mountains and this lost city remained untouched, and the Reaper had slowly faded to a shadow of herself.

Her eyes fell to the stone in her hand. Empty. She shuddered, the spikes slashing into her once more, breaking through her concentration. Breathing heavily, she stood with her eyes closed, seeking the trance that allowed her to escape her bodily torment, to commune with the world as it was beneath all this horrible *flesh*.

It would not come. Not without *atar* to soothe the flames and bring those few moments of peace. Her fingers closed around the ring, trembling. Hours. It would be hours before it charged, even here at the centre of the nexus. A little whimper escaped her lips as the flesh crawled within her.

The chamber still shook gently with the vibrations of the distant landslide. The ancient floorboards groaned gently. Her eyes snapped open and she strode to the window that looked over the mountains. Perhaps she had visitors. Humans never came to this ancient place. The Magisterium didn't like them to see the truths it hid.

But sometimes an Elysian would venture here in search of sanctuary. Fewer and fewer in recent years. Her last remaining crystal she had taken off an older woman…a year ago? The timing felt right. A shame the girl had resisted. It was only a small thing. Hardly worth dying over. And yet her remains lay buried in a shallow grave outside the city.

Dust swirled around the base of the mountains. To the Reaper's eye, it seemed a section of the cliffs had given way. Finally, after all these years, the immortal mountains showed some semblance of change.

She was about to turn away when she glimpsed something on the slopes below. A man in an oversized trenchcoat. No, there were two of them. He had a young woman slung over his shoulder.

The Reaper's heart pulsed. She clenched her fists, uncut nails digging into her palms. The pain drew some relief from the agony in her skull. She watched the man pick his way down the path and enter the city. Had the woman been injured in the landslide? Strange, that it should transpire at the same time as their appearance. The Reaper was not one to believe in coincidence.

Her eyes shifted to the settling dust. Great boulders now filled the pass, closing the ruins to the world. Her eyes narrowed, gaze returning to the man and his injured companion. Even from a distance, she could tell both had seen better days. The man was staggering like a drunk down the broad avenues that formed the spokes of the city's looping streets. His companion must be in even worse shape if she could not walk.

There was something about these two, she was sure of it. Elysian? Elysian with *agimet?*

She warmed at the thought, the pain receding a little. The little crystal had lasted her well, but like all crystals, eventually it would crack from the strain placed on it. And then she would be tempted. Without fresh agimet, could she resist that call…

There was a code amongst the Elysian, generally accepted by all. Hunted by humans, persecuted everywhere they went, the Gifted tried at least to avoid conflict among themselves. It was a sacred, unspoken agreement amongst their kind.

The Reaper followed no code. Not before this curse, and certainly not now, in her most desperate moments. Human or Elysian, both had fallen to her blade over the long years of her life—if the money was good. You survived by your own strength in this world, or you became a slave to another's. She would not hesitate to cut down these intruders if they refused to show good sense.

She lingered long enough in the window to see where the man and his companion went. Then she collected her daggers and slipped from the chamber, beginning the long climb down the stone staircase. She would have to be wary. Without *atar*, she did not have access to her Gift. It placed her at a disadvantage—at least until her crystal recharged. If these strangers were here for the nexus, though, they would have to stay put until the morning. She would use that time to observe them, find out if they had agimet. And then, once her crystal was restored…

… the strangers would discover why they called her the Reaper.

12

The mountains were beautiful when you looked at them from above. The recent storm had dusted their peaks with snow, painting a tapestry of grey and white that stretched as far as the eye could see. There were other colours as well, if she drifted closer, dotted amongst the white…

Boom.

There, a thriving forest. Enormous trees with carmine trunks as broad as houses, their furry branches stretching for the sky…

Boom.

There, the scarlet soil of a volcanic mount, it loomed above the others, the burning heat within banishing the frozen white. Humans toiled on its derelict slopes, raising little buildings of stone and slate. So tiny, from above. So powerless…

Boom.

Wind tugged her restless spirit onward. Over the peaks, across the muddy slopes and gulleys, higher into the rocky crags, until she found herself looking down on that strangest of cities. Here, at least, was a work of man to defy the power of nature. How long had this monument of stone and glass stood against the passage of time, the violence of the mountains?

If only she had such power. If only she had such strength.

Kaila!

The name carried on the breeze like a long-forgotten memory. A shiver passed through the spirit. She drifted closer to the city. There was something about this *place, about those black and green and white buildings, and the mighty tower that stabbed the sky with its slender beauty. There was a power about it, an aura that defied the howling of winds and shifting of the earth, eternal.*

Kaila, wake up!

The world flickered. For a moment, she was in the light again. Theron was holding her, leaning down, pressing his lips to hers. Warmth filled her, pressing back the dark. She tried to kiss him back, to grasp at him, but her strength was gone, and as he withdrew, the darkness returned, swelling back up to claim her…

The light vanished. For a moment, darkness ate everything—and then, colour, ever-changing. Violet to yellow to sapphire and scarlet, and a thousand others with no name. She grew lost in them, trapped amidst the swirling, crackling energies, like she drifted in the centre of something greater, in the eye of a raging storm…

…an eye that could see, that shifted suddenly, turned to stare at her. It saw her.

And then, a voice spoke.

Welcome home, my daughter.

"No!" Kaila woke with a scream.

A shadow loomed above and strong hands grasped her shoulders, forcing her back down. Still half-caught in her dream, Kaila shrieked and kicked out against her captor. A burning pain scorched through her arms as she tried to push him away, but her strength had fled and her assailant was far more powerful than her anyway.

"Easy, easy! It's me. It's Theron!"

Theron?

Something about the name cut through Kaila's panic. She stilled, gasping in great lungfuls of air. Her chest ached as though someone had punched her—*hard*—and there was a tingling in her fingertips. Her head swam as she tried to sit up, only to find her body so weak she barely made it halfway before slumping back against the hard ground. She squinted through the dancing lights, trying to make out the owner of the voice.

Theron's tanned face slowly resolved into view. She groaned.

"You." She closed her eyes again.

The thief chuckled. "Please, hold your excitement."

Kaila muttered several choice words under her breath, before adding, "What happened? Did you…" Her memories were fuzzy, but she couldn't get the memory of the Warden's soul out of her mind. It had burned so strangely, like an inferno trapped in a vase of glass.

Eventually, though, she had to open her eyes again. At first, all she saw were dancing lights, until the rest of the world came into focus. A fire burned gently in an old fireplace, tongues of flame flickering off the shining walls of black stone. *Obsidian*, a piece of her mind finally recalled its name. Volcanic glass. They dug it from the mine sometimes, but there was little use for it, at least in Elgoss. To build from it…

"You're safe," Theron responded, his voice taut. "The pass is closed."

She frowned. There was a strange tension in Theron's voice. In his face as well, Kaila realised as she studied him. He wore his customary smile, but it did not seem to reach his eyes, and his brow was creased with…worry?

"Everything okay?" she asked.

He let out a sigh, dropping the act as his smile faded. "You tell me," he said quietly. "What exactly did you do back there, Kaila? Where did you get that crystal?"

"The crystal?" It took a moment for her sluggish mind to connect the dots. Her eyes widened. "Ah, yes…" she started before hesitating. Her people had hidden this truth from the Elysian for generations. It would be a terrible betrayal to reveal it now…

…except Sister Eurador had already betrayed her. They had turned her into an enemy of humanity, of the Magisterium and the Kingdom of Fresia. Hunted her. Tried to kill her.

If humanity was now her enemy, maybe it was time for Kaila to accept that an Elysian could be her ally.

Starting with telling Theron the truth. About everything.

Gritting her teeth, she tried to sit up again, this time with a little more luck, though not without a groan.

"Easy," Theron said, pressing a hand to her shoulder.

She shook him off. "Theron," she asked, "have you ever heard of an Elysian that could charge agimet? Without a nexus, I mean."

His frown grew deeper. "Huh?"

"That's how I escaped Elgoss," she said, grimacing as a jolt of pain shot up her spine. "I put a little bit of charge into Sister Eurador's crystal."

"Kaila, what are you talking about?" Theron was staring at her now, brow furrowed in concern.

She pressed on anyway. "It's part of the Third Trial—the one to assess potential Wardens," she explained. "Wardens have the power to channel *atar* into crystals, even when far from a nexus."

"But that's…" Theron said, his eyes growing wide, "…impossible," he finished in a whisper.

"Except it's not," Kaila said quietly. "Sister Eurador thought I had failed, but I *knew* I hadn't. I knew the agimet had changed. And then, just now, with the crystal you gave me, I knew I had to do it. Charge it, before the Warden came. And I *did*," she continued, a hint of pride creeping into her voice. A smile touched her lips as she waited for Theron's response.

Instead, he sat staring at her, that strange, troubled look on his face, like the physician back in Elgoss had just diagnosed her with black lung. It did nothing for her anxiety.

"Well?" she said at last. "Are you going to say something?"

She was growing angry now, and shrugging off his restraining hand, she pushed herself up properly. Thankfully, the ground was firm, smooth like the concrete floors in the colonnade, though the veins of crystal in the stone suggested it was natural material, almost like the city's creators had cut these buildings from the bedrock itself.

Sitting back on his heels, Theron studied her. "Kaila, what do you remember?"

For the love of the First Matron…

"I remember seeing you about to be cut in half by Elric Chain," she snapped. "So I charged the crystal you gave me and threw it. Is that enough, or do you need—*why are you looking at me like I'm dying?*"

To her surprise, Theron flinched. His lips drew tight in a narrow line. "Because you *did!*"

Kaila blinked. "What?"

"I don't know what happened exactly. I used that crystal you threw me to collapse the passage on our mutual friend. But when I came looking for you, you were on the ground." He drew in a long breath. "Kaila, you weren't breathing."

"Ha?" she murmured, staring at him. "You're…you're joking, right?"

But Theron was shaking his head. "You didn't have a pulse either." His eyes never left hers. "I…a friend of mine back in Tah'raus, his father was a physician. He…he taught me some things. Chest compressions to help restart the heart and fill the lungs, but for a minute…I didn't think…"

Kaila sat there, too stunned to reply. She had *died*. How? There wasn't a mark on her. It couldn't be true…

"Kaila, if what you're saying is true. If you really *did* somehow charge that piece of agimet…I don't think you should do it again."

"I…but the Wardens…" she trailed off, swallowing the words.

Theron was wrong. He had to be. This power was what made the Wardens special! That meant she still might have a chance to survive. She found herself trembling, though close to the fire's warmth, it had nothing to do with the chill mountain air.

She had almost died.

It was a terrible realisation, to be confronted with her own mortality. The last few days had been filled with danger and near misses, but this had been the closest of all. And it hadn't even come at the hands of the Warden, but her own strange abilities.

Shivering, she reached instinctively for her dagger, only to realise she must have lost it.

"Here," Theron said, holding out the knife he had given her earlier.

Kaila accepted it with a nod, though she ignored the look he gave her as she took it. The look that said at any second he thought she might shatter into a thousand pieces. Her hand tightened around the hilt of the hunting knife. The leather was reassuring beneath her fingers. She closed her eyes, sucking in a short breath. The silence built again. Theron's eyes, Kaila could feel the weight of them, pressing down on her. She couldn't take it.

Though her muscles screamed and tied themselves in knots, she pushed herself to her feet, strangling the scream that rose in her throat.

"Woah!" Theron exclaimed, leaping up after her. "I'm not sure—"

"What happened to the nexus?" she asked. "And the agimet? Aren't we meant to be charging all those crystals you stole?"

Theron stood with one hand outstretched towards her. "We are," he said, then when she only looked at him in bafflement, he gestured to his pack. "The crystals charge themselves once they're inside the nexus. We just have to wait another…eight hours or so."

"Oh," Kaila hesitated. "And the nexus is…"

"All around us," Theron replied with a grim chuckle. "Like I said, the tower is in the centre from what a few Hounds have told me. They can sense *atar* and the Gift when it's used. Its influence extends all over the city, right up to the pass."

"I see," Kaila said, trying to align this information with what Sister Eurador had taught. She had claimed *atar* was everywhere, concentrating around nexus points. Probably, the ambient energy in a nexus was strong enough to charge agimet without the assistance of someone with the abilities of a Warden.

Someone like me.

Shivering, she pushed the thought from her mind. "What is this place?" she asked, staggering to one of the windows. Its edges were worn and pitted, revealing the swirls within the obsidian rock. There had probably once been shutters or perhaps even glass in the window, but now it was empty. Darkness had fallen outside, but the sky was clear. The second moon was just showing above the mountain peaks. By its light, she could just make out the other buildings. They were all single storey, same as theirs. They were in the outer ring of the city.

"The City of the Black Tower, we call it," Theron replied.

Kaila glanced at him from the window. "That's not much of an answer."

He shrugged, moving to join her. "It wasn't much of a question." His shoulder brushed against hers as he leaned against the pitted sill.

She shivered, feeling the heat of his touch, even as she snorted. Outside, the streets were quiet—eerily so. Not an insect chirped or a bird called. Even the wind had died away. Kaila suppressed a shudder. Looking out on that world of stone and volcanic glass, a remnant of her dream resurfaced, of a spirit adrift in the ether. Is that what death was? Cursed forever to watch the world continue without her?

"I never imagined a city could be so…extravagant."

Theron chuckled. "This was the mightiest empire the world has ever known."

"What happened to them?"

"You don't know?"

As he shifted beside her, Kaila looked up to find his gold-flecked eyes watching her. She shivered, her voice suddenly abandoning her at his closeness. Belatedly realising he'd asked a question, she swallowed and shook her head. He grimaced.

"They were betrayed," he murmured.

Her heart stirred at the thought of so great a civilization brought low. "By who?"

Theron shook his head. "There are…conflicting stories," he said, turning away. Kneeling by the fire, he added some branches he must have collected from the nearby forest.

Grimacing, Kaila reached into her pocket and drew out the ring she had taken from Sister Eurador. It was still dead, the crystal facets dim. Theron tensed when he turned and saw her holding it, but she didn't try to charge it like she had the one in the pass, just stared at it, this hated thing. Could she really bring herself to abandon everything she had been taught her entire life?

"I can teach you more about your power in the morning," Theron said gently, "when the agimet has charged. We'll have more than enough *atar* to practice. And with the Warden dead, there's no pressing need to move. We have food for a few days at least."

"You're sure he's dead?" she whispered.

"Unless he somehow survived having a mountain dropped on his head."

A part of her was relieved at the news. For the first time in what felt a lifetime, no one was hunting her. She was safe; she could relax. But there was another part of her, buried deep within, that rebelled at Theron's declaration. A Warden was *dead*. One of their protectors, the men and women who stood against the darkness.

She shuddered. Was this who she was now? A murderer of heroes?

"Something the matter?" Theron asked.

She turned to look into those great blue eyes. "My father would think I'm a monster."

There was silence from her companion before he spoke. "I think Gideon Dwyn showed you exactly what he thought at the end."

Her eyes fluttered closed. "It hurts."

It surprised her when Theron put his arm around her waist. It surprised her more when she did not pull away.

"It always will." His voice was soft. "But each day, it'll get that little bit better. The weight on your chest a little lighter. A little easier to cope with. And then one day, weeks or months or even years from now, you'll realise you went a whole day without thinking of them. And it'll be okay. Because it's not that you don't still love them. Just that the pain went away."

She let out a little sob. Turning, she embraced the strange, stupid, kind man beside her, not even caring anymore that he saw her cry, that for those few moments, she wasn't the brave, bold warrior she pretended to be.

When the tears finally faded, she looked up at him through blurry eyes. "Sister Eurador taught us that Elysian magic is evil because only some get it," she whispered, doubts clinging to her like mud from the river. "That it gives some an unfair advantage against others."

"They're not wrong," Theron replied, his lips twisting in thought, "but everyone is different in their own way. Some are born tougher, or stronger, or smarter. That doesn't make them evil, or that we should force them down to our level. That's just life. It's not meant to be fair."

"Shouldn't it be, though?" she asked. "That's what the kingdom —what Fresia and the Magisterium—is about. Equality. Everyone working together, sharing the burden, to build a greater world for all."

How Kaila longed for that world now, for the sense of peace she'd drawn from being a part of a community. Theron saw duty as a burden, but for her it had been a comfort, to know she had a purpose, that she was bigger than just herself, a part of something grand.

But even as she spoke, Kaila found herself doubting. All her life, she had placed her faith in the Magisterium and Fresia. Now, though, that faith had crumbled, each new revelation another crack in the foundations of her life.

"Yes," Theron said, "but there can be beauty in the struggle, sometimes. In striving to be something more than you already are."

"Maybe," Kaila whispered. The silence stretched out between them as Kaila lingered on his words. She chose her next question carefully. "What I still don't understand," she said at last. "Is *where* my power came from. My father…" Her voice cracked and she couldn't finish get the rest of the words out.

"What about your mother?" Theron asked gently.

"She died—" Kaila began, before her father's words came rushing back, "no, *she's alive*. When my father freed me, he told me that she fought for him, saved his life on the frontlines."

"She was Elysian?"

Kaila frowned. "No…no he said she wasn't."

"Any idea where she is now?"

"No," she repeated, the racing of her heart slowing as reality took hold. "She didn't want me," she continued, the void swirling in her chest. "She appeared at my father's camp a year later with me as a babe. His captain helped cover up where I'd come from."

"So not Elysian," Theron muttered, "a Warden then?"

"Once they take their oaths and their armour, they're bound to celibacy."

Theron raised an eyebrow. "It would explain why she gave you up," he mused, "and maybe their other abilities really do come from a bloodline connection to the Elysian."

She swallowed. It did make a certain kind sense. But there were so many questions still left unanswered. Like what her mother had been doing on that mountainside in the first place when she'd rescued her father—and why afterwards she hadn't taken him back to their camp immediately. And…

"It still doesn't explain how I passed my Trial."

"No," Theron agreed.

He didn't say anything further, however, instead allowing the silence to return. His eyes never left her, still glinting with that soft concern, before he finally pushed himself away from the windowsill. "Well, think you're recovered enough for a bit of a walk?"

She raised her eyebrows in surprise. "It's night outside."

"Oh, sorry. Didn't realise you were afraid of the dark."

She snorted, finding a smile on her lips despite her pain. As it slipped away, she sighed. "Where are we going?"

"Better you see for yourself," Theron said as he stepped out into the night.

The Reaper slipped into an alcove as the pair emerged from the house. She waited, breath stifled against the silence of the night as their footsteps tap-tapped past her hiding place. The girl looked a great deal more alive than when the man had carried her into the city. That was unfortunate.

The man was alert too. While he wore an easy smile, his eyes were everywhere, darting from shadow to shadow, alert. This was someone for whom danger was an old friend. She would not take him unaware.

His companion, however…the Reaper knew an easy mark when she saw one. Probably the man's paramour. She was pretty enough, with that long, raven-black hair, though her skin had the sun-kissed tan of the Fresian working class. She looked around the ruins with eyes wide in awe—with no hint of the caution that came so easily to her friend. The only sign she could be anything more was the hunting knife on her hip; a large, wicked-looking thing. But could she use it?

The Reaper's lips pressed in a thin line as she slipped from the shadows to follow them. Two then, and both armed. Tackling them without *atar* would be risky. Especially with her condition. The withdrawal was well advanced now, the needles of its fire digging deep into her flesh. She could feel *everything.* The grinding of her bones, the burning pulse of blood in her veins, the tearing of her tendons as she moved. It was like her body had become a foreign thing to her own mind. Truly, the Trickster had cursed his chosen ones with a most cruel Gift.

It was unbearable, intolerable. Anything more than a few hours would drive her mad. That was why she had not left these ruins in all these years, not with the tiny crystals she gathered off the unfortunate travellers who passed her way. The closest nexus was a week's journey from the hidden city. She would collapse on the roadside within a day, lost to the withdrawal.

But now an opportunity had revealed itself. The man spoke of agimet. *A lot of agimet,* if he thought they could waste their *atar* helping the young woman practice. The Reaper wondered how much, exactly. Enough for her to finally escape this place?

She would find out soon enough.

Wrapping the dark cloak around her muscular frame, the Reaper stalked her prey.

13

Kaila found herself nervous as Theron led her into the heart of the ruins. The air was cold, the sun having set hours ago, and now a white mist crept down from the hills to swallow the city. She drew her coat tighter about herself with a shiver, though the gesture was only partly in response to the cold. Whatever Theron's reassurances, she couldn't shake the fear that had settled in her gut, the whispers that she was still in danger; that the Warden was out there somewhere in the mists, stalking them…

"You sure you're okay?"

Her head jerked up at the question. Irritation touched her to see the concern written across Theron's face.

"I'm *fine*," she snapped with a little too much force. To be fair, it was the third time she'd had to reassure him.

It didn't help that she didn't *feel* fine, of course. Her entire body ached from what she'd done with the agimet and the wild ride up the mountain, and she felt strung out, like a shirt beaten one too many times on the rocks of the river. Worst of all, a piece of her remained in the darkness, or perhaps it was the void itself, that peat-black emptiness inside.

But Theron's worry wasn't going to change any of that. She wanted to snap at him, to tell him to leave her alone. But she couldn't. He had saved her life. Heat stirred inside her as she recalled how she'd risen briefly from the darkness to find him leaning over her. Kissing her. Had that been real? If so, she should have been outraged!

Instead, she found a piece of her yearned to know what it had been like, to feel his lips against hers again, the heat of his breath as it mingled with her own…

Her face flushed and she thrust the thought away. He had saved her life, yes, but only after she'd saved his! In fact…

"You know," she said suddenly, her voice hoarse from the cold. "I'm still waiting for a thank you."

"Huh?" Confusion replaced the concern on Theron's face.

"That's right," Kaila continued, nodding to herself. "You know, for saving your butt."

This time Theron stopped in the middle of the street. "I'm sorry," he said finally, "but I'm pretty sure it was *me* who saved *your* butt."

"Oh, yes." Kaila snorted. "You were teaching Elric Chain quite the lesson when I got there."

"I…he…you…" Theron spluttered.

"Yep," she continued, flicking an imaginary piece of dust from her cuff. "You would have been toast without me."

Kaila grinned. It was forced, but she needed him to believe it, to stop seeing her as the person who had almost died. Because if he didn't, she wouldn't be able to stop seeing it herself, from remembering that darkness, and the void, and the voice that had spoken.

Theron wore a strange look on his face. He squinted at her, almost as if he knew. As if he *understood* even.

"Hey," he said suddenly. "I was the one getting my hands dirty!" He grinned, throwing up his hands. "And besides, let's not forget who was brought back to life by whom!"

She almost winced, almost ruined it, as the darkness touched her and she recalled the cold…

…but then she remembered him holding her close in the night, and the warmth of the blanket he had given her, his embrace as she grieved her father.

"Exactly!" she said. Her voice was raw, cracking. "I heroically sacrificed my life to save the day!"

Theron raised his eyebrows at that one, before he chuckled. "Damn, you got me there," he said, holding his hands up in mock surrender. "Okay, Kaila Dwyn, you win this round. *Thank you* for saving our lives."

A smile touched Kaila's lips, genuine this time. "You're quite welcome."

Snorting, Theron gestured to the street ahead and they continued, wandering through the stone buildings and archways, and while Kaila's body still ached, she found its burden no longer quite so heavy to carry.

The city rose around them, growing taller, grander as they ventured deeper into the ruins. They passed an enormous archway that would have dwarfed her entire block of flats back in Elgoss. Despite its size, it seemed to serve no real purpose.

"Why *did* you come back for me?" Theron asked suddenly.

She looked around, surprised at the question, then looked away when she saw him watching her again.

"I…I don't know," she said quietly, recalling the sense of doom that had come over her as she fled the pass. "Why did you come back for me in Elgoss?"

A pause. "You were brave back in the mine. Trying to save them all," he said quietly. "I couldn't leave you to face a Warden alone. You deserved better than that."

She nodded to herself, eyes on the ground. "And now the Warden is dead, what now?" she asked. "Where will you go?"

The pause was longer this time, and Kaila was surprised to find herself holding her breath, waiting for the answer. Why? He had saved her life, but he was still the selfish thief, the antithesis to everything she believed in, wasn't he?

Everything you used to believe in, a voice whispered.

"To Tah'raus, I suppose," he said at last.

"Not to your people?" she asked, surprised. "What about the agimet you stole?"

Theron snorted. "The agimet I stole will be sold to the highest bidder," he said, before hesitating. "As for my people…I have never been a warrior."

There was a tug in his voice, as though he was leaving something important unsaid, but after finally getting him to lighten up about her near-death-experience, Kaila decided not to press the matter.

"Will you go alone?" she said instead, surprising even herself. Her head jerked up, lips parted as though to take it back. Where had *that* come from?

"Did you want to join me?" Theron said before she could.

"I…" She murmured, emotions warring inside her.

Fortunately, she was spared answering as Theron's eyes suddenly widened. Before she could react, he lunged towards her, shoving her to the ground, while a dagger appeared in his hand. Crying out, she rolled and reached for her own blade. The weakness in her body betrayed her, however, as cords of fire burned through her legs. She collapsed, crashing to the paved street. Even so, she managed to swing in the direction of the danger—only to lower her blade as the *clip-clopping* of hooves carried through the mists.

Laughter burst from Theron's lips as the stallion approached. Sheathing his blade, he reached out a hand to pat its nose. Grumbling to herself, Kaila picked herself up from the ground— slowly this time—and brushed the dust from her clothes.

"First Matron, what was that for?"

Theron smiled sheepishly. "Sorry, guess I'm still a little on edge."

He ran a hand down the stallion's neck and it trembled at the touch. Kaila grimaced. The poor beast had gotten a rough deal since they'd stolen it.

"I thought you said we were safe here," Kaila said.

"Safe from the Warden," he murmured. "There may be…other dangers in these ruins."

"Such as?" Kaila muttered. Her eyes flickered to the surrounding buildings.

Theron shrugged. "My friend never saw it, but he spoke of a shadow that followed him while he was here last. It didn't act against him, but others have disappeared in this place in recent years."

"*Now* you mention that?" she snapped, her irritation at the fall getting the better of her. "While we're out in this soup with hardly a sword between us? Where are we going anyway?"

"The Black Tower."

"Why there?"

"You'll see."

Kaila gritted her teeth, but it was clear that Theron wasn't going to offer any answers until they reached the tower, so she gestured for him to take the lead. Soon after, the streets widened into a broad avenue she was pretty sure led to the base of the tower. With the mists, however, the tower itself remained out of sight.

"How is this place so *big*?" she muttered as they drew closer to what she hoped was their destination.

"This may surprise you, but Elgoss is hardly the largest place in the world."

"What about Tah'raus?"

"Tah'raus is twice as large," the thief said, "but these ruins are the grander of the two. Grander than *anything* we have built in a thousand years."

"We?" Kaila asked with a frown.

Theron nodded but did not elaborate. They marched on, the mists closing in around them. Their noises became muffled, even the *clack* of the stallion's hooves on the stone road. Kaila soon found herself trembling again and wishing they hadn't left the comfort of the house and the fire in its hearth. Whoever had created this city obviously hadn't cared for its inhabitants' comfort, building it all the way up here in the mountains. And why here in the first place, unless…

It had to be the nexus.

Her eyes darted to the ruins, suddenly seeing them in a whole new light. How they'd been built, the sprawling halls and towering ceilings, the intricate designs carved into the facades, and arches that seemed to serve no purpose. All of it so extravagant, so wasteful, an architecture so different from her own people's as to be almost alien.

And she heard Theron's explanation again. *They were betrayed.*

She stumbled to a halt and the stallion stopped with her. Her hands clenched tightly around the reins. Her skin crawled.

"This is Iselador, isn't it?"

The Hidden City. The place where T'iana had first learned the Elysian's secrets and freed humanity from their evil masters. Almost forgotten to time, it was the secret stronghold of the Elysian. Fresia had been searching for it for centuries.

And here it was—a ruin long forgotten, its mysteries, its *power* lost to the sands of time.

Theron was watching her, his eyes dark in the mist, lips drawn tight.

"It was T'iana, wasn't it?" she continued. "The one you were talking about, who betrayed them."

And still, he watched her, silent. The mist curled between them and the pale fingers of cold stretched out to brush against her skin. She trembled; she couldn't help it.

Theron's face tightened. "Come on. We're close now."

Turning, he plunged into the mists. Kaila longed to call him back, to demand he answer her questions, but instead, as the silence of the night swallowed her up, her chest tightened and she plunged into the darkness after him.

Don't leave me alone.

She rejoined Theron, and with the stallion in tow, they entered the innermost loop of the city. The night seemed to grow darker and despite herself, Kaila found herself slowing as she saw the Black Tower emerging overhead. There was something about it that tugged at her, like a tingling in her spine that whispered it was dangerous, that they should be going nowhere near it.

The cloud swirled in the street, forming visions that seemed to take on a life of their own. Here, a ghost with a knife slowly distended towards her from the ether, and there, a flicker of steel in the moonlight.

Realising she was gripping the hilt of her dagger, Kaila exhaled and forced herself to release it.

You're jumpy now you know what this place is.

Iselador. She could hardly believe it. But Theron hadn't denied it. What was it he wanted to show her, though?

And then from the mists before her appeared a man. He stood tall—taller than any human—imposing in black armour and a heavy broadsword clenched in one fist.

Kaila cried out and was already scrambling for her dagger before she realised it wasn't real. A statue stood before her. No, two statues, each cast from the same black obsidian as the tower. The other was of a woman. Each stood twice, maybe three times the height of even her father.

Her eyes lifted to take them in, wondering how anything so grand could have been crafted by human or Elysian fingers. The artist must have spent weeks detailing just their weapons, etching every nick and scratch in the metal, and weeks more on the man's face, shaping the harsh jawline and sharp cheeks, even the wildness of his hair. And yet, his efforts had been rewarded, for he had captured the raw power of the man. Even the eyes, though they were the same stone as the rest of the statue, seemed alive, as though they watched from the depths of the black glass.

Beside her, Theron chuckled. "*These* are what we came for."

Kaila swallowed, glancing at Theron and then back to the pair of statues. Despite the man's sheer size, it was the woman who drew her attention now. Even carved from weather-worn stone, she was easily the most beautiful woman Kaila had ever seen. Beside the man, she was small and delicate, the swirls of her dress pouring down around her shapely figure. Just as the artist had captured her partner's feroc-ity, so too had he laboured over the details here, chiselling out the lines of her dress, the curve of her hips. Long, flowing hair framed her face, half covering her ears, while wide eyes gazed out through the mists, her expression serene alongside the bottled rage of the man.

Standing there in the dark, even trembling as she was from the cold, Kaila found she could have spent hours watching the woman. There was something about her. The wonder in her eyes, perhaps, or the way her lips were parted as though to speak.

"Who are they?" she asked at last, tearing her gaze from the masterpiece.

Theron smiled, approaching the plinth on which the pair stood. There were words on the base, written in strange letters she did not recognise.

"What does it say?" she asked, joining him.

"Your Sister didn't teach you this language?"

She shook her head. "I'm learning there are many gaps in my education."

"The Magisterium teaches that their world is immutable. That their facts cannot be questioned," Theron grunted. "They don't want people thinking for themselves. Otherwise, they might find there are questions their facts cannot answer." He lifted his head to study the pair. "Questions like why, in the heart of Iselador, our once-great-city, would a statue honouring your First Matron stand side by side with an Elysian king."

"What?" Kaila breathed.

"It says," Theron continued, lowering his gaze to the writing, "that this man was Oberon, king of Iselador." He turned to face her, a grimace on his lips. "And beside him is T'iana. His queen."

Kaila's blood pounded in her ears as Theron spoke the words. She listened, but did not hear. Her mind was already far away, deep in the stories whispered by Sister Eurador when she was still a child, in the words she had read from old papyrus scrolls and the essays she had written. She had spent entire afternoons in daydreams, imagining herself as T'iana, liberator of humanity.

T'iana, who a millennia ago had stolen the Aegis of their enemy and used it to break the chains of their servitude. To free humanity from their Elysian masters.

And now here she was, or her likeness at least, standing proudly in the heart of the enemy's most sacred city.

Her heart was pounding, her lungs screaming for air. She realised she hadn't taken a breath for several heartbeats. Gasping, she swayed, and stars danced before her eyes. When they faded, she saw that Theron was looking at her with concern again. She found she no longer cared.

"How?" she croaked. "How can this be Iselador? It was *lost.* How can it be *here?*"

Theron's lips thinned. "Not lost," he said, still studying her. "Hidden away by your Magisterium."

"Why would they do that?"

The thief glanced at the statue. "Because sometimes the truth doesn't match the stories."

"What does that *mean?*"

Ice crunched beneath her boots as she shifted where she stood. By the First…*gods* it was cold. Her cloak still smelt of must and dampness, but she pulled it tighter anyway, warding off the mists.

"It means our stories are different," Theron said. "In yours, T'iana is a human who freed herself from Elysian chains and raised a rebellion." His pale blue eyes drilled into hers as he spoke. "In our stories, she was Elysian. The queen who betrayed her king. The traitor who stole our most precious artefact and brought about the fall of our people, our entire civilisation."

"That's…that's…"

Her eyes were drawn to that noble face. Now Theron had spoken her name, she saw the resemblance to the old paintings of the First Matron.

"It's…she's…" Kaila couldn't find the words. "That's not…"

"That's why the city was 'lost'," Theron murmured. "They could have destroyed the statue, of course, but T'iana is a holy figure. Not even the Magisterium could commit such sacrilege. So, they hid this place away, burned all record of its location, making sure no one ever found it. The Elysian, though, we have never forgotten."

Kaila couldn't tear her eyes from the statue. The blood was *thundering* in her ears now, roaring like a flood that would sweep her away. How many times would her world be turned on its head?

"So, T'iana was…"

"Elysian," Theron said. "At least, according to our stories."

Shivering, Kaila said nothing, only wrapped her arms around herself and looked at the sky. The clouds had gathered, hiding the moons from view, and the night was dark. Above them loomed the Black Tower.

"Was it all lies?" she whispered at last. "Everything they taught us?"

"I wish I could tell you otherwise."

Her eyes slid closed and she whispered, "Take me back."

"Kaila…"

"Please," she croaked. "Theron, please, take me back to the fire."

She sensed his eyes on her, but didn't look up. Didn't even open her eyes. How could she? After a long while, she heard him exhale. A warm hand touched her shoulder.

"Okay, Kaila. Let's go."

The journey back was silent and long. Kaila's mind was far away. Lost. It was all too much. The past few days she'd been trapped in the currents of a raging river that had washed away her entire world. It was all gone now, stripped from her, every story, every duty, every scrap of dignity the world had given her. She was alone, and the river raged on.

She hardly noticed when they arrived at the house; just stood, staring at the red glow of the embers, lost. Theron must have gone to stable the stallion in the adjacent building because she was alone. A lump lodged in her throat. *Alone.* She trembled. Crossing abruptly to the fireplace, she tossed a handful of sticks into the coals. A few heartbeats later, the flames reappeared, licking along the length of the wood.

Warmth washed across her face. It didn't help. Another shudder shook her body. The void within was everything now, a terrible, all-consuming mass. She needed no Psionic to feed her despair. The void had already taken everything else; her hope, her love, her *light.*

Even if she survived this place, even if Theron brought her with him to Tah'raus, what place was there for her in this world? For the girl who had dreamed of being a Warden, of serving her kingdom and the Magisterium, now turned outlaw and Elysian, enemy of everything she had believed.

Nothing. There's nothing.

"Kaila…" Theron's voice came from behind her. "Are you all right?"

She rose from beside the fire. He was watching her with those eyes again. "No," she whispered, trembling still. "I don't think I'll ever be all right again."

"It gets easier, eventually, this life."

"And what if I don't want it?" she asked quietly.

His frown deepened, his lips setting in a line. "You think any of us want this, Kaila?" he whispered. "That they gave us a choice?"

Kaila swallowed the lump that had formed in her throat. "There's always a choice."

"Ay, you're right," he said, "and people like us, we have to make it every day. Whether to lie down and give up. Or to *fight,* to struggle on, remind them we *exist*, however much they might want to exterminate us."

Her eyes returned to the fire. The gentle blaze cast back the dark and the cold, embracing them in its comforting glow. "What did you want, then?" she whispered, the words springing unbidden from her lips. "Before all this?"

Silence was her answer, but she did not turn to face him, to press the point. She only waited.

"I wanted to grow up," he said at last. "To go on adventures with my sister, to see the world."

She glanced at him, surprised at his answer. "What happened to her, your sister?"

"She failed her Trials," he murmured. "They killed her for it. And then they came looking for me."

"How…" Kaila didn't know where to start.

"She told me to run. So I did."

"Theron…"

He stood with his head bowed, only to shake himself and grimace. "Come on, let's get some sleep." Crouching, he pulled the blanket from their pack and held it out to her with a smile. "You take it tonight. After all, you did save our lives today."

She took it absently, still watching Theron as he drew his trench coat around himself and added more wood to the fire, before lying down beside it. She wondered how he could still find it inside him to smile after everything he had just said, knowing the world for what it truly was.

The fibres of the blanket were coarse in her hands as she held it to her. She couldn't smile. Could hardly feel anything now, knowing the truth, knowing the people she had trusted most in this world had deceived her, manipulated and lied to her, *used her*. It was like a bloody wound inside, constantly bleeding, tearing at her soul.

Trembling, she lay down on the cold floor. Pulling the blanket close, she tried to forget, to escape the truth for a little while and pretend she was home, that it was her father who lay nearby and not one of the enemy.

But she couldn't. No matter how she tried, her mind kept returning to the truth. To that statue in the centre of this lost city, to the power within her. And to the man who had stolen it all away. The enemy who had saved her life.

Elysian.

The blanket whispered as she rose. It gave her away. Theron's eyes blinked open. The golden flecks in their crystal depths shimmered in the firelight. His brow creased as he saw her standing over him.

"Kaila?"

She swallowed, feeling the pain of the void. And a single spark, a little bit of heat that burned against the emptiness.

"I don't want to be alone," she whispered.

His eyes widened. For a heartbeat, he sat looking up at her, lips twisted strangely, as if…

…he rose slowly, the coat slipping from his shoulders to reveal his skin beneath, and then he was stepping towards her. Those strong arms went around her waist, holding her tight, pulling her against him. There was a real fire in his eyes now, more than reflection, or embers, but a smouldering inferno. She wanted that heat, to feel it against her, to feel *him.*

And then he was leaning down and his lips were pressing against hers, and the spark burst to life inside of her. In that instant, the void was washed away, fleeing before the heat they shared. The taste of him filled her, sweet and earthly, while the musk of him filled her nostrils. Her entire body trembled, but it was no longer from the cold, or the pain and fear, but for his closeness, for the heat of him, for the firestorm within, and a terrible, all-consuming *need.*

And then they were on the ground, the blanket forgotten, but he was atop her, and the cold no longer mattered.

All Kaila wanted, all she needed in the world at that moment, was him.

ELRIC CHAIN WOKE IN DARKNESS. IT WAS NOT A PLEASANT sensation.

Then again, he had thought he would not wake at all.

His ears still rung from the roaring of the mountain. *A mountain!*

The abomination with his cursed magics had dropped a gods' cursed mountain on his head. The Nameless himself must be watching over Elric, that he still lived.

Though, as he tried to shift around in the dark and found himself trapped, Elric realised the Nameless was not yet done testing his spirit. Stone. Stone pressed in on him from all sides. He could feel it against his armour, suffocating, *crushing* him. A boulder must have lodged somewhere above, shielding him from the vast weight of rock, but smaller stones and soil had filled the space, entombing him.

The Nameless shall not test you beyond your strength to bear.

As his panic rose, Elric repeated the old scripts. Calm returned, yet he grimaced. The Nameless was challenging him, making his fate seem inescapable, to see whether his faith wavered.

I will not perish here!

Their forgotten god would not abandon his most devout servant. Not while his task remained incomplete. The Elysian spies could not be allowed to escape. He must keep the faith, find the path the Nameless had left for him.

He reached first for the power in his crystals, but they were empty. His armour must have consumed their *atar* while protecting him from the collapsing rock. A shiver ran through him, panic rising once more. Elric struggled to maintain control. Like all Wardens, he could replenish the crystals from ambient *atar*. But the process was slow, particularly when far from a nexus. And these mountains were like an *atar* desert, barely a drop of the energy to be found.

Already, he could feel the space warming around him. His head began to ache as the air grew thin. Gritting his teeth, Elric sucked in another breath, then sought for the energies of the world. They flickered—then flared to life around him. Stars swirled, bright pinpricks connected by strings, joining the world together. *Atar*. The energy of the universe. Now, if he could—

The breath caught in Elric's throat as he sensed the burning wellspring of energy nearby. A nexus. *So close!* He was unfamiliar with the maps in this territory. He hadn't realised there was one so close! Hope bloomed in his chest. The Nameless had truly blessed him. A nexus changed everything. The Elysian fiends would have to wait hours for their crystals to charge, but so close to the nexus, it would take him only minutes to restore his agimet to life.

A smile touched the Warden's lips as a light bloomed in the darkness. *Atar.* He clenched his fist, feeling the cold steel form between his fingers. A dagger for now, small enough to swing with his limited movement. A few swipes of the blade and the rock began to crumble, the connections holding them together consumed by the weapon.

One cut, then another, and another. One cut at a time, Elric Chain would free himself of this silent tomb and breathe again the fresh mountain air.

And then…

Vengeance.

14

*D*arkness smothered Kaila's senses. All was silence. In the otherworldly ether, there was…nothing.

But she was not alone.

Someone stood before her. The man from the statue. Except, he was no longer stone, but flesh and blood and iron armour. Only the eyes remained the same. His cold eyes seemed to strip away her defences, laying her soul bare, and she stood, unable to move, to do anything but wilt before the blizzard of his gaze.

"My, my, what lamb dares disturb my solitude?"

The words were softly spoken, and yet thundered with terrible power. They pierced her like a bolt loosed from a crossbow, cutting deeper than steel, striking deep into her soul. The pain tore a yelp from her lips as she sank to her knees before the king, choking on her weakness, on failing this most powerful of men.

"Please," she gasped. "I didn't mean…"

A snort came from the figure. "How far my children have fallen, that you cower like shadows before the night."

His words dripped scorn, stirring something within her. She had faced more than just darkness up here in these lonely peaks, Wardens and death, and perhaps something more terrifying than either. Would she really kneel here, cowering before some long-dead king?

Somehow, she found her feet. "I am Kaila Dwyn. And I am no lamb!"

The figure glanced back with those burning eyes, and this time, she met his iron gaze. She thought she detected something flicker in his face. Surprise?

197

Then laughter rumbled through the dark. "Perhaps you are a child of mine after all," he growled. "Tell me, though, Kaila Dwyn, why do you cower in the dark? Where is your power?"

"I..." Kaila clenched her fists. Even here, she sensed the sharp edges of agimet against her flesh. Empty. The nexus still had not replenished its atar. *"My crystal is dead."*

"In Iselador, no child of mine is ever without power..."

The voice faded into laughter, and something changed within Kaila, an understanding blossomed. She clutched for it, but the dark was fading now, and the giant of a man was turning away, the light returning, and with it a distant warmth...

Kaila woke with a start, surprised to find herself back inside the ruin of the old house. The cold and dark had vanished, banished by the first rays of dawn's light streaming through the empty window frame. The embers of their fire glowed nearby, still warm enough that they gave off heat when Kaila extended a hand towards them. The blanket lay beneath her naked body.

Her face flushed as memories from the night came rushing back, washing away the last remnants of the dream. A pulse came from her heart as she looked around, but there was no sign of Theron. Surely he hadn't left. The saddlebags still leaned against the wall.

A frown replaced the swirling emotions left over from the night. Outside, the sun was still low in the sky, just peaking above the horizon. Strange to see its brilliance so early. Nestled amidst the mountains in Elgoss, at this time of year the sun only appeared towards midday.

Elgoss. Her home. She lay back on the blanket, thinking of everything that had passed these last few days, the events that had swept her from a life of duty and service, to whatever it was she had now.

At least in the light of day, she could look on the world with a little more optimism. The terrible despair of the night had melted away in the heat of their passions, and now for the first time since she had woken in chains, Kaila wondered whether this new world might hold something better for her. Something more than endless war and duty.

I wanted to see the world.

A lump lodged in her throat as she thought on Theron's words. She rose from the blanket, pulling on her clothes as she did so, and then moved to the doorway and looked out over the city. Iselador. A city of wonders. Hidden all along amidst the jagged peaks of her homeland. Surrounded by verdant forest and rolling hills and the distant rumbling of water. Looking upon its beauty made her wonder what other marvels the Magisterium had hidden from her.

She stirred from her daydreams as the whinny of a horse carried from outside. Shaking herself, Kaila pulled on her jacket. Strangely, the aching in her body had vanished and she felt refreshed, as though she'd had her first full night's sleep in days.

Definitely not a full night's sleep, she thought, cheeks growing hot again.

Stepping into the street, she found herself blinking, her eyes watering in the bright dawn light. It was a moment before her vision cleared and she could go in search of the horse. She found him in the shelter of the alley alongside the house. The stallion shied away from her as she approached. She supposed she couldn't blame it. They'd treated the poor beast terribly to reach the city.

Returning to the house, she fetched the bag of grain. This time, the stallion still nickered at her approach, but its fears dissolved when she revealed a handful of grain. It stretched out its head, cautiously at first, but within minutes was eating happily from her hands. She smiled, running her fingers along the horse's spine, feeling it tremble.

"Thank you," she said quietly. "You saved us both."

Without the mighty Fresian charger, she doubted either of them would have escaped Elgoss, let alone made it to the pass before the Warden caught them.

Slowly, her mind returned to the statues and Theron's revelation. T'iana and Oberon. Who had they been, really? The king and queen who had ruled this city a thousand years ago, this woman who had turned against her people, and the man who haunted her dreams. There had to be more to their story.

A wet tongue across her face brought Kaila back to the present. "*Yuck!*" she exclaimed at the stallion, which nickered its amusement.

Shaking her head, Kaila scratched the horse's chin. There was still one thing she didn't understand. If this was Iselador, where were the rest of the Elysian? Clearly, this was not their secret stronghold. But Theron was still nowhere to be seen, so her questions went unanswered for now.

Her stomach gave a rumble. She was starving. Well, if he wasn't going to show his face, Kaila would just have to help herself to some of his food. After what they'd shared last night, she was pretty sure he wouldn't mind.

Kaila was turning to go back into the house when she heard the noise behind her—the scrape of a boot on stone. Instinct and years of training with her father kicked in before her mind had even registered the danger. Her hand was closing around her hunting knife when cold steel touched her throat.

"Drop it," a harsh voice whispered in her ear.

Her heart practically tore itself from her chest as she turned and found herself face to face with a pair of glowing eyes.

Elysian.

She was older than Theron, in her fifties at least, with more silver in her hair than its original auburn hue. Her cheeks were hollowed out and her eyes were sunken pits in her skull. The faded leather pants and dirty bodice hung from her skeletal frame, while the scars of old battles criss-crossed her arms. She carried the pungent odour of someone that had gone unwashed for more than a few weeks. A ring on her finger shone with the telltale glow of *atar.* Most terrifying of all, the hand that held the dagger to Kaila's throat was shaking.

The knife slipped from Kaila's fingers, striking the ground with a heavy *thud.*

The woman smiled, revealing rotten teeth and an even nastier stench. "Good girl," she sneered. "Now, hand over your agimet and no one needs to get hurt."

"My…my agimet?"

Kaila stared at the woman, struggling to comprehend where she had come from. She tried to retreat a step, but a hand caught her by the wrist and dragged her back. Despite her deprivation, the woman had a wiry strength—made all the more terrifying by the *atar* burning in her eyes.

"Yes, I know you have it! Give it to me, *now!*" The last word was screamed instead of spoken.

Only then did Kaila realise her peril. It wasn't fear or anger in those eyes, and it wasn't hunger that made this woman shake.

It was madness.

She tried to withdraw again, but the Elysian woman followed, burning eyes filled with a desperation Kaila couldn't begin to understand. Then she heard it; the *thud* of a hoof on stone as the stallion stomped. The woman's head snapped up, eyes widening as a shriek came from behind Kaila.

And then the stallion was there, hooves flailing, eyes wild, teeth bared as it lashed at the Elysian woman. For a desperate second, Kaila thought the knife would slip and cut her throat, and it would all be over.

Instead, the hand around her wrist loosened. Only for a second, but it was enough for Kaila. She lashed out with her boot, catching the woman in the hip and sending her crashing backwards. Twisting, Kaila bolted for the street, desperate to escape what she'd glimpsed in those eyes.

Kaila had almost about reached the light when she felt it. She held no *atar* inside her, but a piece of her must have been attuned to this place, for she sensed the energy burst from the woman. There was a *popping* in her ears and she tensed, expecting some unseen force to lift her and slam her into the wall.

But the woman, as it turned out, was not one of Theron's Movers.

Something flickered in the corner of Kaila's vision. *And then the woman was there,* seemingly materialising from nothing. There was no time to avoid her. A fist thumped into Kaila's stomach, the breath exploding between her teeth. Gasping, she crashed to the ground, where she tried to crawl away, but fingers of steel closed around her ankle and began to drag her towards the house.

Desperately, Kaila lashed out with her boot, but the madwoman seemed to flicker, and the blow missed. Again and again she tried, each time to the same result.

The shadows of the house swallowed them up. Kaila cried out

as the woman tossed her across the room, striking the wall with a *thump.*

The woman was on her in an instant. A knee slammed into Kaila's back, sending pain shooting through her kidney. Rough hands grabbed her. She fought back, bucking against her assailant, but the madwoman had *atar.* In short order, her hands were bound behind her back with their own rope. The woman patted down her pockets, coming up with the ring Kaila had taken from Sister Eurador. The tiny gemstone remained dark.

"That's it?" she gasped, sounding desperate. "*Where is the rest?*"

Shoving Kaila hard into the ground, she darted to their bags and rummaged inside, eyes wild, lips drawn back in a desperate snarl. Kaila gritted her teeth and strained against her bindings, but they didn't budge. What would happen once this woman found Theron's crystals? What would *Theron* do if he lost them?

After a few moments of desperate searching, however, the stranger stilled. "It's not here," she whispered. She stared at the torn-up bags for a few heartbeats more, face stricken, tears streaming down her cheeks.

Then her head snapped around, staring straight at Kaila. She cried out and tried to roll away as the woman lunged, but it was hopeless. The icy fingers closed around her throat with a terrible strength. Burning eyes leaned close.

"Where. Is. The. Agimet!"

"*I don't know!*" Kaila gasped, struggling to force the words out. "He must have taken it!"

The woman stilled, her eyes darting to the doorway, then back to Kaila. "Ah…" she hissed. "A clever one. He doesn't trust the girl." An awful smile twisted her lips. "But does he care enough to save her?"

"Please, I don't think, let's talk—*ah!*" Kaila's plea turned to a scream as the woman grabbed a fistful of her hair and dragged her to her feet. "*Witch!*" she spat, wriggling against her bindings. If she could get her hands on that crystal, maybe she could stop this.

A harsh laughter sounded in her ears. "So, the bunny finally shows her teeth. Come here, girl."

There was that strange sense of movement and blurring, and

then the madwoman was behind Kaila. She growled as her head was yanked back by the hair, exposing her throat. Cold steel touched her skin. "Careful." Withered lips brushed her ear, and the putrid stench of the woman's breath filled her nostrils. "Wouldn't want to have any accidents before your friend gets back."

"By the First Matron," Kaila snarled, setting aside all pretence of compliance. "Who the hell are you?"

"That statue out there ain't gonna help you none." The woman cackled. "And they called me the Reaper, long ago. Perhaps they will again, with all that agimet your friend is hauling, ay, girl?"

Her stomach twisted but she dared not struggle now. With her head pulled back by the hair so her eyes faced the ceiling, hands bound behind her back, and the dagger at her throat—not to mention whatever Elysian cursed magic the woman had at her disposal—Kaila was utterly powerless.

"The Reaper?" she replied, glaring at the woman. "What kind of name is that? Gods, are you all as bad as him?"

A scowl twisted the woman's face. "Hundreds have died by my blade, girl," the Reaper snapped. "I suggest you don't try my patience."

Kaila gasped as a trail of fire sliced her flesh. A shallow cut only, but she took the warning to heart and fell silent. Her mind whirled as the minutes ticked passed, trying to figure a way out of this. Who the hell was this woman anyway? From her appearance, she must have been living in the ruins. A chill spread through her veins as she remembered the story Theron had told, about other travellers who had gone missing. Silently, she cursed herself for letting down her guard. This Reaper must have been watching them, waiting for her opportunity. She had handed her one on a silver platter.

All that remained was for Theron to return. Where was he, anyway? And why had he taken the agimet? Clearly, he still didn't trust her, despite what they'd shared, what they'd done for each other. Another emotion touched her. Doubt. What if…

Needles prickled her scalp as an idea came to her.

"He's not coming back, you know."

A moment's silence, then: "What?"

"Isn't it obvious?" Kaila croaked, attempting to inject a quiver into her voice. Given the situation and her own fears, it wasn't hard. "That's why the agimet is gone. He's taken it and run."

Even as she said the words, Kaila found herself wondering if they were true. Still standing over her, she saw the same doubt enter the Reaper's eyes, that moment of panic as she realised the crystals she so desperately desired might have slipped through her fingers. Her eye twitched, yellowed teeth appearing as she drew back her lips. The hand in Kaila's hair seemed to loosen.

"*No!*" the woman hissed. Her head shook back and forth with a violence that had Kaila holding her breath, feeling the steel at her throat waver. "It can't be! I saw you together. He wouldn't have left without you!"

"The bastard used me," she croaked. "Abandoned me. But…he can't have gone far. The pass is blocked…"

She trailed off as the Reaper's eyes fixed on her. "This is a trick."

"No!" Kaila exclaimed. "I swear, the agimet is all he's ever wanted. That's how we met. He was stealing those crystals from my village!"

The woman's eyes grew narrow. She seemed to be considering her words, weighing up their truth. Kaila held her breath, heart thundering in her ears. A piece of her yearned to lunge for the ring and use its power for herself, but caution won out.

Please believe me.

She saw the moment the Reaper made her decision. Glimpsed it in the slight softening of her expression, the parting of her lips, the loosening of the fingers that gripped her hair.

"You'll learn quick enough, girl," she muttered. "Not to trust them. Not to trust *any of them.*"

Exhaling, she seemed about to release Kaila…when a soft crunch carried from outside. *Footsteps.* Theron had returned.

THERON WHISTLED TO HIMSELF AS HE WANDERED THROUGH THE ruins of Iselador. The sun was just beginning to peek above the horizon. He'd woken early and, taken with a restlessness after the long night, had wandered to the edges of the city in search of firewood. Kaila he'd left to sleep—the Trickster alone knew, the girl needed it after what she'd been through. On a whim, he'd taken the agimet with him in the pockets of his coat. It wasn't that he didn't trust her…

It was just that he didn't trust anyone.

Some things never change, hey, brother.

A chill ran down his spine as the words whispered in his mind. He stumbled to a stop, swinging around for the source of the voice, but the ruins were empty. He shouldn't have been surprised. Freya was dead. She had been dead for fifteen years. And yet a part of him had still hoped, for those brief seconds, this time the voice might be real.

Shaking himself, he started off again. The twelve hours was almost up and soon the six large crystals he'd taken from the mine would light up with *atar*. It would be quite the sight to behold, and despite his distrust, Kaila should be there to witness it. And then he could do as he'd promised and teach her, show her how to use her Gift, so when they reached Tah'raus…

She's a liability, brother. You're going to get her killed. Just. Like. Me.

With a sharp inhalation, Theron came to a halt. He shuddered as the pale face appeared in his mind. Not Kaila this time, but Freya as he had seen her last, hanging from the noose, glassy eyes staring, even as her final plea echoed in his mind.

Run, Theron! RUN!

Laughter echoed in his ears. He ground his teeth together, trembling, willing the presence to leave him. He hadn't heard her in years, this phantom of his lost sister. He had thought himself finally free; that he had a chance to be happy.

But of course, their kind could never really be free.

"What do you want, sister?" he grated.

You know I only want to help you, brother, her voice purred. *Things cannot work with her. You know it, even as you try to hide from it. They will take her from you. I am only trying to spare you the pain.*

Theron closed his eyes, breathing deeply, and then shook his head. "No," he said quietly. "No, I won't listen to you anymore. We're done, remember. You're gone." Growling, he set off again through the ruins.

Laughter chased after him, but blessedly, the voice fell silent.

The sun was fully up as he approached the house and his mind was still lost in the pain of the past. So he only noticed the footprints in the mud as he approached the front door. He froze, a chill spreading down his spine as his eyes scanned the ground. One set belonged to him, easily identifiable by the heavy tread. And a second, lighter with barely any print, he recognised as Kaila's. But there was a third set. Not so heavy as his own, but larger than Kaila's, with the edges scuffed and overlapping, as though they'd been involved in a struggle.

The chill expanded to a tingling on his scalp. He reached for the agimet in his pocket, but as his finger brushed the stone he sensed its emptiness. It couldn't be long now until they charged. Minutes? Seconds even? But until the nexus filled them, the agimet would be useless to him.

Holding his breath, Theron slipped forward on silent feet, pressing himself against the wall. There he held his breath, straining his ears for any hint of noise from within. Silence. He silently cursed himself for a fool. After seeing nothing all night, he'd finally dismissed Quintin and the other stories as just that—stories. Now Theron feared he'd made his judgement too soon.

"I know you're out there!" A voice rang out from within—a woman. Older, rougher than Kaila's. "Why don't you come inside from the cold and join us? Your little friend would *love* to see you."

This time, Theron didn't reserve his curses for his own enjoyment. This was bad. *Very bad*. Whoever this was had made Elysian disappear. Obviously they had a powerful Gift. He had to find a way to stall the woman, until his crystals charged. Then he was confident he could take her, *whatever* she was.

But there was nothing for it now. Whoever it was had heard him. Time to move. Stepping out from the shelter of the wall, he entered the doorway. And there they were.

Kaila's face was pale, her chin pointed at the ceiling, exposing her neck to the blade pressed against it. A bruise was already swelling black on her cheek and there was anger in her eyes, but beneath that, he saw the fear. Her hands were tied behind her back, while the filthy fingers of the stranger held her by her long black hair, rendering the young woman helpless.

The owner of the blade loomed behind Kaila. She was older than he had expected, but the rest of what he saw bore a fresh terror in Theron. Sunken cheeks and a skeletal body, even the high pitch of her voice. He recognised the symptoms.

Atar addiction.

He'd told Kaila it was the lucky ones who died after using broken agimet. Well, the unlucky ones became addicted to the rush of the pure *atar* provided by the cut crystals. Consumed by desire, they would waste away to nothing. Eventually.

"That's far enough," the woman said, the pitch of her voice wobbling erratically.

She pulled Kaila hard against her to emphasise the point. The girl yelped as the steel point nicked her chin and a trickle of blood streaked down her throat. Theron clenched his teeth and came to a stop, raising his hands.

The woman's eyes began to glow with the silvery light of *atar*. A tiny stone was set in a ring on her hand. Fear touched Theron—not for her power, but what would happen if that crystal ran dry? *Atar* addicts were unpredictable at the best of times. One suffering from withdrawal…

"Is that fear I see in your eyes?" she rasped, her voice steady now, but cold as mountain ice. "Don't worry, your little friend is fine. We were just having a chat about whether you were coming back. I'm *so* glad you decided to return."

He nodded slowly, his face grim. "It would seem you have me at a disadvantage. Please, why don't you tell me who you are and what you want, and we can come to some sort of agreement."

A crooked smile revealed yellowed teeth. "They used to know me by the Reaper."

Theron sucked in a sharp breath. *The Reaper.* She was just a myth. A story told to Elysian youth when they misbehaved. No one could even agree if they were a man or woman, or what type of Gifted they were. Only that the Reaper was an assassin for hire, one who wasn't fussy about who hired them—or who their targets were.

Most Elysian tried to avoid conflict amongst themselves, but not this one. If the price was right, the Reaper would come for you, and not stone walls or iron blades or the power of a dozen agimet crystals would prevent the black blade from finding your heart.

If this was really the Reaper, then Theron had made a gross miscalculation in coming to Iselador.

There was only one thing for it. He needed to stall for time.

Plastering his trademark smile on his face, he spread his hands. "I've heard of you!" he exclaimed, dipping into a bow. "Why, it's always an honour to make the acquaintance of a fellow professional. My name is Theron. They call me the prince of thieves. Perhaps you've heard of me as well?"

A frown planted itself on the Reaper's lips. "I have not."

"No? I was behind the Diamond Deception."

The woman shook her head.

"The Vanishing Vault?"

No response this time. Just a slight thinning of her lips

"Surely you've heard about the Coswell Larceny?"

"Theron…" Kaila croaked, interrupting for the first time. "I think she gets it."

"Just trying to establish a repour between two legends of the underworld," Theron said, stepping into the room as he did so. "Anyway, surely we can come to some kind of arrangement—"

He broke off as Kaila gave a strangled cry, his foot still raised to take another step. Another trickle of blood ran down the young woman's chin.

The burning eyes of the Reaper met his. "You'll forgive my distrust," the Reaper said, "but I wasn't born yesterday. Stay right where you are, thank you."

"What do you want?" Theron growled, discarding the charade.

"These ruins belong to *me*. All who pass this way must pay my toll."

"And what toll would that be."

Her eyes glinted in the sunlight streaming through the window. "All the agimet that you have."

The words closed like iron jaws around Theron's chest. He

swayed where he stood, ears ringing, stars filling his vision—and not the *atarlight* variety. Panic touched him. He tracked another drip of blood as it ran down Kaila's throat. She had barely said a word, but those hazel eyes of hers watched him, pleading…

You're going to get her killed, just like me…

He shuddered, fists clenching into balls. *Fool, fool, fool.* How could he have let this happen? Why had he ever gone back for her in the first place? He had been free and clear. And now…now…

You hardly know her, he tried to tell himself.

But it was a lie. He had known her from the day he'd seen her tackle the runaway in Elgoss. From the way she had strutted through her village, that proud lift of her chin, the sparkle in her eyes as she confronted him in the mine. They were the eyes of a believer.

And then after, the pain she wore about her like a cloak, the betrayal and hurt of finding out her entire world had been a lie.

It was the same look he'd worn as a boy fifteen years ago when they'd strung up his sister as an Elysian collaborator.

I'm sorry, Theron.

"Well, *prince of thieves*, what will it be?" the Reaper sneered. "Your agimet or your lover? Choose."

Freya was right. Everyone close to him died. But they didn't have to. Not this time. He had a chance to save her. His fingers tightened briefly around the agimet in his pocket. Then, slowly, he drew it out and placed it on the floor before him. It remained dark, but there could only be minutes left before it filled with *atar*. Sucking in a long breath, he waited another heartbeat, but the crystal remained dim, so with a final exhalation, he rolled it across the floor towards the pair. It bounced a few times before coming to a rest at the Reaper's feet. She made no move to pick it up.

Instead, she raised an eyebrow. "What about the rest?"

"Consider that a down payment," Theron said.

Could this really be her? It scared him, not knowing exactly what he was up against. And those eyes…the *atar* addiction would explain why she had disappeared. But how had she come to be here, of all places? And what madness had possessed her to use broken agimet in the first place? He could see the longing in her eyes as she stared at the crystal he'd thrown. It was ten times the size of the one on her finger. He waited, breath held, waiting…

"A down payment for what?"

He nodded to Kaila. "Take it and let her go."

"And why would I do that?" The Reaper snorted. "You're in no position to bargain. Hand over the rest, and maybe I'll let your little friend live."

"You don't need it," Theron argued, desperation creeping into his voice. "That crystal will hold enough *atar* to last you a day. Maybe more. No more withdrawal. No more pain."

"But not enough to leave this place," the Reaper said. "Now stop stalling. I'm beginning to think you talked your targets into giving up their riches. Hand over the rest—"

The Reaper broke off as light filled the room, not from the window, but the crystal lying at her feet. So bright, it shone like the sun had risen inside the little house.

Theron was already reaching for his pocket as the Reaper cried her rage, his fingers closing around the stone hidden there. *Atar* flooded through his veins and he let out a little sigh. Relief. His magic had returned just in time. The world filled with *atarlight* and he sent a thread of power shooting out, ready to snatch the ring and neutralise the threat—

The magic died.

He staggered, caught off balance by the sudden shift in the world. One second, *atar* was surging through his veins—the next, it vanished. Gaping, he stared at his hand. It was empty. A second ago, he'd been holding the largest piece of agimet he'd ever seen in his life. Now it was gone, just gone…

He looked up, surprised to find Kaila standing alone, eyes wide and looking as stunned as he was.

Laughter whispered in his ears and he spun to find the Reaper standing in the doorway. Her face had changed again. Before her eyes had glowed with the faint trace of *atar;* now they *burned.* The sunken shadows and lingering pain had fled as well, and there was a smile on her lips that spoke of ecstasy, pleasure, and unhinged joy.

"Thank you, *prince of thieves,* for stalling. You weren't the only one waiting for the nexus to fill your crystals."

She tossed a crystal in the air. At first, Theron thought it was the one he'd thrown her. But then another appeared in her hands. And another, until she was juggling six enormous pieces of agimet. Several smaller pieces joined them as well, before vanishing one after another into her pockets, until she held only one again.

Theron could only stare. All of the agimet, she had it all. *How… She's a Wraith.*

The answer came to him with growing horror. That was why no one had seen her coming, how she had evaded the most skilled of guards, entered the most impenetrable of fortresses. She was a Wraith, using *atar* to move at terrible speeds. She had used the last of the power in her ring to claim the crystal from the floor, then helped herself to the contents of his pockets. All in the time it had taken Theron to draw on the *atar* to attack her.

"Well, I think I'll be going," the Reaper said. Her voice was cheerful, now she had what she wanted.

"Wait," Theron croaked. He stood alone, defeated. But he couldn't just let her go. Not like this. Elysian didn't last long in this world without their power. "One crystal. Please. Or we're as good as dead."

The Reaper paused, eyes narrowing as she studied them. "Why?"

He swallowed. "I offered you one, didn't I?"

Her lips pursed at that, and she studied him for a long time, those silver eyes of hers eerie with the glint of *atar*.

"Very well," she said at last.

Removing the ring and its tiny piece of agimet, she offered it to Theron. Before he could step forward and take it, though, her eyes grew brighter still, burning with a terrible intensity. She seemed to blur, and even her skin took on a silver glow, as though she had *inhaled* the energy of the crystal. For a second, he thought she was about to attack, but not this time. She burned brighter still, her brilliance filling the room until even the obsidian walls shone white…

…and then just like that, the power died away.

The crystal in the ring was now empty. The Reaper tossed it to Theron.

"There," she said as Theron blinked the stars from his eyes. "Now I know you won't follow me."

A shadow flickered at the edge of his vision, followed by the crunch of footsteps.

And then the Reaper was gone.

15

S *ilence.*

Kaila stared at the doorway where the Elysian woman had vanished, heart still pounding hard in her chest. She had been frozen, petrified by her panic, helpless in the grasp of the madwoman.

The Reaper.

She shuddered. The woman had been like one of the evil Elysian from Sister Eurador's stories, like she'd stepped right off the pages of her books and into real life. An evil force that left only despair and destruction in her wake.

Kaila's hand went to her throat and she winced. The cut was shallow. Any deeper…

Her hands shook. *Everything* was shaking, she realised, and though she clenched her fists, it would not stop. She kept seeing those eyes again, the raw madness, the desperation. She would have cut Kaila's throat without hesitation if it meant getting her hands on their agimet.

"It's all gone."

Her head jerked up. Theron swayed on his feet, cradling the empty ring the Reaper had left them. His eyes were distant, his face pale. She recognised that look. Despair. It sent a tingling down her spine. She had expected anger, grief, *hatred* even. In the brief time she'd known him, Theron had never wavered. Even when he'd faced the Warden alone, there had been a spark in his eyes that said he still *believed.*

Not now. The Reaper's victory had left him a hollow shell. A knife twisted in her chest. She swallowed, torn between relief and a painful guilt that she had played a part in his loss.

"At least we're alive," she said, laying a hand on his shoulder.

"Alive?" he snapped. "She took everything." He shrugged her off. "Do you know what it cost me to find Elgoss? How much I owe for that information? Now I have *nothing!* And why?" His lips drew back in a snarl as his burning eyes fell on Kaila. "Because I decided to go and save an ungrateful godsdamn *child* from her own stupidity."

Kaila recoiled as if she'd been struck. Heat crept across her face, anger and shame boiling to the surface. She opened her mouth for a retort, but found no words. The room seemed to close in on her, the silence pressing in, until…

"I'm sorry." Theron looked away, his lips pressed in a line. "I didn't mean that."

A shiver ran through Kaila, but she couldn't look away now. "I never asked you to come back for me," she said quietly.

He nodded curtly. "I know."

She swallowed. "I never said thank you either," she croaked. "Thank you. For everything."

Blinking, Theron glanced at her again, and this time when he nodded, the anger had drained away. "You're welcome."

The silence returned, less tense than before, but it was awkward now. Strained. Gone was the easy rapport from the night before, the warmth and sheer *fun* of their company. A frigid barrier had leapt up with the cruel words, and the disaster, and the terror.

Kaila didn't know how to begin to defuse it. Cold touched her heart and suddenly the void was back, its terrible filaments spreading through her soul, swallowing up the little blaze of hope they had lit together.

"So…what do we do now?" She finally ventured a question.

"Now?" he asked, grimacing. "Now I go back to Tah'raus and hope Ambrose doesn't take my head for losing his money."

The words were another bolt of ice to her heart. *I*, not *we*. The call of the void whispered, demanding her surrender, to give in to the darkness. Stiffening, Kaila shook her head. She couldn't let things end like this. But all she had left was her anger.

"That's all you ever cared about, isn't it?" she snapped, the words pouring from her. "*Money*. You wanted to come to Elgoss and make your fortune and ride off into the sunset." She jabbed him in the chest. "You might mock me for believing in honour and duty, but at least I believed in *something* before you came along."

"Something?" he asked, staring at Kaila like she was a stranger. "You were a *slave*. Just because they didn't lock you in chains, make no mistake about that." His face hardened, jaw growing tight. Always before, Theron had offered a smile and a laugh when talking about the world and his life. Now he wore a grimace as he continued. "And as for *my desires*, yes, I wanted the money. What else is there for our kind? What else does the Magisterium leave for us but this miserable, godsforsaken existence."

She swallowed in the face of his anger. "There has to be a way to fight back."

"There are some who like to play the hero. I've seen it before." His eyes were grim. "It always ends the same way."

"This can't be it," Kaila whispered. "There has to be something more. A reason I was given these powers. Why my life…" Her voice grew hoarse. She couldn't finish.

"That's just the way the world is sometimes, Kaila." Theron's face softened as he looked down on her, but what he said next, she sensed he was no longer talking about the Magisterium. "Sometimes things…happen, and they don't mean anything."

Bastard!

She was trembling again, wanted to hurl a fist at his face for those words. She clenched her hands into balls, barely able to contain her rage. A burning red filled her vision and Kaila was sure if she'd held a crystal, she could have charged it with the heat of her anger alone.

But she said nothing, only kept her eyes fixed on the floor, so he wouldn't see them shining. She drew in a breath. If that was the way he wanted things, so be it. Another inhalation, and an exhale. Several seconds ticked past before she regained the composure to speak.

"What about the Reaper?" she said, grasping at straws now, but she couldn't give up. Not yet.

"Even if we had *atar*, I'm not sure I could take her."

Kaila hesitated. "What *was* she?"

"You remember I told you some kinds of Elysian are more myth than reality these days? Well, our good friend the Reaper is a Wraith."

"That was a lot more than just *fast*," Kaila snapped, recalling Theron's earlier description.

Theron grunted. "Like I said, I don't know anyone who's actually met one until now." He hesitated. "Explains a lot, actually."

"You knew who she was, didn't you?"

"Most Elysian have heard of the Reaper. She was an assassin; and not particularly choosy about whether her victims were humans or her own kind. That's frowned upon amongst our kind. She hasn't been active for more than a decade, though. I suppose now we know why."

"She was insane." Kaila swallowed. "Is that what happens to Elysian, to us, if we use the magic too much?"

Theron shook his head. "You remember when I told you not to use a broken or cut crystal?"

"Something about death being the preferred outcome," she muttered, unable to keep the bitterness from creeping into her voice.

Grunting, Theron didn't seem to be able to meet her eyes. "Well, *that* is what happens if you're unfortunate enough to survive. *Atar addiction*."

"Oh."

That answered one question, at least. A shiver ran down her spine at the memory of the woman's eyes, the pain, the *need* as she demanded to know where their crystals were hidden. What must it be like, to have your mind torn to fragments by something so out of reach? Recalling the rush she experienced whenever she drew *atar* from a crystal, Kaila wondered too if Theron was telling the whole truth. After all, she could still see that despair in his eyes, could almost imagine it as a reflection of the Reaper's cravings.

But those concerns would have to wait. The silence had resumed between them. Theron shifted on his feet, his eyes looking anywhere but her. Her scalp tingled, and not just where the Reaper had almost torn her hair out by the roots.

"What about my other ability?" she said, grasping at anything that might fix things between them. "I could charge the crystal the Reaper left. She would never expect it."

Theron's eyes finally found hers. "The last time you tried that, you died."

"We don't know that it will be the same this time…"

"No, Kaila," Theron said softly, placing a hand on her shoulder. Somehow, the gesture didn't have the same familiarity as the night before. She had to steel herself not to shrug him off as he had done to her.

"It's okay, this is not your fault," he paused, "I…never should have said that about you."

If it's not my fault, why are you looking at me like that?

She wanted to scream at him. Instead, she looked away. She had to fix this, to find a way to mend not only the chasm between them, but return the lost crystals.

"We could go back to Elgoss." She said it more to stall than with any real hope.

"They'll be waiting for us," Theron said hollowly.

"Then what, Theron?" she snapped, finally relenting to the anger within. "What happened to the Prince of Thieves? Are you really going to just lie down and give up?"

"I was never the Prince of Thieves," Theron muttered. "I said that to scare you. Besides, I don't hear you offering any suggestions."

"We go after her."

Theron snorted. "Oh yes, because our first encounter went so well."

"Are you really so afraid of her?"

"I'm not afraid of anyone."

"Then why are you running away?" she asked quietly.

"Because I'm not a fool, Kaila," Theron muttered. "You saw

what she could do. She took my crystal before I even knew she had moved. I can't fight that."

Instinctively, Kaila's hand went to her throat again. The nick the Reaper had left still stung. He was right. They didn't stand a chance against that power. Her body grew cold, leaving her with an empty feeling in the pit of her stomach. Fear. She didn't want to die. And she had a feeling the Reaper wouldn't be half so forgiving if she saw them again.

But then she remembered her father in Elgoss, facing down the Warden. And she recalled the words he had often spoken.

A true warrior finds a way to win.

There had to be a way to beat the woman. Reverse their fortunes and steal back the agimet. She looked at Theron, at the so-called Prince of Thieves—

The hairs on her scalp stood on end as an idea came to her. "Then don't."

"What?" Theron asked, looking around with a frown.

Exhaling through her teeth, Kaila stepped in close to him. "We don't fight her," she said quickly. "We do what the Prince of Thieves does best."

"And what exactly would that be?" Theron grunted.

Somehow, Kaila found it within herself to smile. "Well, to start, you could stop with the moping."

He scowled.

"And then…" she said quickly, "we can figure out how we're going to rob the witch blind."

The Reaper paced the high chamber of the Black Tower, the whisper of her leather boots against hard stone counting down the minutes. Outside, the setting sun lit the sky a brilliant red, while in the city below the shadow of the mountains crept across the streets, approaching her isolated perch. Nightfall was not far off.

Unless she wished it to be.

The pack on her shoulder seemed to grow heavier with the thought. Her hands shook, her eye twitching. Agimet. *So much of it.*

But was it enough? How many days was the journey to Tah'raus? A week, normally. But with her condition…now she had her hands on the precious crystal, she couldn't stop herself. *Atar* buzzed in her veins, setting her eyes aglow. She would have to avoid the roads. If only she'd had a Weaver handy, they might have knitted an illusion to hide the tell-tale glow.

But she had nothing. Not even the old, uncomfortable lenses she had used long ago to mask the strangeness of her eyes. They'd been lost, tossed away in the throes of withdrawal.

Her eye twitched again. She allowed herself another sip of *atar* and her hands stilled. A sigh slipped from her lips. Outside, the creeping shadow drew to a stop. For several long heartbeats, she looked down on a frozen world, savouring her renewed sense of power. The world was once more hers to command.

Her fingers tightened around the stone. *A lie.* Had the world ever really been hers, she wondered. She had been feared, sure. Her legend had kept Fresian nobles and Elysian alike trembling in their beds, wondering if she would come for them.

But her victims had never been hers to choose. The Magisterium had paid handsomely to see their enemies removed. But ultimately, she had only been another pawn in their games. A *rich* pawn, but a pawn nonetheless.

In the end, she couldn't even stop them from taking her daughter.

A stone settled in her gut. Would he even remember her now, after all these years? Did he even still live? This was a harsh world, especially without her protection.

With a sigh, she relented her hold on the world.

As the shadows below crept on, a burning fire lanced through her skull. She doubled over from the pain. The crystal in her hand was empty. *Already.* A groan rasped from her throat as withdrawal rolled through her. The throb of blood in her veins was like razor-blades, cutting her up from the inside. Sinking to her knees, she clutched her pounding head. Several minutes passed before the pain receded, at least a little. She sucked in great lungfuls of air. The solid feeling of the wooden floor steadied her. Slowly the lights dancing in her eyes faded.

Her stomach twisted and if it hadn't already been empty, she would have vomited.

The withdrawal was getting worse. It wasn't so bad when she just touched the *atar*, but that was like holding a glass of ice-cold water on a hot day and not drinking it. More and more, she *needed* to use her power, longed for that feeling of invincibility, knowing the world couldn't touch her.

But every time she used it, the aftereffects grew worse. And now she had already burned through an entire crystal. She started to shake as she looked over the valley beyond the city. *Six crystals.* Were they really enough to reach another nexus?

And even if she did make it to Tah'raus…she couldn't return to her old ways. The addiction and subsequent withdrawal were crippling. What good would she be to her daughter, in her condition?

She trembled as an old emotion spread through her veins. Fear. It was a bitter taste. But she couldn't lie to herself. It was the reason she was still here, why she had lingered in the ancient ruins. Because the Reaper wasn't sure if she was strong enough to face what waited outside. If she could defeat her enemies, or her own weakness.

Gritting her teeth, she crawled across the floor to where she'd left the bag of agimet she'd taken from the Elysian pair. She sighed as her fingers closed around a fresh crystal. Drawing it from the bag, she cradled it to her chest. Fresh energy filled her, granting her the strength to stand. The fear burned away. She would not be cowed. She was the Reaper. The world feared *her*.

She had only returned to the Black Tower to gather her possessions. She did so now, collecting the few scraps of food that remained from her last scavenge in the surrounding woods, along with an old pair of clothes. Last of all, she took the little stuffed rabbit from the pile of furs that served as her bed. She held it close to her chest, before placing it in the pack and sinching the straps tight.

And then it was time to go. The Black Tower had not been her home, but a prison from which she could now finally escape. She would not miss it.

She had just started towards the stairs when a silhouette moved in the shadows. A second later, the thief appeared. His hands were raised to show them as empty, but nonetheless, the Reaper was instantly on alert. Snarling, she drew *atar* from her fresh crystal, filling her veins to bursting.

"There…"

The world froze as the Reaper activated her Gift. She took three steps, drew her blade, and pressed its cold edge to Theron's throat before he could get out the next words."

"…you are—"

He broke off, lips still parted as though he dared not close them, lest The Reaper take it as a provocation. Which she very well might.

"What are you doing here?" she said. "I warned you to stay away."

"I like to live life on the edge."

"Well, you got your wish. You're standing on the bloody precipice. Give me one good reason why I shouldn't send you to meet the Trickster."

Theron slowly lowered his hands, steady eyes meeting her own. "Because then you'd miss out on what I have to say."

"I think I heard about as much as I could stand back in the ruins." Her eyes narrowed. "What happened to the girl?"

"I left her behind."

The Reaper arched one eyebrow. She wasn't about to take a thief at his word. Her instincts screamed that this was a trap. Her eyes darted to the stairwell. Darkness lingered below. Was the girl hiding there, another crystal she had somehow missed secreted away, ready to strike when The Reaper turned her back?

Gritting her teeth, she activated her Gift, stepping around Theron as the world slowed and moved into the stairwell. Empty. She went down several flights to be sure, before returning to examine the thief anew. Another sweep of his person revealed no hidden pockets or compartments, only a single dagger in his boot. She left it there. Steel was no threat to her while she had *atar*.

Returning to her original position, The Reaper considered the man. What game was he playing? But the answer wouldn't come, and finally, she lowered her blade and stepped back. Time resumed. Shards of liquid agony stabbed deep into her skull, but she kept her face a mask.

"Why are you here?" she demanded.

He was lying. She *knew* he was lying. Her hands tightened around her dagger. She should kill him and get it over with.

"Well, that's kind of a long story," he replied. Digging his hands deep into the pockets of his trench coat, he wandered around the chamber. She watched him, eyes narrowed, as he continued. "You see, you've kind of left me in an awkward position. I spent a lot of money locating that agimet you stole."

"I fail to see how that's my problem."

"Yes, yes, of course. Easy come, easy go," Theron said quickly, "but perhaps we can come to some arrangement. It's a long journey to Tah'raus, especially with only one tiny crystal. And if the Wardens hunting the girl catch us before we get there, well, I can say goodbye to my reward money, can't I?"

The Reaper blinked. "Reward money?"

"Oh, did I neglect to mention that part?" Theron asked, looking up from where he stood by the window. "Turns out, the girl is kind of important." A smile spread across his lips. "She could be the key to us both becoming very, very rich."

———

The wind howled around Kaila as she stretched out an arm, fingers seeking the next hold. The grooves between each stone were deep, providing good purchase for her toes and fingers, but the blocks themselves were almost her height. She had to stretch almost to her tiptoes just to reach the next hold. And the black stone was worn by centuries of wind and rain, leaving some edges as smooth as ice, others jagged like broken glass.

So instead, she made use of the vertical cracks as well, wedging fingers and toes for counterbalance, before hauling herself up to the next section. Her body pressed close to the cold stone, maintaining her balance between each movement. It was precarious, but inch by solitary inch, she crept higher.

And the voices from above grew louder.

She could see the windows now, little stone slits that ringed the highest chamber of the Black Tower. It hadn't seemed so high before she started. Maybe she should have paid more attention to Theron's concerns when she'd first raised the idea. She hadn't really stopped to consider what she was getting herself into. She had climbed their building in Elgoss more times than she could count. How much harder could this be?

Quite a bit, as it turned out.

Her arms were shaking as she pulled herself up to the next level. Here, to her relief, a blind arcade had been set in a ring around the tower. The rows of narrow arches provided a ledge where she wedged her feet, taking some of the pressure off her arms.

Sucking in great gasps of air, she took the opportunity to assess her progress. She was maybe two-thirds of the way, at her best guess. Another fifty feet and she would reach the Reaper's nest. What exactly would be waiting for her there, she wasn't sure. Theron was meant to distract the woman, but he hadn't exactly elaborated on his part of the plan.

But Kaila couldn't think about him just then. She wiped the sweat from her brow. Her hands ached and the muscles of her shoulders and chest were burning. One slip, and she was done for—and the climb might not even be the riskiest part of her plan.

The ring weighed heavily in her pocket. Theron had rejected the idea out of hand, at first. She couldn't blame him. The idea of charging the crystal terrified her as well. When she'd last used her strange power, it had quite literally killed her. This time she would have to be careful, only feed it a dribble, no more. Hopefully, it would be enough.

She grimaced, studying the remainder of the climb. Exhaustion had wormed its way inside her. Would she even make it to the top? And when she got there, would she have enough strength left to charge the agimet?

This might have been a bad plan.

But it was too late to turn back now.

Taking a deep breath, Kaila resumed the climb.

"Maybe you and I have different ideas of 'very rich," the Reaper sneered. "Last I checked, the bounty for any old Elysian was a few gold pieces at best."

"That's just it, Reaper," Theron tisked, "the girl *isn't* any old Elysian. Otherwise, they wouldn't have sent a Warden to drag her back to Tah'raus."

The Reaper pursed her lips. "Unusual, but not unheard of."

Theron nodded. "That's only the start of it. When I dug a little deeper, turns out the girl passed her Trial of Agimet."

That finally got a reaction from the stone-faced woman. "Impossible," she scowled. "If there was a way to pass the Trial, it would—"

"Change everything," Theron interrupted, leaning back against the windowsill. "Exactly. Hence why the Magisterium was so desperate to get their hands on her."

The Reaper pursed her lips. "You haven't proven anything yet."

"I'm getting there. Geez, do you have *any* patience?"

"Very little, and it was used up by your earlier babbling."

"All right, all right." He raised his hands, jumping up off the sill. "But aren't you at least a *little* curious? If she really does hold the secret to beating the Trials, the Magisterium would pay her weight in *agimet* to keep that knowledge quiet." Watching the woman, he continued his circumnavigation of the room.

"You really expect me to believe you'd sell out the girl after sacrificing all your agimet to protect her?"

He shrugged. "She's hardly valuable to anyone dead," he said. "Besides, I'm sure the underground would pay well for her knowledge as well. Maybe we can get a bidding war going." He leaned against another window and grinned.

The Reaper's brow creased in a frown. His heart gave a little pulse. She seemed to actually be considering the idea. Finally, though, she shook her head. "If this is true, why come to me?"

He spread his hands. "Insurance. I can hardly bargain from a position of power with that tiny ring you left me. Hell, the journey to Tah'raus would be difficult enough without your help."

"You want me to share my agimet." Her fingers tightened around the bag on her shoulder.

"Just your protection," he said quickly. "You guide us to Tah'raus —keeping quiet about all this, of course. When we reach the capital, I'll negotiate our reward for the girl. With the Reaper herself backing me, no one is likely to try a double cross. Afterwards, we'll split the bounty fifty-fifty."

"Mighty generous of you," she replied, a sneer twisting her lips. "What's to stop me cutting your throat and claiming the reward for myself?"

"Well, for one, the loss of my amazing company."

"I'm not hearing any downsides so far."

"And second," Theron continued, "she'll hardly go willingly with you after what you pulled back there."

The Reaper fell silent, her cold eyes studying him. Theron tried and failed to suppress a shudder. There was something unnerving about those eyes. The glow of *atar* he had seen a thousand times, yet it gave this woman an almost supernatural appearance. Maybe it was the addiction, or some aftereffect of her strange power, but her eyes didn't seem altogether human, or even Elysian.

"Very well," she said at last. "Where did you leave her?"

"I told her to stay in the house," Theron replied, "but she has this bad habit of ignoring orders."

"So, do you know where she is now?"

"Of course," Theron replied, rising from the windowsill with a smile. "She's outside, climbing the tower walls."

ALMOST THERE!

Panting, Kaila hung below the lip of the window embrasure, trying to gather her strength for what came next. She had caught only fragments of the conversation above, as the wind whipped and whirled around the tower, hurling the words away. She prayed to the First Matron—old habits died hard--that everything was going to plan. Theron just had to keep the Reaper away from the windows a little longer.

"She's outside…now…climbing…walls."

Kaila's heart somersaulted in her chest. *What the hell? That wasn't part of the plan!*

Panic needled her skull, threatening to swallow her up. A voice screamed for her to *run*. Something was wrong. Theron had betrayed her…

…but where *could* she run? She was completely exposed here on the side of the tower, a two-hundred-foot drop yawning below.

A true warrior finds a way.

Taking her panic by the scruff of its neck, Kaila shoved it back in its cage. Cold logic returned, clawing its way up from the void. Fingers tightened on icy stone, and then she began to climb, hand over hand, as fast as she could. If Theron was telling the Reaper where she was, he must have a plan. And if he'd betrayed her…

…hopefully she could get a shot at him with her knife before the Reaper snuffed out her fleeting life.

THE REAPER BLINKED. "WHAT?"

"She's a few feet below this window," Theron replied. "I think she's trying to surprise you and steal a piece of agimet."

The breath escaped The Reaper in a hiss. "*What?*"

She activated her Gift and exhaled. Relief. Nothing could harm her now. In this frozen world, the only sound was the thundering of her heart in her ears. Shaking her head, she drew another breath. So, this girl thought she could take *the Reaper* by surprise? Her fingers tightened around her dagger. Raising it in readiness to throw, she stepped up to the ledge.

"What in the name of the Trickster?" she demanded, releasing her power and turning to confront Theron.

As she did so, a fresh wave of pain washed over her body. Pinpricks burned in her retinas, but she still had her dagger and was more than willing to use it on the thieving bastard. She'd had enough of his games. But the man only raised his empty hands and grinned, as if it had all been some practical joke. She swayed on her feet, dagger extended, struggling to resist the flow of pain. Was that why he'd done it? If so, he could screw his reward. She was still trying to decide whether to make a pincushion of the thief, when movement flickered in the corner of her eye. She turned, mind working slowly as it tried to overcome the wave of withdrawal.

She blinked, unable to comprehend what she was seeing. It was the girl; she had appeared from nowhere, alighting on the windowsill on the other side of the chamber. She wore a grimace as she raised her hand. The agimet ring the Reaper had given Theron rested in her palm. Only instead of dull crystal, it glinted with *atar*. As she stared, the girl's eyes began to glow.

Instantly, the Reaper squeezed the agimet in her hand tight. Her head swam, slowing her reaction, but the crystal would be the first thing a Mover went for to disable another Elysian. Or at least, so she reasoned…

She was wrong.

Rrrrip!

Too late, the Reaper realised what the girl intended, as a great rending sound, her backpack was torn in two. Agimet crystals and her scant belongings scattered across the floorboards, glittering with their burning light. Her heart lurched in her chest and she cried out, drawing *atar* from the crystal still in her hand. Power burned through her veins, even as Theron dove for the nearest agimet. Almost in slow motion, his fingers closed around the shining gemstone. His eyes began to glow—

Time stopped.

The Reaper exhaled. Her heart thundered. Theron and his little accomplice didn't move. Slowly, she drew another breath. That had been close. *Too close*. Her fingers tightened around the leather hilt of her dagger. Well, she'd given them fair warning. Smiling grimly she stepped towards Theron with her blade poised—

Wham!

It was like an invisible hand picked her up and hurled her across the room. The Reaper cried out, losing her grip on her Gift as she tumbled through the air, only for the stone walls of the chamber to bring her to an abrupt halt. Groaning, she slid to the floor, eyes fluttering.

"What…what the *hell?*"

Teeth clenched, her fingers tightened around her crystal. The blow—or whatever it had been—had hurled her straight across the room. Bracing herself, the Reaper picked herself up and looked around.

Theron strode towards her, eyes ablaze, a veritable *whirlwind* howling around him. As she watched, discarded pieces of wood and crumbling mortar and parts of the walls were swept up in the vortex, even the other pieces of agimet, drawing them out of reach. Worst of all, she glimpsed the precious stuffed rabbit caught up in his magic.

"*Trickster's Balls*," Theron muttered, a smile gracing his lips, "I can't believe that worked."

"What the hell did you do?" the Reaper gasped. The aftereffects of her magic were still grating through her veins, but she stood poised, one eye on the thief, the other on the girl, who had remained in the window.

"Does your Gift speed you up, or is it the world that slows down?" he said, before shaking his head. "Doesn't matter. I always wondered if that would work.

"You really do like the sound of your own voice, don't you," the Reaper snapped. "What did you do?"

He smiled. "I pushed on the air," he replied. "Tricky to pull off, threading all those tiny stars. You activated your power just in time to get a face full of it." The grin slipped from his lips, turning to a grimace. "So, are you ready to surrender?"

"Be damned, thief," the Reaper said, eyes darting to the girl. Kaila was on her knees and seemed to be relying on the windowsill to hold herself up. Barely any light remained in her crystal. Her attention snapped back to Theron. He was the real threat, but if she could get to the girl, none of his clever tricks would matter.

The pain was beginning to fade. Another moment and she would be ready. "How did you charge the crystal? I emptied it. I made sure of it."

"Did I forget to mention that part?" Theron asked, leaning his head to the side with a lopsided grin. "The *third* reason the Magisterium are hunting her?" As he spoke, one of the glowing pieces of agimet shot across the room to land in the girl's outstretched hand. The spark in her eyes burst into an inferno.

"Turns out," he continued, "that Kaila here can charge agimet without waiting for a nexus to do it. The ability is not without its… kinks, but it works in a pinch."

"At least I didn't die this time," the girl muttered, still looking pale.

The Reaper narrowed her eyes. "The day's not over yet."

16

Kaila sank to the floorboards as Theron and the Reaper disappeared into a whirl of dust and debris. Her chest heaved as she fought for each breath. Sweat pasted her clothes to her skin and the cold wind made her entire body tremble. Her legs, shoulders, and arms burned from the strain of the climb.

But the exhaustion went beyond physical pain. She felt it in her soul, like she'd poured a piece of herself into the crystal. Was this why Elric's *soullight* had been so twisted? A tingling spread down her spine and she clung to the freshly charged crystal Theron had thrown her. Its *atar* flowed through her veins, the fire washing away her lethargy. A little sigh slipped from her lips.

She savoured the sweetness of it, lost for a moment in the thrill of its power—until a *crash* snapped her back to the present. The Reaper and Theron raged back and forth across the chamber, all flashing steel and burning *atar* and breaking stone. A hole was torn in the floor by a piece of mortar as it slammed into the space where the Reaper had stood a moment before, then knives slashed at Theron, only to be deflected by a piece of rubble.

"So much for not fighting her," she muttered.

It was too late to change course now. She had to find a way to help Theron. Her fingers tightened around the crystal in her hand. As she drew on its *atar*, the battlefield changed, a thousand tiny *soul-*

lights appearing. They whirled about the chamber, each connected by a dozen tiny threads, weaving them into a tapestry with Theron at its centre.

It was a masterpiece Kaila could hardly comprehend. She had struggled to connect a few flakes of unmoving snow. Here, Theron worked his Gift on an entirely different scale. Her head hurt watching it—but if she didn't want one of the Reaper's blades buried in her chest, she needed to do more than just observe.

Gritting her teeth, Kaila narrowed her concentration to the *soul-lights* around only herself, first the larger pieces of rubble, then the splinters and crumbling mortar. They trembled as her power connected them, as though they yearned to move, to dance to her tune.

But as she tried to lift them together as Theron had, a sharp pain drove through the base of Kaila's skull. She gritted her teeth against it and continued, but each fresh connection was like a hammer driving a chisel deeper into her cranium. She managed only half a dozen bits of rubble before she could go no further.

Fire pulsed down her spine and her back arched, her legs going numb. Trembling, she clung to the pieces she had gathered. After several heartbeats, the sensation passed. Gasping, she opened her eyes.

And the world moved.

Slowly at first, then faster, the rubble began to spin as Kaila drew the thread about herself like a whirlpool, creating a vortex of debris as Theron had done. Her heart swelled as she saw it was working—

Crack!

She flinched as a brick tore from her control and shot across the room to slam into the wall beside her head. It shattered, spraying her with shards of black glass. Gasping, Kaila raised her arm to protect her face.

Crack, crack, CRACK!

Roaring filled the chamber as her half dozen other pieces of stone and mortar smashed into the walls, the floor, even the ceiling. Stars burst filled Kaila's vision and a blinding pain seared behind her eyes. Groaning, she sank to one knee. It was several moments before she realised what had gone wrong. First, one projectile had slipped from her control, then another, and then all of them at once —each hurtling off in the last direction he had been moving them.

She coughed as dust billowed around her, choking her lungs. Red filled her vision and the terrible weakness was upon her again. It took a moment for Kaila to realise she'd consumed all the *atar* in her system. Relief was immediate as she drew a fresh sip from the crystal.

The crunch of gravel warned Kaila she had company. Her head snapped up to see the Reaper regaining her feet—she looked to have been struck by one of the lost projectiles. Her eyes narrowed as she took in Kaila, still on one knee.

Kaila swore and lifted her crystal. Mentally, she fumbled for something to hurl at the woman. A sense of futility took root in her gut as a glow flickered in the Reaper's eyes.

And then Theron was there. He stepped between them, a tempest of dust and stone and wood moving with him, a maelstrom that seemed to fill the entire chamber. He had claimed a second piece of agimet for himself; two chunks as large as his fists blazing with the light of tiny suns.

"This fight is between us, Reaper," he said quietly. "There'll be no taking of hostages this time."

Beyond Theron, the Reaper glared at Kaila with eyes of fire. Then she blinked, and the Reaper was gone. Her heart stilled. She opened her mouth to scream a warning—only for a *crash* to come from across the room as the Reaper slammed into the wall. She hadn't even made it halfway across the chamber.

Theron tisked. "Come on, Mover against Wraith! Don't you want to find out who's better?"

A growl came from the Reaper as she picked herself up off the ground. "Did you just call yourself a Mover?"

"Yes, that's what—"

"That's a terrible name."

Kaila swallowed as Theron's face hardened. "Oh, you've done it now."

And then the two went to war.

Kaila could hardly follow what came next. She had thought she was beginning to understand her Gift, but Theron…

He was unlike anything she had ever seen.

The Reaper could move through time. By all rights, this fight was hers to lose. But somehow, Theron always seemed one step ahead. Whenever she vanished, his whirlwind spun faster, and then the Wraith would reappear, struck by a rock, or a pebble, or any of the thousand pieces of debris Theron used to protect himself. Sometimes the objects only seemed to disrupt her concentration and make her stagger, while others hurled her across the room.

Not that the battle was entirely one way. Several times Theron tried to move the woman herself—to lift her and hurl her into the wall or out a window. But each time he tried, the woman would simply disappear, reappearing almost instantly someplace else. Apparently, her Gift allowed her to slip from Theron's control.

Hurling projectiles directly at her was equally ineffective, though when Theron tried this, it did give the Reaper an idea of her own. The next time she reappeared, it was to hurl a chunk of stone the size of her fist straight for Theron's head. Her momentum must have carried from the time skip, for the stone shot from her hand with enough force to drop a Fresian charger. Tearing through Theron's maelstrom, it would have taken off his head had he not deflected it with a flash of *atar*.

Even then, the field of rubble orbiting the thief did not waver.

Kaila swallowed as she watched the masterpiece of magic unfold. There was so much debris, so many threads of atar, even with her *atarsight* she struggled to follow it all. And she wasn't the one controlling it, directing it against her enemy. How could Theron manage it?

As for the Reaper, the woman was a force unto herself. She had given up attacking Theron or Kaila directly, but darted in and out of the debris field instead, only coming close enough to hurl a fresh projectile. Most she directed at Theron, but a few shot towards Kaila. Theron blocked them all.

Kaila studied the woman, looking for some insight into her power, how they could finally put an end to her. The lights of the universe dimmed whenever she vanished, then burst like firecrackers when she reappeared, scattering *soullights* in every direction. And her own *soullight*; there was a way it flared when she drew *atar*, in the moments before she vanished—

Boom!

A crash rumbled from the window behind Kaila, loud enough to be heard over the battle. Intent on each other's defeat, the pair did not pause. Now, they were taking shots at each other with various sharp objects they found around the chamber. Kaila hesitated only a heartbeat before darting to the window.

At first, she couldn't locate the source of the disturbance. The width of the windowsill blocked her view of the city below. A glance over her shoulder confirmed the two Elysian were still going at each other like a hammer against an anvil. Gritting her teeth against her fatigue, Kaila climbed up onto the windowsill for a better view of the base of the tower.

Below, the statue of Oberon and T'iana had fallen. Shards of obsidian lay scattered across the courtyard. For a second, Kaila couldn't understand what she was seeing. After all these centuries, how could it have fallen, now of all times.

Then something shifted amidst the rubble. Shining blue steel, so dark it was almost black, rippled in the dying light of sunset. A figure straightened, agimet bursting to life across his chest, casting back the shadows. As the dark visor lifted to stare up at the tower, slivers of dread slid down Kaila's spine. Even from there, she sensed those dark eyes, followed by the brush of power against her mind.

All the life, all the fury and ecstasy and grief of the past few days vanished. She choked, sinking into the despair that lurked beneath it all, the void rising to swallow her up. Drowning, Kaila swayed on the edge of the windowsill, feeling the hopelessness, the inevitability of that dreaded gaze. Death came for her. There was no escape. Why not embrace it—

"Kaila!"

"Gah!" she screamed, hurling herself backwards as she found herself standing on the ledge.

She drew *atar* from the crystal in her hand, its fire cutting through the emptiness the Warden had left.

With its clarity, though, came a terrible, irresistible fear.

The Warden was alive. *And he was here!*

"Theron!"

RAGE.

Elric burned with it, consumed by its red-hot fire, by its hunger, its *need* to be unleashed. It had begun in the pass, sparking to life as he fought with the cursed Elysian. The battle to free himself from his tomb had fed it. But only as he emerged into the sunlight and looked down on the ancient ruins, had the true rage possessed him.

Iselador.

The lost city, cursed of the enemy. He had found it. He knew then why the Nameless had spared him, why he had passed through this trial of fire and strife. To strike at the heart of the enemy.

Only as he wandered through the streets and found them empty had he begun to doubt. To question. This was the secret fortress of the enemy, the source of their vile magics. Yet rubble filled its streets and dust lay thick on the ground. No one had lived in this place for a long time. It made no sense, and slowly, his rage turned to confusion.

Until the sounds of battle had drawn him to the dark tower.

There, at last, he saw the true evil of these creatures, their desecration of the First Matron. Such an unspeakable crime could not go unpunished. *That* was why the Nameless had drawn him here. To be their avenger and correct this ancient blasphemy.

His blade formed without thought. The enemy dared present this terrible lie to the world, this stain upon the sacred memory of T'iana? Fury overcame him, stealing away his control. With a single swing of his avenging blade, Elric undid their falsehoods.

Then, as shards of obsidian crashed down against his armour, Elric finally looked up.

And there she was, high in the window of the Black Tower, *watching him.* A smile crossed his lips as he saw destiny unveiled. This would be his reward; the cursed Elysian would die screaming by his own hand.

Even so high above, she was not beyond his reach. Not with the power of a nexus flowing through his armour. And so he stretched out a dark fist and wrung the emotion from her. Fear, anger, pain, and love. Elric took it all, leaving her an empty vessel—into which he poured dread and despair. With satisfaction, he watched her waver on the ledge, consumed by the terror all her kind must feel, standing before their executioner and knowing they were doomed.

But the girl proved tougher than expected, for at the last second, she tore herself free of his control. She swayed, caught in the swirling winds, before diving backwards into the chamber, out of sight.

No matter. Elric was undaunted. She and her foul companion would not escape him now. Better, really, that the cursed one die by his hand, rather than her own.

A grim smile stretched his lips as he entered the Black Tower.

THERON WAS IN THE FIGHT OF HIS LIFE. A MATCH OF STRENGTH, WIT, and skill, and if he was honest, no small degree of luck. Going up against a Wraith was as difficult as he'd imagined. No wonder none of the Reaper's victims had ever walked away. Even with his makeshift forcefield of odds and ends, she'd come perilously close to sinking that dagger of hers in his flesh on more than one occasion. And when that failed, she had started throwing projectiles of her own, hurled with deadly precision and force.

Most he'd deflected, but with the concentration it took to keep his other threads of *atar* in place, some made it through. He was bleeding from a dozen places now. Nothing serious—or at least, he hoped not. He could hardly ask for a timeout to check.

As for the Reaper, the early blows he'd struck didn't seem to have slowed her, and now she'd cottoned onto his tactics, he struggled to match her ferocity.

Worse still, his maelstrom was consuming a *ridiculous* amount of *atar*. The chunks of agimet he'd stolen from Elgoss were as big as they came, but he'd already emptied an entire crystal and was steadily eating through his second.

His only blessing was that the Reaper hardly seemed much better off. Whether that was down to her addiction or the drain of a

Wraith's Gift, Theron was not certain, but he wasn't about to start counting his blessings now. With Kaila holding the last charged crystal, this had become a battle of attrition.

Unfortunately, his opponent realised this as well. She had settled into a pattern, hurling a few sharp projectiles, and then retreating to watch him bat them away—or not, depending how well-placed her aim. It was galling. Theron had to maintain his forcefield or she'd be on him in seconds, while the Reaper could sit back and wait for his *atar* to run out.

It wasn't looking good.

So the sight of Kaila swaying on the window ledge was not a particularly welcome distraction.

"Kaila!" he screamed, heart lurching in his chest.

Thankfully, the cry seemed to snap the woman from whatever madness had overcome her, as she threw herself back from the ledge.

Unfortunately, that was only the start of their problems.

"Theron!"

Something in Kaila's voice struck a chord inside him, the sheer terror of her cry. Kaila stood, hair wild, face pale. A stone caught her boot, causing her to stagger, but her eyes never left the window, as though at any moment she expected a demon to come swooping from the heavens to fall upon them.

"It's him," she moaned, finally tearing her gaze from the scarlet sky. Her eyes were so large he could see flecks of blue amidst the silver *atar*. "The Warden…I don't know how…*Theron, he's coming!"*

It was like dunking his head in ice water. He took a step towards her without thinking—before a snarl reminded him of the more present danger. The Reaper. Spinning, he reeled as a shard of black glass sliced his cheek. One of the threads connecting his maelstrom stuttered, sending several objects whirling into the obsidian walls.

"Reaper!" he roared as she reappeared, a fresh shard of obsidian already drawn back to hurl.

Anger boiled up within him. With a pulse of *atar*, he caught the projectile and sent it hurtling back in her direction. She blinked out of existence as it slashed the space where she'd been standing, reappearing a few yards to the right.

"Enough!" he bellowed, risking another glance at Kaila. She had regained her feet, but the panic in her eyes had not abated. A clear sign a Psionic had gotten to her. Unless there was *yet another* Gifted hiding in these thrice-cursed-ruins, it could mean only one thing.

"Reaper, a Warden is outside!" he continued. "He's coming for us."

That finally brought a pause to the Reaper's attacks. "What's this?" she demanded, a scowl wrinkling her face. "You must be desperate if you think I'll fall for your tricks, thief."

"Damn you!" Nearby, Kaila swayed on her feet, beads of sweat on her brow. She still held the crystal he'd thrown her tight in one hand. It was probably the only thing keeping her upright.

"Look at her!" He glared at the Reaper, willing her to believe. "Can't you see…"

But she couldn't. He knew it already. Because *he* would not have believed *her* if their positions had been reversed. There was only one way he could convince her of the truth. A curse slipped from his lips.

Abruptly, he cut the flow of *atar* to his whirlwind. The sound of crashing stone and glass filled the room as hundreds of objects smashed into one another or went crashing into the walls and floor. His protections dismissed, Theron turned to the Reaper and raised his hands—though he did not release his crystal.

"No tricks," he grated through clenched teeth. "See?"

The Reaper studied him with the paranoid eyes of a junky scared for her stash, and for a second, Theron wondered if he'd made a terrible mistake. *Atar* was still flowing from her crystal into her *soullight*, as though she was readying herself to step through time…

"Please," Kaila croaked, "he's telling the truth. A Warden is coming."

Her eyes narrowed, fingers clenching so tight around her remaining stone that veins showed through the pale flesh of her wrists. "More lies."

"No. His name is Elric Chain. He followed us from Elgoss."

The woman's eyes flickered to the stone in Kaila's hand. "How did you recharge the crystal so quickly?"

Kaila hesitated. "Theron told you the truth. I have an ability. That's why they're hunting me, I think. Because I can charge the crystals myself." She grimaced. "Not that I'm very good at it."

The Reaper seemed to consider this, before switching her gaze to Theron. "You sure you don't want to claim that bounty?"

Kaila's eyes widened, but Theron grunted. "I dropped a mountain on the man. Pretty sure he's not in the mood for negotiations."

As if to punctuate his point, a *roar* echoed from the stairwell. They all spun to stare at the darkened passageway. Theron suppressed a shudder. The sound had been barely human. No words, just raw, primal fury.

The Reaper grimaced. "You might be right."

"What do we do?" Some of the panic had left Kaila's voice. She was still pale as a ghost, but that was probably the aftereffects of her ability.

"Don't suppose there are any secret passages out of this tower?" Theron asked.

The Reaper scowled at him.

He sighed. "Well, how much *atar* do you have left then?"

"Enough."

"Let's hope that's true." Theron gritted his teeth. "Will your powers work on a Warden?"

"Of course," she grunted, then waved her dagger. "But this pig sticker will break long before I can make it through that armour."

Theron nodded. He glanced at Kaila. She was back on her feet with crystal in hand, but this battle was well beyond her capabilities. It was on himself and the Reaper to face the monster. And this time, there were no mountains to drop on him. And even if he *could* bring down the tower, he'd be dropping it on their own heads as well. The Reaper was right; their blades would never penetrate his armour. But maybe…

"Okay, I might have a plan."

17

Elric slowed as silence fell above him in the tower. They knew he was there. The thought drew a smile to his lips. He crept up the stairs, blade and *atarsight* extended before him. The stone walls dulled his vision of the other world, but at least the creatures would not take him by surprise.

How many waited for him? At least the two from the village. Maybe more. But he was prepared. The agimet that powered his armour was already charged, but he drew another loop of energy from the nexus anyway. The light of his crystals brightened, while fresh energy crackled through his veins, sharpening his senses.

Only as he approached the top of the tower did he catch the glint of *soullights* from above. His enemies awaited. There were three of the Elysian, two positioned near the stairwell—no doubt thinking to catch him off-guard, while the last lingered near the back. Probably the girl, given her obvious inexperience.

He paused, considering his options. The stairs wound around the circumference of the tower one final time to where his foes waited in ambush. Elric did not doubt he could withstand their tricks, however, these particular creatures had proven resourceful. The last time he'd underestimated this Theron, the foul thing had collapsed half a mountain on his head.

Upon consideration, it was time Elric sprang a surprise of his own.

There was a doorway on the landing, leading to a dark, windowless chamber. It had probably been used for storage a millennia ago, when humanity had still served as slaves to the Elysian of this city. Stepping into the darkness, he studied the ceiling. Heavy wooden beams propped up the floorboards of the chamber above. They creaked as his enemies shifted carefully on their feet.

Elric's smile grew. The greatsword in his hand changed without a word, becoming a massive double-headed axe. Taking a firmer grip of the weapon, he crouched and fed *atar* to his armour. There was a soft sizzling as energy gathered in the strange steel.

The armour of a Warden was a terrible thing, a responsibility only granted to those worthy of its power. Elric had worn it with pride for decades. Its abilities came as second nature to him, granting power to his limbs beyond any mortal.

So it was that the wooden beams gave way easily before him as he came crashing and tearing through the floor of the chamber.

It was gratifying, to see the looks of terror that twisted the faces of his enemies when they turned to find a Warden in their midst, vengeance finally come to claim their evil souls.

But these were no regular enemies, and their surprise was brief. Even as he alighted between them, they were already leaping into action. He sensed a crackling of energy as the thief from the pass threw up his hand. Several shards of broken stone hurtled in Elric's direction. More concerning still, the third member, a woman unfamiliar to him, vanished.

Wraith!

Fortunately, Elric knew how to deal with her kind. Wraiths were exceedingly rare nowadays, but those Wardens who had come before him had passed down their knowledge. His training kicked in before his mind had even finished registering the new threat. Psionic power bubbled from his armour, delivering a pulse of anguish to every living soul within the crumbling tower.

Darkness flickered, and then the strange woman reappeared, face drained of colour and blade extended to stab at his visor. Snarling, she recovered almost instantly and hurled herself at him, but Elric threw up an armoured hand. Steel grated against steel as the dagger was deflected, before he traded a blow of his own, smashing her with a gauntleted fist. She went tumbling, ending up in a heap of broken rubble and debris.

"So much for that plan," the Elysian man muttered.

Elric grinned beneath his visor and pointed his axe at the man. "The judgement of the Nameless has come for you, Elysian. Will you submit to his penance?"

"Not bloody likely," his foe swore.

"So be it," Elric said and started forward.

The Elysian threw up his hand and the foul light of corruption burst from his eyes. A piece of rock hurtled at Elric. He met the projectile with the dark steel of a Warden, shattering first one rock, then a second. A third slammed into his shoulder, but the armour protected him and he continued his advance.

"I will not allow your lies to leave this place," he growled.

"Ah, saw the statues, did you?" his opponent taunted, dodging a swing of Elric's axe. "What, the workmanship wasn't to your liking?"

"Does your blasphemy know no limits?" Elric snapped back. "That you would twist even the sacred image of our First Matron."

"You call her sacred, we call her a treacherous cur. Potato, potato, am I right?"

"*Be damned!*"

Elric hurtled forward, swinging his axe with the borrowed power of *atar*. No mortal could have evaded him, but Elysian were unnatural devils and the thief somehow managed to hurl himself aside. His axe sank deep into the floorboards. The wood creaked and shifted as he tore the weapon loose, but Elric didn't pause, springing instead after his prey, unwilling to let up now the battle was joined.

Light burst from his foe and a chunk of rock slammed into the side of Elric's head. Most of the impact was deflected by his armour, though, and he barely broke his stride. The Elysian was not to be deterred. More debris joined the fray, slamming into Elric from every direction, pushing him one way, then another. He gritted his teeth against the assault, but endured, knowing these puny attacks couldn't truly harm him. They were a distraction, a delaying tactic until they found a way through his armour.

Elric would have none of it.

Bellowing, he unleashed another Psionic blast that sent the Elysian man reeling. Relishing the sight, Elric pressed his advantage, lashing the thief's mind with tendrils of despair. The man clutched at his skull, a groan hissing from his lips.

"Kneel, abomination," Elric mocked. "Accept your fate."

His smile grew as the thief crumpled to his knees. The axe shifted in Elric's hand, becoming the greatsword that was his preferred weapon. With the Elysian helpless, he took a moment to savour the victory. The tower was silent, the girl from Elgoss watching in petrified horror. He raised his blade high.

At that moment, though, his victim found some hidden strength. His head jerked up, meeting Elric's iron gaze.

"Do…your worst…bastard."

In other circumstances, Elric might have been impressed. But this was the man who had dropped a mountain on him. An abomination who had cursed the name of the First Matron herself…

…he lowered his sword with a growl.

"A quick death is too good for the likes of you."

Gripping his Warden's blade, Elric slammed it into the floorboards, lodging it in place. The Elysian flinched, but his mind was befuddled by Elric's power, his movements uncontrolled. Elric's fist caught him in the forehead, driving him back to his knees. There, he swayed, eyes foggy, helpless as Elric wrapped a gauntleted hand around his throat.

And the Elysian began to scream.

THERON KNEW IT WOULD HURT. IT WAS THE ONE RULE EVERY ELYSIAN knew when it came to Wardens—don't let them touch you. Like their swords, the touch of that armour was deadly.

Hopefully, this would be an exception. Though as the steel fingers closed around his throat, Theron had his doubts. The pain was instant, but it went deeper than flesh, like someone had poured ice water down his throat. The glowing torch that was his *soullight* guttered, as though something was draining it away.

Theron didn't know when he had started screaming, only that it reverberated through the tower chamber. He *did* notice when he began thrashing, desperation overcoming cold logic. He clawed at the Warden, trying to dislodge him, but the man had the strength of a Bruiser and nothing Theron did could move him. He could have crushed Theron's throat whenever he wished, but instead, the man behind the black visor seemed to savour his suffering, stretching out his death.

Theron had been counting on it. He just hadn't thought it would go on for *quite* this long.

Trickster curse her, where was the damn Reaper?

She had better pick herself up, or they were all done. He could *feel* himself dying, the acidic power of the armour eating into his flesh, the corruption spreading through his *soullight*. The *atar* in his body was gone, consumed by whatever foul magic had wrought the armour of the Wardens. Some remained in his crystal, but he was loathe to touch it. He needed it. But if he waited any longer, he wasn't sure he would remain conscious.

It was now or never.

He sucked the *atar* from the crystal like a man dying of thirst. All of it, every drop, until it blazed from his eyes and he felt the pain relent. Teeth bared, he directed his Gift at his foe and *pushed*, trying with everything he had to separate them.

The energy gathered between them, before with a silent *twang*, it rebounded from the armoured monster back onto Theron, striking him with enough force to send a man hurtling several yards across an empty field.

It almost wasn't enough.

Theron felt his bones creak, limbs stretching as his power pushed him one way, and the inexorable strength of the Warden tried to hold him in place. For a second, he thought he would be torn in two, but then the iron fingers relented, and his precious neck slipped from the Warden's grasp.

A moment of exultation followed, before Theron slammed into the wall of the chamber.

This time, something *did* break, as something went *crack* in his shoulder. Pain followed, a sharp stabbing sensation in his collar that joined the burning around his throat. But Theron couldn't rest. The Warden was already advancing, fists clenched, *soullight* broiling. If Theron could have seen the man's face, he imagined it would have been a twisted mix of rage and hatred.

Thankfully, the Reaper chose that moment to carry out phase two of their plan.

Step one—separate the Warden from his sword. Step two—stick it in him wherever was convenient.

Theron preferred not to kill—most people were just doing their best to survive in this wretched world. But he made an exception for servants of the Magisterium. As far as he was concerned, bastards like Elric Chain had earned death a thousand times over for their crimes against the world.

So it was with enormous satisfaction that he watched the dark blade tear through his enemy's chest, driven by a well-aimed thrust by the Reaper as she stepped through time.

Unlike regular weapons, this sword had no trouble piercing Warden's armour. But even with the terrible blade piercing his chest, Elric Chain showed he was no ordinary human. He staggered, tearing the blade from the Reaper's grasp, and continued towards Theron. Theron experienced a moment of panic as the monster loomed above him, fist raised to cave in his skull.

But even a Warden had his limits, and here Elric Chain found his, as his knees collapsed, sending him crashing to the floorboards. The light of his agimet flickered, dying to dim sparks. A wet wheezing came from inside the dark helmet as he sagged forward.

Letting out a gasp of laughter, Theron sank onto his back. *They'd done it!* He could hardly believe it. After dropping a mountain on the man, he'd started to believe the bastard was immortal after all.

Footsteps approached as the Reaper moved wearily around the fallen warrior. A faint glow still shone from her own last piece of agimet. She watched the Warden with narrowed eyes, but he lay still, the dark armour unmoving.

"You okay?" she grunted.

Theron was anything but *okay*, but he nodded dully. "I think I'll live."

The Reaper's lips pressed into a thin line as she glanced at him.

The faint glow of *atar* still shone from her eyes. He was completely out. "Well then," she said, "I guess we pick back up where we left off—"

She broke off as a flash of *atar* turned the room white. The Warden moved like a viper. He didn't bother with weapons, but hurled himself at the Reaper. She had no chance to react before the terrible arms wrapped her in an iron hug.

"*No!*" Theron cried, but it was already too late.

The Reaper stiffened as the Warden dragged her onto the bloody point of the blade in his chest. Her eyes went wide, a burst of *atar* swirling in their crystal depths. Her body trembled, as though she was trying to activate her Gift, but this time nothing happened. The glow flickered and died.

The Warden held her in that crushing grasp for several long seconds before he released her. Her body toppled forward, limp, and crashed to the ground alongside Theron. Blood seeped out around her, running across the floorboards toward the hole the Warden had torn in the floor.

Drawing in a gurgling breath, Elric Chain towered over Theron. The crystals embedded in his armour sputtered, shining brilliant one second, dying to a spark the next. The black blade in his chest shrank, dissipating into his body—and then reforming in Elric's fist.

Theron let it happen. His last piece of agimet was empty anyway. Despair settled on his soul. This time he knew it had nothing to do with Psionic power, but the cold certainty of defeat.

And then Kaila's voice carried across the chamber. "*Theron!*"

Something in her tone cut through the desolation. He swung towards her. Her face was wan as she drew back her hand. She held the crystal he'd given her earlier—the only one left still shining with *atar*. His heart swelled. Injured as the Warden was, maybe Theron had a chance after all. He rose as Kaila threw the stone, stretching out his hand—

A dark blade arced through the air, intercepting the crystal mid-flight. A sharp *wrenching* sound followed, like nails on a chalkboard, as the stone shattered into a dozen pieces.

"No more of that," An iron voice grated from inside the helmet.

Slowly, as if it took a great labour, the Warden reached up and pressed a hand to his ear.

The blue metal shimmered, pulling away to reveal the face of their tormentor. Blood dripped from purple lips and his eyes were bloodshot, his hair slick against his pale skull. *Atar* ran in rivulets through his skin like veins, as though the power of the crystals was all that kept him upright. As the helmet faded, the sword in his hand grew larger. He no longer seemed to have the strength to manifest both. Baring bloody teeth, he lifted the dark sword over Theron.

"And behold," he whispered. "I am the blade of the Nameless, his eternal light against the darkness."

18

"And behold, I am the blade of the Nameless, his eternal light against the darkness."

Kaila experienced a strange moment of disassociation looking upon the face that had hunted her all the way from Elgoss. Here, at last, was the man who had destroyed her life. He loomed over the chamber, more force of nature than a man. A weapon of vengeance that could not be stopped.

But she had to try.

"*Stop!*" Something was breaking inside of Kaila as she stepped towards them. It was all wrong. A few days ago, this man had been her hero, and Theron the monster beneath her bed. How had things gotten so mixed up? "It's me you're after."

To her surprise, Elric paused and turned towards her. His eyes did not glow like an Elysian, though she could see it pulsing beneath his skin, nourished by the remaining gemstones in his armour.

"You will both feel the wrath of the Nameless before this day is done." His voice was terrible now, metallic despite the removal of his helmet, as though he were more metal than flesh himself.

Despite her terror, Kaila took a trembling step towards him. She still had the ring from the Reaper, though it was empty again. Why had she thrown away their last piece of charged agimet? She had thought giving it to Theron was their best chance, that the prince of thieves must have one last trick up his sleeves.

Instead, she had tossed away their last chance of survival.

Her hand tightened around the ring. She was trembling all over now, contemplating what she was about to do. If she even could. *So weak.* Her entire body ached from the climb and the weariness in her soul had not abated. She was in a worse state than back in the pass. If she used her power now, would there be any coming back this time?

What other option did she have? Elric had the upper hand. Her only chance was to take him by surprise, strike with what he least expected.

The truth was, she had no choice. Gritting her teeth against the pain she knew would follow, Kaila called on the strange, trancelike state she had practiced a handful of times now. This time, though, she dug deeper than ever before, down to her own *soullight.* It already felt stretched and twisted, and chunks had been torn from it. The colour was all wrong, like cheese that had been left to ripen a few weeks too long. She had already asked too much of herself these last days, she knew.

One final push.

With that thought, Kaila tore another piece from her spirit and pushed it into the agimet. Her legs immediately turned to jelly. She staggered, almost going down. By some scrap of will Kaila never knew she possessed, she managed to remain on her feet long enough to feel the tingle of *atar* in her hand.

It was satisfying, to witness the shock on the Warden's face. The man behind the iron mask was finally revealed as human. Grimly, she lifted a hand, feeling the power gather.

Sometimes it was good to be underestimated.

Unfortunately, her satisfaction proved fleeting. Her body chose that moment to finally give in. The glow of *atar* stuttered, and then the darkness descended. She tried to hold it at bay, willing her body to resist, just until the job was done and the enemy lay dead at her feet.

To no avail.

The last Kaila knew before the emptiness swallowed her, was relief. Relief, as her broken spirit was taken, swept away to a place beyond pain and worry and grief, to a world where she no longer need care for vengeance, or fear, or anger; if she lived or died. A place where she could be…nothing.

Only a tiny part of her resisted. A final, spluttering candle amidst the void. A guttering flicker of *soullight* that pled to the darkness for mercy, for someone, *anyone*, to help her.

"And so the sheep returns."

A part of Kaila knew she should be frightened. She was a spirit, standing in the dark, and she was not alone. Before her loomed the man that haunted her dreams. Oberon, the ancient king. If anything, he was larger even than the statue lying broken in the tower square. His chin was like marble, his arms great saplings that sprouted from his barrel chest. In his eyes burned a fire, terrible, hungry, the sort that had consumed nations and seen worlds tremble.

Yet as the giant from their forgotten past loomed above her, this time Kaila felt no fear.

Instead, she looked around and was surprised to find not only darkness, but shapes amidst the void. Walls pulsed with a faint, otherworldly glow, enclosing them in a quiet room. Strange contraptions lay on tables, wheels and elongated spirals, dark boxes and cylinders and spheres of unknown purpose. It reminded her of the blacksmiths workshop back in Elgoss, where old Tomas had tinkered day and night. In the centre of the room, an ornate pedestal had been adorned with runes and crystals that might have been agimet, except they were dark. Empty.

"Where are we?" she asked, returning her gaze to the ancient king.

"A place neither of your world, nor that of the spirit."

"Then I'm…" She struggled to get out the last word. Here, absent of pain, she finally felt grief for the life she would never live. "…dead."

The king surprised her with a chuckle. "If you wish."

A rush of hope filled the space where her heart would have been, had Kaila still possessed a body. "And if I don't?"

"That depends on you, child."

She shivered. Oberon spoke in an almost fatherly tone, as though guiding a toddler on their first steps.

"What do I need to do?"

"Use your power."

"I tried!" she gasped, her hope wilting. "But I'm not like the Wardens. My soul isn't strong enough to fill a crystal."

Laughter shook the darkness. "Foolish girl. No soul in this world, nor any of the Seven, is strong enough for the Gift of the Elysian."

Kaila stared into the dark eyes. "Then how?"

"I already told you: no child of mine is ever without power in Iselador."

Understanding, like a lantern lit at the stroke of midnight, bloomed in Kaila. "The nexus!"

A smile cracked the granite face. The king nodded.

Kaila shuddered, looking again around the dark place. For the first time, she realised there were no windows or doors, nor any other passageways to leave the strange place.

"How…do I go back?"

The ancient king's smile faded. He studied her with those dark eyes. "Only you can decide that. Enough power remains in your soul, I think, to return. You must will it with all your strength."

"And if I can't?"

"Your spirit cannot remain in this place. Eventually, it will fade, and you will make the final crossing, beyond which even I do not know what awaits."

She swallowed. "Then…why, why are you still here?"

The dark eyes regarded her a while longer, as though considering something, before he spoke: "I wait…" he said. It seemed he would go on, but instead the king fell silent, watching her with those dark yes, until at last. "Time for you to go, I think. Your world calls."

Nodding, Kaila turned to go, before hesitating. "Thank you, Oberon."

"You are welcome, my child."

"Why do you call me that?"

"I consider all who carry my blood to be my children. Now, go, Kaila Dwyn. Prove you are a lion."

Kaila's heart swelled. Something about the king, the power of his spirit, gave her confidence where even she doubted. She closed her eyes, blocking out the strange chamber and the ancient spirit, the cool silence, the emptiness of the void. There had to be a way back to her body and the world and…and to Theron.

The thought of him made her heart pulse, the emotions tangling, the heat and the pain and the fear. She saw him lying on the floor, helpless and broken, the Warden standing over him, dark sword in hand. She had to go back, return for him, just as he had returned for her…

…and like that, Kaila saw it. A thread of light that grew from her beaten soul. It wound its way through the ether, finding the tiniest of slivers in the stone prison, and stretched away into the night. A part of her feared it was the path to that other place, the one beyond the veil that not even Oberon could know. She had no way to discern it; only belief that her soul would not lead her astray.

And so Kaila grasped the thread…

…and woke on the floor of the tower. The pain was immediate, as lances of fire tore into her lungs, stealing away her voice, her breath. Every inch of her body burned, her muscles cramping, her blood pulsing like liquid fire in her veins. Her head screamed like it had been split in two. She swayed at the edge of a precipice, and knew that this time if she fell, there would be no return.

But Kaila had the answer now, the solution to her problem. Gathering what little strength remained, she pushed herself to her hands and knees. This time as she sought the trance, she reached *outwards*, instead of in. And she saw it, blazing like a second sun, filling the Black Tower and spreading over the city, a thousand threads of colour, entwining, binding, gathering to form a node of power.

The nexus.

It had been there all along, waiting for her call. Agimet attracted the threads naturally, drawing them into its crystal facets like water across an osmotic barrier. Slowly, ever so slowly. But it could move faster—infinitely faster. It just needed a catalyst. *She* was the catalyst.

Opening her eyes, Kaila looked around the room. Only a heart-beat had passed, for the Warden still stood with sword raised, poised to spear Theron and finish the job he had started a few minutes ago. She had to stop him.

Teeth clenched, unsure exactly what would happen next, Kaila grasped as much of the nexus as she could and hauled it into the crystal.

And a brilliant flash of light filled the Black Tower, casting them all in her shade.

Elric stood over the twisted body of the Wraith. Each breath was a burning agony. He could feel himself slowly drowning in his own blood. It took all of his willpower to move, to take one step, then another towards the Elysian thief.

Only the armour had kept him alive this long. Even as its crystals guttered and threatened to die, he drew more power from the nexus, filling them and feeding fresh strength to his failing body. He knew this was yet another test. The Nameless would not abandon him, not while he served this sacred duty.

Then he sensed the fresh power fill the chamber, the terrible glint of a new crystal. His head jerked up, his bodily reactions not entirely under his control now.

"How?" he growled when he saw the girl.

She had been a spent force, her *soullight* dying to dull embers. Now it blazed once more with life. Threads swirled within her, stretching out, connecting with a crystal on her finger, and now it too shone with *atar*, where before it had been dead.

"You're not the only one with a trick up their sleeve, Warden."

The girl smiled, and despite himself, something shivered inside of Elric. It couldn't be. He had seen the girl wielding the magics of the enemy. She could not possess the sacred power as well. Such a thing was impossible. And yet…

"You're one of us…" he breathed.

Smirking, the Elysian girl shifted into a fighting stance, a knife stretched out before her. "Something like that."

Elric trembled, two forces doing battle within. She was of the cursed blood, those who used the foul magics of the Elysian. But she also possessed the power of a Warden. A chosen of the Nameless.

"So it's true," Elric cursed. Lowering his blade, he bowed his head. "Had Sister Eurador not already paid penance for her crimes, I would drag her before the Sanctum to be burned for blasphemy." Meeting the girl's eyes, he saw her confusion, the doubt and distrust. He grimaced. "Kaila Dwyn," he continued, "a great injustice has been perpetrated upon you by the former Sister of Elgoss. For that, you have my sincere apologies."

The girl blinked. "What?"

"I cannot undo the damage her crime has caused you," Elric

continued, "but I can offer you what should have been yours by right—to be a Warden of Fresia."

She was staring at him now, eyes so wide they filled her face, like she couldn't quite believe what he'd said.

"What did you say?"

19

Blood was pounding in Kaila's ears, but even over its thundering, she still heard the words of Elric Chain.

Warden, Warden, WARDEN!

Her chest hurt. She couldn't breathe. Her head was pulsing, *pounding* like it was about five seconds away from bursting. Stars filled her vision as she swayed.

"What did you say?" she whispered.

"I would make you a Warden, Kaila Dwyn."

He stood in the centre of the tower, iron face hard, twisted, scowling as he had before…but there was something more there now. A glint of respect? Surely not. Not for the foul Elysian monstrosity he had hunted all this way.

"Why?" she rasped. Her mouth was so dry she could barely get out the words.

"It always should have been so," the Warden replied. He gestured to the ring. "You have attuned to the sacred crystal. It makes you one of *us*. A servant of the Nameless."

"No," she croaked, vision blurring. She felt the hot streak of a tear on her cheek. *Why now?* This couldn't be happening. Not now. Why, not a week ago, before her entire world had been turned on its head. Before she'd seen Iselador and the statue of T'iana and spoken with the spirit of the void. Before her father had *died*.

Before she'd met Theron.

Shuddering, her eyes were drawn to the man who had led her on this terrible journey. The thief that had destroyed her life—and then saved her life again and again. The man who had removed the blindfold that had been placed over her eyes her entire life.

He crouched, gasping on the floor, but he looked up then, as though sensing her gaze upon him. Their eyes met and his jaw hardened.

"Kaila," he rasped, "don't listen—"

An iron fist smashed him across the face, cutting off his words. He lay still while the Warden glared down at him, before returning his attention to Kaila. He stretched out a hand towards her.

"Come," he spoke again, voice soft now, without the metallic grate of earlier. "Join me and we will smite this foul creature together."

Her chin hardened as she looked at the hand. "What about my power?"

For a second, his fist clenched, and she saw his tension. But then he shook his head. "We will keep it secret," he said, dark eyes meeting her own. "No one has to know the truth."

Kaila swallowed. He was offering her everything she had ever dreamed of. Somehow, she found herself walking towards him, her treacherous legs carrying her across the rubble-strewn floor. It was madness to walk towards the man, and yet she did, until she stood before him, looking up into that twisted face, the hero of Fresia.

Someday you will be a hero. You will make us proud.

Tears were streaming down Kaila's face. She could hear her father's voice, feel the love that had shone from his eyes. The Warden still held out his gauntleted hand. The steel rippled, twisting, a dagger forming between his fingers.

"Take it," he whispered, "claim your rightful place in the order of Wardens."

The blade glinted black in the light of their agimet. Her hand shook as it closed around the steel hilt. A tingling sensation leapt across her flesh, shooting through her fingers and up her arm. She gasped but did not let go as every hair on her body stood on end.

"The armour recognises you," Elric said. With his other hand, he closed her fist more tightly around the blade. "Now use it on our enemy." He pointed at Theron.

The Elysian thief stared up at her, his expression unreadable. A shudder swept through Kaila, a crack in her broken soul. Something strange was happening inside her, like her crystal and the blade were reacting to each other. Another image appeared in her mind. Her father, lying on the floor in Elgoss. Her hand shook.

Could she really forget all of it? Her father. Theron. The magic inside of her. Could she set them all to the side and pretend none of this had ever happened? All her life, she had dreamed of becoming a Warden, of serving the Magisterium, defending their kingdom from the enemy.

But that dream had been built on a lie. The enemy was not some monster, but human too, just like the rest of them. Duty had only ever been a tool to control them. Even the Wardens themselves had been a lie. The man before her was no hero, sworn to serve the realm, but a monster that rejoiced in the pain he inflicted.

"What do you want to be, girl?" Elric was watching her with those terrible eyes. "One of us, or one of *them*?"

It was a fair question. She looked at the Warden, at the *atar* coursing through his veins, encased in metal. Her hero. This was not the dream she had nursed since childhood, but a perverted distortion of it.

Her eyes went to Theron. The man who lived for nothing and no one, who stole and lied and cheated, only ever looking out for himself.

One served a higher purpose, the other none.

In that moment, she realised the truth.

"I'm not sure," she whispered.

Kaila didn't know what she wanted. Elysian or Warden, soldier or thief. She didn't know. And that was okay. Before, she had known with *absolute certainty* what she would be. For the first time in her life, it was nice to just…not know.

Elric wore a twisted scowl. "How can you not be sure? You must decide."

Her face hardened. "Oh, I decided," she said, voice growing cold. "Or at least, I decided what I *won't* be."

She was shaking now. Not from joy, or relief, or fear, or even doubt. Kaila Dwyn shook with *rage*.

"I will not be a monster!"

The words tore from her throat as she unleashed her fury. All the pain and anger and injustice of the last week, *of her entire life*, came rushing from her. She breathed in the power from her ring, feeling her veins flood with *atar*. The sheer strength of it was like nothing she'd felt before. It burned as she consumed it, like she'd snuck a sip of her father's hidden whiskey.

Gasping, she gathered her strength, so that when she let fly with her Gift, it would strike like an arrow from a bow. It was gratifying to see Elric retreat from her, his courage wavering in the face of her fury. His dagger was heavy in her hand. Its power prickled her flesh, clashing with the *atar* from her agimet. *Wrong*. She tossed it aside. The Reaper had tried to kill Elric with his own blade. It hadn't worked; Kaila would not make the same mistake.

Armed only with her crystal, she advanced on the Warden.

Seeing Kaila discard the weapon seemed to snap Elric from his cowardice. His face hardened, *atar* pulsing brighter in the veins of his neck. The liquid armour came flowing up his neck to encase him again entirely in steel.

"So be it," he growled.

Striding to his dagger, he gathered it and held it high. Kaila didn't care. She was a lamb no longer, to be led by the wolves to the slaughter.

She was Kaila Dwyn of Iselador, heir to the powers of an ancient king, and she would *destroy* this pretender.

Atar lit the room as she called on her Gift and grasped the armour of the Warden, just as she had all those days ago in Elgoss. Again she was rebuffed by the strangeness of Elric's *soullight*. She sensed the energies gathering between them. She let it grow. Back in Elgoss, the force had rebounded on her, throwing her in the opposite direction she'd tried to move him.

This time though, Kaila wasn't trying to push the Warden away.

She was pulling him towards her.

TWANG!

With a shriek like wire on a chalkboard, the power *snapped*, pulling Kaila from her feet—*towards* the Warden like she'd just been shot out of a catapult. She braced herself, *atar* bolstering her, but the *crash* as they came together still sent spikes of pain jolting through her body. Red light flashed before her eyes—and then they were tumbling backwards, propelled by her momentum, straight for her target.

A target with only the slightest bit of irony.

The window.

Elric cried out as his legs hit the rim. For a moment they windmilled, trying to recover his balance, but there was only empty space behind him. Desperately, Kaila twisted away, grasping for the ledge, but her foe was too quick. Iron fingers wrapped around her bicep hard enough to crush bone.

She screamed as his weight dragged her with him through the empty window.

And then she was falling…

THERON'S HEART LURCHED IN HIS CHEST AS KAILA DISAPPEARED through the window, dragged down by an iron hand caught around her arm. For a second, he experienced what it must be like as a Wraith, as the entire world seemed to freeze.

Run, Theron! RUN!

Suddenly he was moving, *sprinting* for the window. The agimet in his hands was dead, empty, but shards of crystal were scattered across the floor. They blazed now with *atar*, charged in minutes by the nexus. Broken agimet. Cursed, tainted, *deadly.*

Theron scooped up a shard, fingers tightening around the terrible fragment. For a moment only he hesitated. Using it meant death, or something even worse. Addiction, condemned to the same terrible fate as the Reaper.

You're going to get her killed. Just like…me.

With each passing heartbeat, Kaila fell further away from the high chamber, further towards the point of no return, beyond the reach of his Gift.

Atar crackled in his veins as he drew from the shard. Theron knew then why no one who started down this path ever returned.

It was glorious.

Light filled him, searing away his weakness. Ordinary *atar* was like watered ale compared to the sweetness of this nectar. What a fool he'd been not to use this power before. *Atar* flowed from the crystal, flooding every fibre of his being in a way it never had before, like he could draw on this one tiny shard forever and never run dry. With this power in his hands, he could do anything.

Reaching the window, he looked out and saw the glint of Kaila's *soullight* below. Thirty feet and falling quickly. Simple. It took no effort at all to use his Gift and catch her tumbling body, slowing her descent, then reversing it entirely. Her eyes were closed as she rose to his perch in the tower. She must have lost consciousness in the fall.

He retreated from the window, his power carrying her easily inside, and set her gently on the floor. Safe. He exhaled before returning to the window. Far, far, below, the Warden had already hit the ground. He had landed amidst the ruin of the statues, and the obsidian had torn great chunks from his body. Looking with his *atar-sight*, Theron confirmed what was obvious to the naked eye. Elric Chain lived no more.

Satisfied, he grunted and stepped back from the window. *Atar* still flowed in his veins. He looked at the crystal, surprised to find its energy undiminished. Incredible. He sucked in more power, savouring it, and then more still, until his veins prickled and the world blazed.

He could do anything.

Then let go…

From somewhere deep within, a voice pleaded with him. Theron shuddered, fist tightening around the fragment.

Anything but that!

Then you're weak!

Weak! I'm not weak! He was more powerful than he'd ever been. Even had the Warden survived, Theron could have crushed him now, torn him limb from limb with this little piece of agimet. Why had he been searching for pure crystals, when a broken shard offered *this?*

He drew on more *atar*. It *burned*. The sensation was amazing, like the entire world lay at his fingertips. Everything was a blaze of white.

Please, you have to let it go.

Something in the voice cut through the ecstasy, the silent plea in it, the desperation. Suddenly, Theron choked, tasting blood on his tongue. There was a burning in his nostrils, and pain in his belly, a searing in his veins.

It was too much.

Shuddering, trembling, he clung to the crystal, feeling its power, the sheer *purity* of it. He couldn't let it go! Not now. With this, the Magisterium were nothing. He could take them all on, challenge their naked evil, even steal their most prized possession…

Please…

The voice seemed further away, like it was fading, dying. He recognised it then, the distant whisper.

Freya.

He couldn't lose her. Not again!

A part of him cracked and tore, but somehow Theron forced his fingers to open. He released the crystal shard.

The sudden loss of *atar* was like the blow from a hammer. He gasped, reeling away from where the crystal had fallen, and sank to his knees, sobbing. For a long time, he remained that way, or perhaps it was only a few minutes. He didn't know. All sense of time had fled. All he knew was the agony of withdrawal and the craving to get back what he had lost.

When Kaila finally stirred, minutes, seconds, or hours could have passed. Panic touched him when he saw her eyes flicker. She couldn't see him this way, couldn't know what he had done. His eyes settled on the agimet ring on her finger, still glowing with the light she had given it.

He darted forward and slipped it from her finger. A sigh escaped his lips as he drew on its *atar*. Not like before. Not enough to sate the hole that pure, wonderous light had burnt inside of him. But enough, for now.

"Theron?" Kaila's eyes fluttered open. A brow creased her forehead as she pushed herself up on one elbow. "What happened? I thought…"

Theron lifted the ring with a grin as false as his own name. "Caught you," he replied. "Couldn't let you sacrifice your life and end up owing you *again.*"

Her eyes flickered to the crystal, before returning to his face. Slowly, the frown faded from her lips, only to return as she glanced at the window.

"Elric?"

"Dead," he replied, and this time the relief in his voice was not feigned. "You did it, Kaila. Congratulations. You killed a Warden."

"Congratulations. You killed a Warden."

He said it so casually, like she'd won a gold star from Sister Eurador instead of committing the most heinous of crimes known to Fresia. A sense of disgust rose in Kaila's throat. How many times would she face this truth before it grew easier?

You killed a Warden.

"And the Reaper?" she asked, pushing the images in her head aside and struggling to stand.

"I haven't checked."

They both looked in the direction of the woman. Blood pooled around her body, so much of it that Kaila doubted anyone could have survived. Nevertheless, she stumbled to the woman's side. Theron hung back, moving slowly from his wounds. Kneeling, Kaila checked the woman's pulse.

To her surprise, the woman's head rolled towards her, her eyes flickering open. Kaila's heart lurched in her chest and she reached out to turn the woman on her back, so she could get a better look at her wound.

"Don't." The command came out as barely a whisper.

"But your wound—"

"I know…wounds…" the Reaper rasped. "Nothing…to be done."

Cold spread through Kaila's stomach. The woman might have been their enemy, but she had also saved their life, fighting at Theron's side, wounding the Warden, *resisting*. She hadn't deserved this.

"I'm sorry," Kaila croaked. "Reaper…

Laughter rasped from the woman's throat. "Call me…Mora," she whispered. "Can you…the rabbit." Her eyes flickered.

For a heartbeat, Kaila didn't understand. Then her eyes fell on the pack the woman had discarded before their fight, the one that had contained the agimet and her other possessions. Lying nearby, ignored in the skirmish for larger projectiles, was a stuffed rabbit. Her heart twisting, she rose and retrieved it for the woman.

"Who…"

"My daughter," she breathed, a tear streaking from her eyes as she clutched the rabbit close. "I…wish I could have…protected her…from them." Her eyes flickered. "Arg, hurts…so much…*atar*… any…left?"

Kaila nodded. Mora still clutched a piece of empty agimet. That, at least, she could do something about.

"Here." She laid her hand on the stone and sought the nexus. It was easier this time, feeling out the power. It flowed like a cool river through her hands and light appeared in the crystal.

"*Ahhhh*," the Reaper sighed. A second later, the crystal's light reflected from her eyes. "Thank you."

Her eyes flickered closed, and the world seemed to fade; the sound of the wind and the groaning of the building, even the breath of air against her face. Kaila held the Reaper's hand—Mora's hand —feeling the warmth of life and *atar* against her skin.

"I'm sorry this happened to you," she said at last.

Mora's eyes fluttered open at her voice. Surprise glinted there. "How…" she began, before pursing her lips. The moment drew out, the silence heavy in the quiet of the tower. "So, you can really do what they can."

Kaila nodded, struggling to keep the tears from her eyes. Pain flashed across Mora's face. She clenched her jaw, teeth bared. Only when it passed did her eyes flicker to something over Kaila's shoulder. Someone.

"You can't trust…the thief," Mora breathed. "Hasn't told you…everything."

Kaila frowned. "Theron?"

"Don't know…what you…are," Mora continued. "Different… dangerous to them. Maybe to…us as well." Her eyes flickered closed. "Good…"

"What are you talking about? Mora? *Mora!*"

It was too late. The woman who had been the Reaper was gone; her spirit carried away at last to whatever lay beyond the darkness. Kaila crouched there for a while longer, head bowed, hands still wrapped around the piece of agimet. Finally, she released a breath she hadn't realised she'd been holding and rose.

Theron waited, his face grim. Kaila approached him.

"What did she mean?"

A frown touched his forehead. "What?"

"What she said at the end, about you hiding something from me?"

If anything, Theron's frown only deepened. "What do you mean, at the end? You crouched beside her, and then she died."

Kaila opened her mouth to call him a liar, then remembered the silence that had swallowed them up. Her heart pulsed in her chest and she glanced at the fallen woman. Had she…had *they* somehow shared a moment of the Wraith's power? Was that even possible?

She started to ask the question, but something made her hesitate. *He hasn't told you everything.*

Theron was watching her with a faintly concerned look. Swallowing what she'd been about to say, Kaila shook her head.

"Never mind. I…" Her gaze was drawn to the window. "You're sure he's really dead this time?"

Theron grimaced. "Dropping a mountain on him might not have done the trick, but the obsidian he landed on…he's no longer in one piece down there."

She nodded, allowing herself some small measure of relief. Part of her would probably always wonder what might have happened if she'd accepted his offer, if she'd rejected her Elysian half and turned her back on Theron…

…but Kaila also knew she did not regret what she had done.

You will make us proud.

Even if it wasn't how her father might have imagined, she knew he would be happy with her choice. Trapped between two worlds, she had chosen to walk her own path. And there was no going back now.

"So, where do we go now?"

A grim smile touched Theron's lips. "Well, we've recovered *most* of our agimet." His eyes found hers. "What do you say I finally show you the wonders of the capital?"

EPILOGUE

The journey to Tah'raus took the better part of two weeks. They waited a day before setting off, sufficient time for their remaining agimet to charge naturally. Kaila could have tried to do it herself, but with the Warden and the Reaper both dead, the need for urgency was removed. There was no point placing further strain on her already exhausted body.

During the journey, Theron did as he had promised and began instructing Kaila on her Gift, teaching her to use it as both a weapon and a shield. It would take much more than a few weeks practice to become a master— or anything like what the thief had displayed in the Black Tower. But in the meantime, she would practice every evening after they prepared camp.

Eventually, they settled into an easy rhythm, taking turns in the saddle or walking the trail, collecting firewood towards the end of each day, setting camp and cooking meals made from a mix of the rations and whatever they scavenged from the lush forests through which they travelled. There were no roads in this part of the world; this valley was on no maps; and so they didn't see another soul until they stood at the top of a great waterfall and looked out at the distant line of the coast.

But while they were courteous with one another, the fire they had shared that dark night in Iselador did not return. It hurt Kaila to feel the distance between them, knowing they had shared something more. She yearned to span the chasm words had torn between them, but she didn't know how to bridge it.

And, of course, there was the Reaper's final warning.

He hasn't told you everything.

So they completed their journey to the capital, together in many ways, but alone in those that mattered. A day before they neared the great city itself, Theron took the stallion into a settlement and returned a few hours later alone. Kaila would miss the great beast, but she understood the need. It carried the branding of the Magisterium and was worth a small fortune. Its presence would draw questions they could not answer.

And Theron did not return emptyhanded. Apparently, all manner of crimes could be had for the right price, and he handed Kaila a set of papers that declared her to be the only surviving daughter of a merchant family, journeying to Tah'raus in search of a suitor. An orphan. Hopefully, it would get them passed the city guards.

They arrived in the predawn to find a line of wagons already waiting to enter the city. Vendors for the most part, nearby farmers come to sell their crops, along with merchants travelling with goods from further afield.

As they waited with the men and women and carts outside the gates, Kaila's nerves returned. It began as a small thing, a tiny ball of anxiety in her chest. But as each shuffle of the queue drew them closer to the gates, it grew larger. By the time they neared the front, it had become a raw, furious thing.

The stone walls of the city rose above, casting the new arrivals in shade even as the sun crept higher into the sky. The empty hours were no friend to her sanity. A voice kept whispering in Kaila's mind, reminding her what she'd done. She had killed a Warden. At any moment, she expected soldiers to charge from the gates with swords levelled and that familiar hatred in their eyes.

The line edged forward. Kaila could almost make out the front of the queue now. Shifting on her feet, she tried to catch a glimpse of the guards. A tension hung over the crowd, a kind of seething frustration. A few yards behind them, two men began shouting at one another. Fists soon followed. Three guards raced forward, armour rattling as they drew clubs and laid into the dissidents. Both were dragged away a few minutes later, unconscious.

The crowd shifted again, slowly creeping towards the towering concrete walls that ringed the ancient city. She stared up at those great blocks of stone. The air had cooled since leaving the secret valley, but there were still plenty of signs of life. Lichen and ivy grew in the cracks between the blocks and a low scrub had grown up around the base of the wall, branches naked in preparation for winter.

It was strange, comparing this place with the ruins of Iselador. Majestic, soaring, defiant the Lost City might have been, but there had been no life in that ancient place. It was like a tomb, a memorial of another time, to a civilisation that had long since departed this world.

Finally the great gates came into view, all polished mahogany, iron, and brass. Beyond lay the Fresian capital and seat of the Magisterium. Her heart began to thud with a mix of dread and excitement. Despite everything that had passed these last weeks, there was a part of Kaila that wanted to believe in her kingdom, this last bastion of human civilisation.

Then the crowd shifted, the guards coming into view, and the fear came rushing back. This was no checkpoint on the gates of a tiny mountain village. There were dozens of them, each holding a spear and shield and wearing the scarlet uniform of the Fresian army. Several were looking over arrival papers, while others searched the wagons and carts. Yet more stood atop the wall, crossbows loaded and pointed at the crowd, ready to fire at the slightest hint of danger.

Kaila didn't even notice herself reaching for her agimet, when Theron's cold hand closed around her wrist.

"Easy," he said softly. His eyes remained fixed on the guards. "You're an orphan, remember?"

The words did little to calm her, but Kaila managed to drop her hand—just. As they neared the final checkpoint, a guard waved them over. Looping his arm through hers, Theron practically dragged her with him.

"Quite the security you've got today," he said cheerfully, adopting a slick southern accent as he handed over their papers. "Something we should know about?"

The man looked bored as he flicked through the pages. "Just the usual rumours. Elysian resistance. Dead traitor and the like…"

Blood pulsing in her ears, Kaila struggled to follow the conversation. Her eyes were fixed on the falsified documents as she shifted from foot to foot, straining to contain her nerves. What would happen if he realised their details didn't match? Could Theron deflect a crossbow bolt with his power? Could *she?* She'd practiced deflecting projectiles with Theron, but the bruises on her arms and torso were proof enough of her inexperience.

She need not have worried. The guard barely cast a glance over their papers before the grumbling from the queue had him handing them back. Theron thanked him with a clap on the shoulder, and then they were on their way. She was still wondering at the ease of their passage as they stepped into the gate tunnel.

Darkness swallowed them up, the grey of the winter morning replaced by the humid dampness of stone and dirt. The travellers in front of them had already hurried through, but as they reached the darkest point of the tunnel, Theron grasped her by the shoulder, drawing her to a stop. For the moment, they were alone. The next group was travelling with a wagon and the guards would take a few minutes to check over it, if the rest of the morning had been anything to go by.

"Listen, Kaila," Theron said, his voice tense, "there's something you should know, something I should have told you by now…"

The words set her heart to racing. Was this it, the secret the Reaper had warned her about? A lump lodged in her throat, and she glanced from Theron to the passage ahead.

"Is this really the place for this conversation…" she started, before the words abandoned her.

There was something ahead. Something…unnatural. A chill spread down her spine.

"Kaila…" Theron tried again, but she was already shrugging off his hand and stumbling forward a step, then another and another, until she emerged from the dank tunnel into a new world.

Light blazed, radiant, dazzling, as though the clouds that had filled he sky had suddenly been cast away. Yet she felt no heat on her skin, only a strange…bubbling sensation, a tingling that crept across her flesh. She squinted against the brilliance, waiting for the stars to face, and bit by bit the dark silhouettes of buildings took shape. The flicker of movement followed, and the buzz of voices above the pounding in her ears. The rumble of traffic finally broke through, the busy streets filled with people and carriages. Tah'raus was the centre of everything. Over a million people lived within its concrete walls.

Kaila had expected a place larger, grander than anything she could imagine.

But nothing could have prepared her for what she saw now.

It was not sunlight that filled the city.

It was agimet.

Agimet, those precious, forbidden crystals, was everywhere. Shining from street corners, hung above every doorway. People wore it as their jewellery, on great pendants around their necks and strange devices strapped to their wrists. It was even set in the wheels of the strange, horseless wagons that thundered through the perfectly straight streets, seemingly as of a will of their own.

"How?" she whispered.

This wasn't supposed to be possible. Agimet was perilous. It was a capital offence to carry a single crystal in Elgoss. Yet here it was, so much of it, the very crystals her father and the villagers had risked their lives to dig from the earth. A precious resource, they'd been told, vital for their soldiers on the frontlines, to protect them from the magics of the enemy.

A lie. Another lie.

"I'm sorry, Kaila," somehow, Theron's voice cut through the ringing in her ears. "I…wanted to tell you, but I wasn't sure you were ready…"

Kaila looked at him through blurry eyes. There was no stopping the tears once they arrived. They burned hot streaks down her face.

She didn't bother to wipe them away. "But…the crystals here…you…"

All this agimet, it would be a veritable arsenal for the Elysian, wouldn't it…

She knew the answer, even before he said it.

"Useless to us," he said softly. "It's been cut, polished, ground into pleasing shapes. The perfect energy source for their machines—but deadly to the Gifted. The raw crystals never come anywhere near the city."

Kaila was still trying to process what her eyes were telling her. "People *died* for those crystals," she rasped. "Buried in the dark, burned, suffocated, entombed." Her voice cracked. "They died thinking it was for a reason. So that others would live."

Theron pressed his lips in a thin line. "You see it now."

"We…" Her voice broke. "We really are slaves to them." She squeezed her eyes closed. "Why? Why would they do this?"

An answer did not come. When she opened her eyes again, Theron was no longer looking at her, but into the distance. She followed his gaze and saw the concrete dome rising above the rooftops of Tah'raus. She recognised it instantly, knew it from her books and Sister Eurador's loving tales.

The Sanctum.

"You want to know why?" Theron said at last. "Why they spin these tales of impending doom? Why they filled you with fear and anger and set you upon yourselves? Why they laugh as we murder one another? It's all for one reason. Power. Agimet is the most precious resource in the world. Without it, Tah'raus would grind to a halt."

"But why keep us in the dark? Why play games with us?"

Theron's eyes were hard as they turned to her. "Because if your people knew what they had, they might decide to take it for themselves," he said softly. "Easier to keep a slave compliant if they never know they're slaves in the first place."

Kaila was trembling now, great waves of anger shaking her body. There was a *roaring* in her ears. She didn't even realise she was reaching for her crystal until Theron grabbed her. She flinched, then instinctively tried to pull away. He refused to release her.

"Stop, Kaila," he said gently. "If you use it, they'll see you."

"Let them see!"

In that moment, she didn't care. Let them think her a traitor—if this was the truth of their world, she wanted nothing to do with it. She would make them pay for their complicity, for what they had done to her, and Caellum, and her father…

Lies. All lies.

"And then what?" Theron hissed. He dragged her into the shadow of a nearby alley, away from the passing traffic. "You'll throw your life away and nothing will change. Is that what you want, Kaila Dwyn? Is that what your *father* would have wanted?"

"I don't care!" she snarled. "This…this is too much. I won't, I can't…" She closed her eyes. "Nothing changes. Isn't that what you said, back in Iselador? That we can't fight them, that we can't…" she broke off with a sob. "I can't…"

"I know," Theron replied, his voice softening as he released her. "But there's more than one way of resisting the Magisterium."

"How?" she whispered, lifting her head to look at him. "The war?"

Theron's lips tightened. "If there are really those who still fight, I have not met them. Maybe on the frontier, across the wastelands, there are still those who resist," he paused, then shook his head. "No, Kaila. We do the same thing we did back in Iselador. What a thief does best, like you said. We rob them of everything they have."

Kaila stared at him for a long while, her mind still swirling, struggling. Finally, she looked away, gazing out over the rooftops, to where the white dome loomed above everything and everyone. The Sanctum. The seat of the Magisterium. The people that had trained Sister Eurador, and given Elric Chain his armour, where the lies had first begun. The power that had spread them to all four corners of Fresia. All her life, Kaila had worshipped them, the peace and unity they had created for humanity.

"What do you think?"

Kaila thought about his words. She wanted more; to destroy them, to burn down this city and everything it represented.

But she couldn't fight back that way. The Magisterium and its

Wardens were too powerful. That path could only lead to death. And then it would be as Theron said—nothing would change.

We rob them of everything they have.

A smile touched Kaila's lips. She couldn't destroy them, but maybe she could make them hurt. For now, that would have to be enough.

"I'm in."

****Continue the story in Rogue's Gambit****

A NOTE FROM THE AUTHOR

Well happy 2024 everyone! I hope you enjoyed this very special story I've been working on the last 8 months. This thing had without a doubt the longest outline of any book I've worked on before - coming to a 100,000 words at one point, before I decided it needed to split into two books. This allowed me to not only spend more time exploring Kaila's awakening to the truth of Fresia, but also delve into the next part of her journey as she seeks vengeance.

Oh, and have the second book in the series half finished by the time this one gets published, which is always a bonus ;-) Means you shouldn't have too long to wait until Rogue's Gambit comes along. In fact, it should already be up for preorder! Make sure you grab a copy so you an continue Kaila's story later this year.

Anyway, that's it from me for now. If you're new to my work be sure to check out my other books, I recommend ***The Legend of the Gods*** for something of a similar vein to this.

Oh and before I forget, don't forget to leave a review for Warden's Justice.

Write on!
Aaron Hodges

FOLLOW AARON HODGES...

And receive TWO FREE novels and a short story!
https://aaronhodgesauthor.com/newsletter

ALSO BY AARON HODGES

Trials of the Aegis

Book 1: Warden's Justice

Book 2: Rogue's Gambit

The Sword of Light

Book 1: Stormwielder

Book 2: Firestorm

Book 3: Soul Blade

The Legend of the Gods

Book 1: Oathbreaker

Book 2: Shield of Winter

Book 3: Dawn of War

The Knights of Alana

Book 1: Daughter of Fate

Book 2: Queen of Vengeance

Book 3: Crown of Chaos

The Evolution Gene

Book 1: Reborn

Book 2: Havoc

Book 3: Carnage

Descendants of the Fall

Book 1: Warbringer

Book 2: Wrath of the Forgotten

Book 3: Age of Gods

Book 4: Dreams of Fury

<u>**The Alfurian Chronicles**</u>

Book 1: Defiant

Book 2: Guardian

Book 3: Conquest

<u>**The Swords of Heaven and Hell**</u>

Book 1: <u>Darkstrider</u>

Book 2: <u>Voidlight</u>

<u>**The Four Circles**</u>

Book 1: Help! My Wizard Mentor Had A Heart Attack And Now I'm Being Chased By A Horde Of Giant Spiders!

<u>**The Untamed Isles**</u>

The Path Awakens